TWICE AGAINST THE DRAGON

STEFON MEARS

Thousand
Faces
Publishing

Also by Stefon Mears

Cavan Oltblood Series
Half a Wizard
The Ice Dagger
Spells of Undeath

Spells for Hire
Devil's Shoestring
Zombie Powder
Spirit Trap
Dragon's Blood (coming December 2019)

The Rise of Magic
Magician's Choice
Sleight of Mind
Lunar Alchemy
Three Fae Monte
The Sphinx Principle

The Telepath Trilogy
Surviving Telepathy
Immoral Telepathy
Targeting Telepathy

Edge of Humanity
Caught Between Monsters
Hunting Monsters

Power City Tales
Not Quite Bulletproof
No Money in Heroism

Devil's Night
Portal-Land, Oregon
Stealing from Pirates
Fade to Gold
With a Broken Sword
Twice Against the Dragon
The House on Cedar Street
Sudden Death
On the Edge of Faerie
Confronting Legends (Spells & Swords Vol. 1)
Uncle Stone Teeth and Other Macabre Poems
The Patreon Collection, Vol. 1-4 (Vol. 5, coming soon)

Published by Thousand Faces Publishing, Portland, Oregon

http://1kfaces.com

ISBN: 978-1-948490-08-5

Twice Against the Dragon

PROLOGUE

TEN YEARS AGO

The great wyrm rose up on its back legs, wings spread wider than the cattle pen beside it. Its scales glistened black even under the threatening rain clouds, without so much as a seam Larek could see. Nothing for Taran to sink an arrow into. Foreclaws so long and sharp. Made Inga's sword look like a dagger.

The dragon reeked of sulfur, ash and death. Larek's breakfast of cold, rushed mutton stew threatened to taste even worse if it came back up.

Dragons only strike where you're weak.

A single line, from a single history text in the vast library of Larek's master, but it stood out in the chaos of the young wizard's mind. Death looming above him. Spells chasing their way around his brain. But Larek did not dream of glory or wet himself with fear.

Instead that single line dominated his thoughts.

Perhaps because the dragon's presence here confirmed it.

Three weeks ago the dragon first struck. Rumor had named it Blackflame, the dragon whose fire burned as dark as its scales.

One week ago, royal scouts reported that they had successfully traced the wyrm to its lair, in a cavern to the east.

Two days ago the king had gathered a company of thirty knights, plus the royal wizard and two ducal wizards.

Yesterday that company set out to slay this Blackflame once and for all.

And yet here, this morning, among dozens of farms better known for their grains and peas than for their cattle — well west of the capitol, much less the dragon's reputed lair — the beast came to feed.

No knights here. Not even a militia. Only three willing to take up arms. Taran, the tall, handsome archer who made his living by shooting through the eyes of his prey, then selling their hides and furs as well as their meat. Inga, the strong and stocky farmer who gained a reputation as a swordswoman when she slew a pack of six bandits.

And Larek, red of hair and red of eye, a wizard in his first official robe, pale blue with gold trim. Too young to grow a beard and thin enough to hide behind his staff.

Larek only meant to pass through on his way to seek a court position. If he could find a court small enough to match his inexperience. But at dawn the dragon had been sighted, and Larek's ablutions had been interrupted by Inga, kicking open his door at the inn.

Taran, smiling, stood behind her, leaning on his longbow. Inga insisted that the three of them could slay the beast.

That was the stuff of songs. And Inga had such charisma and enthusiasm that Larek had been proud to set out beside her. Taran even sounded confident of their victory.

Together they rode wide circles through the wheat fields, following the route the dragon flew above them.

But now the beast had landed, here beside a pen of a dozen cattle.

Inga screamed a charge, great sword held high in both hands, knees guiding the roan that had served her better against bandits than it ever had with a plow.

Taran pulled up short and loosed an arrow. Not for any of the seams Larek had sought, but for the eye of the beast.

Larek halted his borrowed piebald gelding and raised his staff, desperately incanting a spell that might protect them from dragonfire.

Should protect them from dragonfire.

Larek knew the spell. Had practiced it often, in secret. He had to practice such spells in secret because his master would have disapproved. "A wizard provides support. Guidance. Counsel a king, don't slay his enemies. Enchant a sword, don't strike the blow. Heroes die young, but a smart wizard can live forever."

Yet those were not the words Larek heard over and over in his head as he chanted his spell. His thoughts fixated on that single line from that one old history. *Dragons only strike where you're weak.*

In particular, it was the last two words that resounded through his mind. Over and over.

You're weak.

The arrow flew.

Inga charged.

Larek cast his spell.

And the dragon set them all aflame.

1

Larek paced a wide, dusty circle, as close to the boundaries of the tourney ground as he could, without the risk of anyone interfering with the small, polished stones he set down every two paces. Stones that would mark the edges of the spell he would work.

Not one onlooker, not even the youngest of children, would have been foolish enough to interfere with the spells of a wizard. But in Larek's case, well, the whispered comments he heard as he passed gave him the measure of the crowd's respect.

"He's a wizard? He looks like a merchant, and a fat one at that."

"Do you think he really got all those burn scars from a dragon?"

"More likely he drank too much and fell into some tavern's hearth."

Worse were the comments from other wizards, their voices full of derision.

"No robe? No staff? Shameful. And those *red eyes*. Obviously yet another failed spell."

"I hear he gets by selling spells to peasants."

"Gives us all a bad name."

The too-loud mutterings continued, but Larek did not dispute them. He had earned their scorn and he knew it. No doubt the stories and songs had been circling again, since the rumors of Blackflame's return in the north.

Claims of the dragon's black fire had reached the capitol, but the king had learned something from his previous effort. King Harlan III and his advisers had concluded that last time he had called together too large a company. The dragon had seen and heard them coming, and simply chose not to be there when they came for it.

Cowardly, many called it. A dragon willing to slaughter the defenseless but avoiding any serious threat.

But that behavior suited the old tales, the ones believed to be true histories and not the inventions of skalds. The dragons in those stories always had to be hunted down before they were inevitably slain by a handful of knights with a single wizard after a wonderful battle.

Larek could have been that single wizard, but he failed. And no one — least of all the kingdom's wizards — would allow him to forget that.

As though he could.

And so this time the king called for volunteers to form a party of six, the number of the largest party in any of the old histories. His Majesty would let the hopefuls prove their worth in a tournament that would also help distract the peasants.

That part, at least, had worked so far. It seemed that the tournament had called together half the kingdom of Aeralfast. Peasants had come from days away to share in the spectacle, to buy and sell at the great market, to witness the competition, or even simply to see the royal castle for the first time.

High the palace stood, on a hill above the tourney ground, with three rings of high, gray stone walls and eighteen towers. So grand and glorious that it was rumored that the king who built it, Tordale V, had married three queens who had all lived and ruled with him for thirty years — each without ever knowing about the others.

"Larek!"

Larek paused in his stone placement at the sharpness of the tone, but needed a moment to realize someone actually addressed him, instead of simply talking as though he could not hear. He turned his head and saw a wizard apparently about his own age, though her dusky skin was smooth and her eyes their natural deep brown color. Her robe was pine green, and flattered her. Her staff was almond brown, and twisted near the top.

Suspicion kept Larek's mouth shut. He had no time for mockery. He had to prepare the tourney ground for the contest of magic. The finest job he'd been given in half a year — by the king's seneschal no less, even if only to save the crown costs during the week-long tournament — and he would have a hard enough time chanting the right spells with his tongue and teeth covered in grit and the hot spring sun beating down on him.

Larek had loathed heat ever since the dragon incident.

So he turned and stared at the green-clad wizard until she spoke again, her words less certain this time.

"Will you be joining us in the tournament?"

Larek waited for the punchline. A crowd of peasants surrounding the green-clad wizard, smiles hiding just behind their eyes, waited with him.

"You *are* the only one of us to have faced a dragon." Her voice grew more certain, and was that mirth flashing in her eye? "And you lived to tell of it."

"So did the dragon." Larek's voice was quiet, but silence hung on the air as conversations died so that others could hear his bitter words.

"But Inga is dead. And Taran is dead. And the farmers. The ones who owned the cattle Blackflame consumed. They're dead. And their farmhands are dead. And their neighbors are dead. Everyone for near a mile around the dragon that day is dead."

Larek met her eye, but where he expected mirth he saw something else. Something that might have been sympathy, had Larek been open to seeing it.

"And yet I survived. I managed one spell to ward off dragonfire, and I could scarcely save my own life with it. So what good could I possibly do the party going after Blackflame this time?"

Larek turned away.

"I've faced enough dragons for a lifetime."

Larek placed another stone, uttered the right word to tie it to the others, and continued on his way before the jeering could reach him. Before any of them could see the tears forming in his eyes, starting to trace their way down the dust on his face. The guilt was bad enough to live with. The shame. The failure.

He did not need to hear their taunts.

Soon enough the crowd would have real wizards to gawk over. They would see spells the like of which they would never see again.

And the wizards themselves would worry over triumph and defeat, and the task they will gloriously face or narrowly avoid.

And as they did, Larek would get to slip back into the obscurity he so devoutly craved.

Larek stood under the hot sun, trying not to think about the sweat in his eyes or the dust on his skin and in his mouth. He wore his finest shirt for this moment, blue, with toggles up the front, and his finest pants, also blue, with an actual leather belt instead of a cord of rope to hold them up.

The working he was about to perform might not be difficult, but a wizard who looked impressive could charge a better rate. And a royal commission — even a small one — might remove some of the stain on his name.

However much he deserved it.

Perhaps Larek should have worn a robe for this. He might not have held a formal post, or a position in any order of magic, but he *had* completed his apprenticeship. He *had* the right to the robe, and the staff.

Except for the expectations that would follow.

Other wizards might jeer him now for dressing in a fashion that brought shame on the profession, but if Larek truly dressed the part, their treatment would be far worse. He would forever have to prove that he deserved the formal garb to any wizard who had doubts.

He had already heard new rumors that he had failed his apprenticeship. And Larek's old master had not come forward to dispute the rumormongers.

Even old Grendis was ashamed of him.

Larek took a deep breath to stop the flow of such thoughts. Leaving a good impression here might remind people that he had failed, but he had failed against a dragon. A dragon that no one had slain since.

Perhaps he could earn some measure of respect. Perhaps he could even begin to forgive himself.

And it all started with this.

The spells to establish boundaries for the contest of magic were simple enough. Larek had prepared the stones in advance, polishing them all together and connecting them magically as he did. Then he had arranged them in a wide circle, with so large a diameter enough that even the most flamboyant of the contestants would have more than enough room for fancy spells. And in placing each stone, Larek whispered the word that would remind the stones of their connection.

And now the final stone had been placed, and Larek stood at the beginning and the end of the circle, right under the judges' platform. And not coincidentally the point furthest from the crowd. This was not the time to have jibes undercutting his confidence.

Larek swept his hands wide, and sang the song in ancient Aarkadian that called down the power of the sun itself, bright and hot, to beam onto each stone of the circle that connected to the keystone in his left hand. A stomp, a clap and a twirl of the keystone high in the air, and the beams flared wider until they touched each other. A chant in a singsong lilt tied them together, solidified their connection.

Larek now stood alone in a cone of bright, hot sunlight. Just about the least comfortable place he could imagine, but comfort was the last thing on his mind just then.

Larek stretched his hand high above him, the keystone held

between two fingers until it blotted the sun from his vision. Another chant then, this one harsh and demanding, and Larek pulled the stone back down toward him.

Slowly he brought it down, as though the sun itself hesitated to relinquish the stone.

As Larek chanted and pulled, the tip of the cone bowed and bent down toward him, until the bright, hot sunlight formed a dome, anchored at six dozen spots by the stones Larek had prepared in advance.

He now formed a fist around the keystone, and snapped orders at it, still in ancient Aarkadian. *Locked and bound*, Larek demanded. *Sealed within, sealed without.*

As Larek finished his orders, the dome turned bright pine green, as though in tribute to the green-clad wizard Larek had met earlier, though he could not have said himself why it had turned that color. The books had been unclear on the point. The dome's color had something to do with the wizard's focus.

Finally, he slammed his rock-holding fist into the dirt, barking out the final word of the spell as he struck.

Pain jolted up his arm, and the dome faded from sight. But its visibility did not matter. No wizard could cast a spell while within the circle of stones — save for Larek himself — without first touching the keystone and submitting to its magic.

The grounds had been set. Any spells cast within the circle that might pass beyond the stones would be anchored by Larek's enchantment and reinforce the barrier. Wizards could now cast as recklessly as they desired in their attempt to win the contest, without harming so much as a hair on the head of a bystander.

Even better, the stones themselves were now rooted to the spot for seven days. No drunk who doubted Larek's skill could sneak off with one of the stones as a joke.

The work was well done. Larek could sense the spell buzzing about him. He could feel almost proud of the accomplishment. Two dozen wizards had come to the capitol to participate in this tournament, and how many could have cast a containment circle as wide and strong as Larek's?

Probably all of them, Larek told himself.

Still, he knew he had done a good job. Larek felt a smile begin to stretch his lips as he looked up to where the seneschal waited for the keystone.

But the seneschal was not watching. He was staring off to Larek's right.

Larek turned, and saw that four wizards had begun to entertain the crowd with illusions, drawing gasps and applause.

And every eye for hundreds of paces.

Just Larek's luck. Not a single person had watched him work.

Well, a single person. He could see the green-clad wizard from earlier, still standing where she had been when they had their "conversation." She raised her hand, and opened her mouth to say something, but Larek turned before she could offer an opinion about how he could better cast it next time.

Larek turned to the seneschal and said, "Here is the keystone. Remember. Each entrant must touch the stone and offer the oath of submission."

"Yes," said the seneschal, reluctantly turning away from the show. "Does it have to be precise?"

"Yes, but you don't need to memorize it. If any of them get it wrong, their competitor will correct them. No one wants to give their foe an advantage."

"Advantage?" That almost drew the seneschal's attention back from the illusions.

"There are ways to exploit every spell. Suffice to say they'll keep each other in line."

But the seneschal did not meet Larek's eye as he listened. In truth, he might not have even heard the words. He offered no acknowledgment, save an astonished syllable at the sight of an illusory griffin flying low and pretending to snatch at audience members.

But the seneschal did at least hold up the small pouch containing

Larek's payment. So Larek handed him the stone, took the pouch, and wandered off.

No one had watched him work. No one had cared that he had worn his best clothes.

This commission would not lead to others.

———

BY THE TIME LAREK MADE HIS WAY OUT OF THE TOURNEY GROUNDS THE sun had mercifully moved behind a great white cloud, cooling the early afternoon and easing the tension among the burn scars on Larek's face, neck and hands. He had even had a chance to wash the dirt from his face and hands at a horse trough, and splash a little water on his carrot red hair.

The best part about skipping the contest of magic was that Larek would not have to wait for a crowd to thin in order to buy his lunch. The bad part was that almost all the stalls were closed because every-body — *everybody* — wanted to go watch the wizards.

Blacksmiths and woodcarvers, jewelers and coopers and chandlers and weavers and tailors and more, all had locked away their wares, leaving nothing but closed tents and empty wooden displays arranged in rows outside the tourney grounds beyond the outer castle wall.

Not that Larek walked utterly alone. The closed-up tents and stalls were watched over by the occasional strolling or lolling guard carrying a club and wearing boiled leathers notched at the right shoulder with the v-shaped insignia of the tourney.

Larek knew to give these guards plenty of room as he passed. The notched insignia meant that they were not part of the capitol's true city watch, but additional guards hired on for the tourney. Such men were mercenaries at best, thugs at worst, and while they would not dare to rob the stalls they guarded — not when the merchants spoke with such a strong voice in the capitol — a passing disgraced wizard with a pouch of fresh coins in his pocket might prove too tempting a target.

So Larek plodded down the center of the wide lane of dirt and hay and stamped-down yellow grass, which at least gave him an easy time stepping around the leavings of passing horses, mules and dogs. He only wished he could smell something more tempting than those leavings. He had not dined since breaking his fast before dawn, and now the sun was past its apex.

Lane after lane he walked, his stomach's complaints growing steadily louder in his own ears, and the eyes of guards began to linger suspiciously on him. Not as though Larek were a potential victim, but a possible robber.

But Larek could understand that. At a tournament like this one anyone not watching the events, and yet not working, was likely either a nobleman or a thief.

And no one would mistake Larek for a nobleman.

Finally, tucked away among pens of blackfeather chickens and black-and-white saddleback pigs, Larek spotted a stall that was not only open, but sold food and had customers.

Unfortunately, those customers were all tourney guards, either preparing to come on duty or relaxing after finishing their day's shift. Some two dozen such guards, drinking and eating and laughing, at the benches surrounding three broad oak tables in the open air.

Larek considered making his way home on an empty stomach.

Larek's stomach insisted that this was impossible. It had caught a change in the slight breeze that now carried over the smell of roasting chickens with carrots and potatoes, and threatened open rebellion if not filled in the immediate future.

Larek slipped an iron stall out of his pouch — a thin coin, the rectangular shape of a horse's stall — then tucked the pouch away into the seams of his pants alongside the payment for his tournament spell.

The guards noticed Larek as he approached. Stared openly at his burns. Tried to catch his red eyes. He gave them a smile and nod and, thanks to years of practice, avoided eye contact with any one of them.

Instead he shifted his attention to the stall itself. Worked by a family of three, the parents cooking and their daughter — who looked old enough to be running her own stall — handling cleanup and sales.

Guard conversations died and smirks appeared as Larek placed his order for a meal, refusing a flagon of beer in favor of a cup of wine. Despite rumors to the contrary, Larek had not gotten drunk since the early days of his apprenticeship.

And the yellow wines of this region, supplied by the duchy of Terhold, were weak enough to generate the obvious comparison among less discriminating diners.

In fact, Larek could hear a burble of chuckles from the tables behind him that told him the obvious comparison had already been made. Just as well. If they laughed at his drink, they weren't laughing at his magic or his scars.

The guards must have provided steady custom, because Larek did not have to wait for his food. No sooner had he placed his order than the serving woman handed it to him in a wicker basket, obviously trying not to stare at his scars or eyes.

The wine took a little longer while she dug out a small, untapped cask. Tapping the cask took long enough that she forewent finding Larek a wooden cup and filled a flagon instead.

That meant more wine for the money, though Larek knew his wine was likely to be "flavored" by hints of ale.

But on the scale of Larek's problems, he considered that one beneath his notice.

He paid much less than he expected for the food and, lacking any trees to sit under, began carrying his food to the nearest tent that looked unspoiled on the outside.

"Here," called a tourney guard from the last of the tables. "There's room for one more."

More mutters and chuckles from the tables, but for once Larek suspected they were not at his expense. Or at least, not directly. The guard who had called him over was a woman.

Even sitting, she looked at least a head taller than Larek, with strength in the set of her shoulders. She had long, woolly black hair tied behind her into a near-whip with a long leather thong that ended in a small blade. Her nut brown skin and gray eyes told of the deserts of far western Karwale.

She also had a ghost-white scar that carved its way from her right cheekbone, down across her chin and neck, and disappeared into her leathers past her left collarbone.

Something about the woman struck a memory in Larek. A song he had heard in a tavern about an exceptionally tall woman warrior...

But the words failed him just then. Not that they mattered.

Larek stifled a sigh. The last thing he wanted to do was share a meal with a pack of tourney guards. But refusing the offer would have been rude, and being rude to those who had a license to harass him seemed like a poor option.

Larek smiled the way he smiled at a customer who wanted him to brew a potion that would lead to unguarded treasure. If such potions existed outside the tales of skalds, why would Larek sell his spells?

He took the offered seat, ignoring the mumbles and sniggers from further up the bench. Mumbles and sniggers that died the moment the woman spoke.

"I'm Dyrra," she said as though it were a challenge, and not just to Larek. Her words still carried the lift and drop of a Karwalish accent, but their peaks and valleys had been flattened by time or effort. And she met his eyes without staring or flinching. "Yes, that Dyrra. And if hearing my name gives you anything to say, best to say it now and take the consequences."

Dyrra. Now the song fell into place. "The Ballad of Dyrra the Tall and the Merchant of Fent."

The Merchant of Fent
Wherever he went
Left his wife and children behind.
For guarding his hall
Stood Dyrra the Tall
And danger far from his mind.
Tall Dryrra they said
Could cleave a man's head
So fast, his mouth would yet talk.

And her nerve was so sore
She could face down a score
Of bandits and never balk.
But then the day came
When testing her fame
Were two, with swords in the dark.
Desperate men
Banished from Mem
And bearing the deserter's mark.
Tall Dyrra struck true
But between me and you
Her blows were less than she thought.
They left her for dead
And raided the stead.
All the Merchant's gold was for naught.

There were more verses, and a great deal made about the scar he could now see for himself, but Larek had always considered the first verses to contain the crux of the story, and probably the closest to the truth.

That was certainly the case with songs about him.

He held the steady face he used to ignore jibes directed at him and looked Dyrra in the eye. "I'm pleased to meet you."

Suspicion drew down the arch of her eyebrows, but the truth was that Larek meant what he said. How often did he get to meet another person who lived under the yoke of failure?

"Come on, boys," said one of the other tourney guards, "we should give these two privacy. They're made for each other."

No longer attempting subtlety, the whole crowd of them barked with vicious laughter as they cleared out, some congratulating others for one disparaging comment or another.

And then Larek the Burned found himself sitting alone with Dyrra Slow Sword.

And he had no idea what to say.

2

————

Now that Larek and Dyrra had more room, she snatched up her drink and her basket of food and moved to the other side of the oak bench table to face Larek directly, instead of sitting beside him.

Saddleback pigs snuffled and grunted in their pen some ten paces distant, while nearby blackfeather chickens scratched and clucked in theirs. Muted, harsh conversation drifted over from the tent where Larek and Dyrra had gotten their roast chickens and vegetables, not to mention their flagons of wine and beer respectively.

The departing tourney guards chorused fading laughter, almost drowning out the appreciative cheers from the distant contest of magic.

The sky above fit the tourney, with its royal blue and vast white clouds, but not the meal Larek now felt obligated to share.

To share in silence, perhaps, because Dyrra had yet to find words either.

Larek stuffed a chicken leg at his mouth to give him time to think. Did she just want the company of someone else who knew what it meant to live with guilt? Or was she merely pleased to sit near someone who would not be looking down on her for something that must have happened years ago, and probably nothing like the way it was portrayed in the song?

If it had happened at all.

"Don't listen to the muttonheads," she said. "I'm not looking for someone to share my bedroll."

While Larek found that reassuring — striking as she was, he felt quite sure she could break him in half in a fit of passion — the moment he could clear the bite of tasty chicken from his mouth what he said was, "I never thought you were."

"And I'm not going to talk about that thrice-damned song. Any more than I expect you to talk about that dragon. Or your eyes."

"Glad to hear it." Larek swallowed some of the yellow wine. Weak, true, but that was the way he liked it. And honestly, he thought the more subtle flavor added to the chicken.

"So what shall we talk about?"

"Leaving."

"Leaving?" Larek did not have to pretend shock. If he still had eyebrows, he had no doubt they would even now be threatening his hairline. But still... "You mean the tourney?"

"I mean all of Aeralfast."

Larek stared, chicken fat trying to burn his fingers from the piece halfway to his mouth. "How did you know I was thinking of leaving?"

"I didn't. But it makes sense." She paused to rip the roast flesh from a dead chicken's ribcage, then wiped the grease from her chin with her wrist. "Find someplace where your name and face don't inspire laughter. Or worse."

The sound that came out of Larek's mouth was halfway between a sigh and a groan. Odd enough that Dyrra raised one of her very dark and not at all burnt eyebrows.

"You get it. You actually get it," he said. His shoulders slumped forward with relief. "It's not just about the taunting."

"It's the pay," she agreed. "Everyone takes advantage of you because they figure you're happy just to have work."

"Then they spit on you while you help them."

"And sneer when they pay you."

"And try to short you what they promised."

Larek and Dyrra went back and forth like this for some time, warming to the topic of other people's derision, until they'd both finished their meals and their drinks, and even a second round, brought unasked for by the woman who had sold them their food.

Larek had noticed that the saleswoman stood within earshot, just outside of her tent, but he paid her no mind. He was used to serving as entertainment for others. And it wasn't as though any other customers had approached.

"So," said Dyrra, smiling now with the sort of camaraderie Larek had not felt in years. If ever. "The topic was leaving."

"Yes," said Larek with feeling, but then felt his shoulders fall again, for a very different reason. "But what does it matter if we go someplace where no one knows what happened — or is said to have happened? We can't outrun the consequences of what we did, or failed to do. I know that I—"

"We are not discussing the dragon or that song. Remember?"

"Yes, but—"

"Well damn it!" Dyrra slapped her hand down on the table, and Larek saw the saleswoman jump in surprise. "Guilt is a private matter anyway, and no one's business but our own. Whether or not a past failure ruins my sleep and hounds my every step in life, that does not give license to every muttonhead on the street to look down on me. As though any of them could have done better."

The guilt Larek saw in Dyrra's eye as she spoke mirrored his own. He felt sure of it. And he had to admit that even his job preparing the tournament circle looked unlikely to lead to other respectable commissions.

"Velstadt lies far to the south," said Dyrra. "Beyond the Peaks of Fallen Sky. True or false, our tales are old. It's not likely that the skalds still sing them that far south. Here, in front of us? Our mere presence keeps their mockery alive."

"Velstadt?" Larek tried to sip a little more wine, but his flagon was empty. "No caravan will be heading that way until after the tournament. That would give us the better part of a week to—"

"No caravan." Dyrra leaned forward. "That was why I wanted to talk to you. I'm sick to death of these people, and I imagine you must be as well. The last thing I want to do is travel with a company of them, encouraging them to sing that damned song at every stop and spoiling the point of leaving."

"But the roads are dangerous for a traveler alone," said Larek. "Even a warrior…"

"Exactly. But a warrior traveling with a wizard? We could keep each other safe, as well as company. And if we die? Well, at least no taunts reach the grave."

Dyrra extended her forearm, a fierce grin on her face.

Larek smiled and clasped arms with her. "I'll need time to gather a few things."

"As will I."

"As will I," said the saleswoman.

Almost as one, Larek and Dyrra turned to stare.

THE SUN SEEMED TO TUCK ITSELF AS FAR BEHIND THAT HUGE WHITE cloud as it could, lending the air and the moment a chill. A soft breeze drifted past Larek's face in silence.

Even the nearby chickens and pigs hushed as Larek and Dyrra turned from where they faced each other across the oak bench table to look up at the saleswoman.

The saleswoman who had just invited herself along on their journey south to Velstadt.

Larek thought she looked a few years younger than he and Dyrra were, but that might have been her bare height and slender frame. Still, though youth kept the pale skin of her wrists and throat tight, worries and stresses had added wrinkles around her green eyes and full lips, stolen some of the luster from her long, honey blonde hair.

And there was something familiar about the muted yellow kirtle she wore over her white tunic, tied at the waist with a double-length of brown cord. Against current fashions it laced up the front, and had sleeves wide enough to serve as small pockets.

And there was a spot on the kirtle above her heart where embroidery had been cut away. But Larek could not stare long enough at the spot to figure out what symbol once belonged there. Not without appearing to stare at the body underneath.

"Think you're going on a trip, do you?" said Dyrra, in tones so harsh Larek found himself glancing to make sure she wasn't addressing him.

But the sales woman never batted an eye, as though well accustomed to such tones herself.

Interesting.

"I think a chance to start over in Velstadt sounds wonderful."

"And you think the fact that Larek here and I allowed you to stand nearby while we discussed the matter constituted an invitation?"

"I think the two of you aren't alone in having past events you want to leave behind."

Dyrra scoffed. "Whatever his name is, he'll get over it. And clearly your family haven't shunned you. I'd say you'll survive."

Dyrra turned back to Larek, but the sales woman stood there, unmoving. Her mouth had tightened, as though a slice of lemon had soured her tongue, and she narrowed her eyes in frustration.

"You're charges are said to have died," said the woman, more challenge in her voice than Larek would have directed at an armed, irritated warrior. But then she directed that same tone at him. "And perhaps your failure doomed more than a hundred."

She waited until both Dyrra and Larek had turned to regard her again.

"But neither of you..." Her voice broke, but her jaw stayed firm. "But neither of you killed a dozen people you were trying to save."

Larek's eyes widened in shock, and even he had to resist the urge to sketch a ward in the air. Dyrra sat straighter, her right hand falling to the handle of her tourney guard club.

"That's right," said the sales woman in a bitter tone that Larek knew all too well. "I am Sindra."

Sindra. The yellow kirtle. The ruined embroidery. It had to have been the soothing hand sigil of Nilasah, Goddess of Compassion and Patroness of the Order of Healers and Physickers.

"Well, Sindra, called the Poisonous," said Larek, his eye and voice steady as he recited titles he had never used before, "I am Larek, called the Burned, and this is Dyrra, called Slow Sword."

Sindra grimaced at the sound of her own appellation, but still her eyebrows rose hopefully.

Dyrra growled from the back of her throat. "No," she said, and the word came out dangerous. "Do not call me that again, Larek, and do not do what you are about to do. No wonder the meals cost so little. I—"

"If I never utter those kennings again," said Larek, loudly enough to drown out whatever Dyrra would have said next, "I will still blame myself for voicing them even once. And as to what I am about to do—"

"No!" Dyrra slapped her hand down on the table. "A dozen help-less, wounded men in her care! All dead by her hand!"

"So the story goes," said Larek, refusing to match Dyrra's rising tone and volume. "And the story also casts doubt on her true inten-tions when she applied her poultices and prayed."

"Yes!"

"And tell me, Dyrra," — Larek paused just long enough to let the silence add her unchosen title for him — "are the details of your famous song all accurate? Last I heard it was up to six verses about the fight alone."

Dyrra started to draw her weapon, then blinked in momentary confusion, as though the handle she held was not the handle she expected. Sindra took a step back.

But Larek never budged.

"Of course not. I've heard the song, but I don't know the truth of what happened. And since we said we would not discuss your song or my story, you don't know the truth of what happened with me." Larek nodded to indicate Sindra. "And neither one of us knows the truth of what happened with her. But look at her, Dyrra."

"I'll grant that she is pretty, but—"

"Not that. Really look at her."

Larek gave Dyrra a moment to look Sindra over, while Sindra drew a deep breath, held her head high, and pressed her hands against her sides to keep from fidgeting.

Dyrra looked, and looked, and Larek waited. Sindra finally closed her eyes against the scrutiny.

Finally, Dyrra said, "She is haunted."

"She is haunted," said Larek. "As are you. As am I. She sleeps no better than either of us. So how is it that you and I should get to seek an absence to whispers while she should not?"

"You are a wizard and I am a warrior. Our skills will be useful on the road. What can she do? Kill us trying to mend a cut?"

"You can trust my physicking as far as I can trust your fighting or his spells," said Sindra, eyes open and tone calm. "And I'm probably a better cook than both of you."

Dyrra turned to Larek. "You are set on this."

"I am.

Dyrra glared at Larek, and he had to admit to himself that she could probably murder a cowardly man with that glare. But he held still through it.

Dyrra picked up her flagon, but it was empty. She threw it down into the crushed grass, and jumped to her feet, knocking over her bench in the process.

"By the blood spilled at Aranguard, how can I toast my new companions without ale?"

LAREK, DYRRA, AND SINDRA SPENT ANOTHER HOUR AT THAT TABLE, while occasional guards brought their dinners to the other two oak bench tables, and glanced with furtive curiosity at the quiet, huddled trio.

But none of those guards dared interfere or interrupt, any more than they would have thrown open the nearby pens of chickens and pigs to see what would happen. They knew that the results would not have proven nearly as entertaining as they might hope. And the consequences might have proven more than a little dangerous.

Larek wondered from time to time that Sindra's parents did not interrupt them, if only to get their daughter to return to work. But then, they must have handled their work without her while she had been a Healer, so perhaps it was no great stretch for them to work without her now.

It might even have been that they wanted to see her leave and start her life anew in Velstadt.

And so Larek, Dyrra and Sindra had their table to themselves under the cool, cloudy afternoon sky, and together they discussed routes, the latest spots favored by bandits looking for quick money, and how much each of them could, and would, carry.

They worked through most of their questions and concerns about the journey, and had been about to part and go their separate ways, when Sindra said, "Horses!"

"Horses are expensive," said Larek, "and I've traveled some good distances without them myself."

"Horses are too much trouble," said Dyrra.

"They're easy enough to ride, if that's your concern," said Sindra to Larek, excitement beginning to fill her voice. "At least for our purposes. You don't have to be a knight to handle a walking pace for the kind of distance we'll be covering. And apart from extra food and water, plus brushing, they're hardly any trouble at all."

"They're still expensive," said Larek, who decided that talking about his experience in the saddle would prove counterproductive.

"Still too much trouble," agreed Dyrra.

"Not at all!" Sindra was smiling now, more sure of herself. "I know a stablemaster who takes in the horses who falter at combat training—"

"Horses that spook," said Dyrra.

"Horses that can't handle riding full tilt into the chaos of battle carrying an armored, screaming knight. Doesn't mean they can't ride a nice, sedate route south carrying nice ... sedate people."

Larek looked away to keep a laugh from bursting out at the hesitation Sindra showed at characterizing Dyrra as "nice" and "sedate." He could not keep the grin entirely from his face, however. Sindra's cheer was infectious.

"While the horses sound fitting," said Larek, "there's still the matter of cost."

"And trouble," added Dyrra.

"That's the best part," said Sindra. "He sells the horses at a discount to anyone who will not make them pull a plough or a cart. Says that kind of work doesn't suit the horses' spirits. And with all the knights and squires and others training for this tournament, he's more than doubled his stock faster than he can comfortably stable them! He'll practically give them to us!"

"Too. Much. Trouble."

Dyrra's simple objection — and her steadfast refusal to succumb to Sindra's enthusiasm — finally cracked through the ex-Healer's cheer.

"Why?" The word rang out, a hammer on an anvil. Angry frustration in Sindra's eyes, but if Dyrra felt any tension, she did not show it. She regarded Sindra with simple confidence in her rightness.

"First. Horses are too big to hide. We don't know what we're going to face out there, and there may be times that the smartest thing to do is hide while some bigger threat passes us by. Maybe a pack of bandits. Maybe something worse. Either way, three on foot can easily vanish into trees, bushes, or even tall grass in a pinch. But horses can be seen from much further away, and it's much harder to hide a horse behind a bush.

"Second. Horses mean money. It doesn't matter how much or how little we pay for these horses. It doesn't matter if this stablemaster of yours gives them to us for free, along with enough food and water to carry us all the way over the mountains and into Velstadt. They're still valuable to anyone who can take them from us.

"We'd be painting targets on our backs. Targets visible to every bandit and robber between here and the mountains." Dyrra held Sindra's eye as she shook her head. "On foot we may look like too much risk for too little potential reward. But on horseback we'll be riding a good reason to rob us."

"Larek," said Sindra, "you've been quiet during all this. What do you think?"

Larek looked from one woman to the other, then up at the clouds that the wind had splintered from the single massive white structure of earlier in the day.

He looked back at Sindra. "Dyrra's right."

Dyrra slapped the table in triumph. Sindra's mouth drew down in a hard line, but her eyes showed that she was still listening, so Larek continued.

"If we were traveling with a caravan, we'd want horses. If we were sticking to safe, well-traveled roads, we'd want horses.

"But where we're going, we're going to pass through areas where the bandits ride in packs strong enough to hit well-protected caravans. On foot we aren't likely to be worth their bother." Larek wondered about that, but held his voice steady because he felt certain about his second point. "But on horseback? Marauders would kill us just to add our mounts to their stables."

Sindra considered that as she studied the cracks of a knot in the table's wood. "I suppose," she conceded.

"Not backing out of our journey, are you?" said Dyrra, and Larek thought she sounded just a bit hopeful. "Are your pretty feet too tender for so long a walk?"

"Not at all," said Sindra. "I just don't relish having to tend to *your* blisters. And if you get corns, you're rubbing them yourself."

Dyrra's eyes narrowed for a moment, but Larek started laughing. Something about his laughter broke the tension, and soon they were all laughing.

"So, it's agreed then," said Larek as the laughter died down. "We gather tomorrow morning at the southern edge of the tourney encampments at dawn?"

"At dawn," said Dyrra.

"At dawn," said Sindra.

THE SUN WAS CLOSE TO SETTING BY THE TIME LAREK MADE IT BACK through the grove of maples to his house. For many people the orange and red shades that filled the sky around the setting sun were a pleasure to gaze upon. For the desert people of Karwale, who tracked their days sunset to sunset to avoid working during the scalding daytime heat, the setting sun heralded new beginnings.

To Larek, it looked like the sky was on fire. The only way it could have looked worse would have been if the sun itself were black like the dragon's breath.

But as his soft boots crunched through leaves and twigs on the approach to his door that day, the setting sun did not make Larek dwell on burning fields and burning people. Instead, he wondered if Dyrra, whose accent suggested she had not lived in Karwale for many years, still thought of days as starting at sunset instead of sunrise. Did she think of them as starting their journey tomorrow morning or halfway through today?

Larek's home sat alone among the trees, in a location that he liked to tell himself was conveniently close to the capitol as well as to the surrounding farms and three nearby towns. But when he was honest with himself — as he was when he stood and looked that evening upon the little red two-room house with its workroom attic — he knew that he built it there because he had no nearby neighbors. It was his own attempt to build here what he hoped to find in Velstadt — a place free of jeering.

Here the attempt had failed. But in Velstadt he yet had hope. If he could get away from the endless taunts and retellings, he might find a way to begin to forgive himself.

Larek snorted at the thought. A little distance would not absolve him of so many deaths. But even a chance to live quietly with his guilt would be an improvement.

The house, like the trees around it, was all maple wood, and when freshly cleaned and aired its smell retained a hint of the sweetness of its long-dried-out sap.

Larek could see nothing he needed to pack from the front room, but the front room never kept much anyway. Four chairs, one for Larek and three in case of clients. The stone hearth, and a cabinet holding his few dishes, some food, plus his everfull jug of clean water.

Sindra would bring the cooking pans, so his might as well remain behind. Though they could at least provide him one more meal. He woke the embers of the fire and started his beef stew heating, adding a small amount of water from the jug.

The jug, Larek would bring. He was proud of the jug. It was the first object he had ever enchanted, as part of his apprenticeship.

Larek had purchased a fresh, unused jug, and had it fitted with a tight copper lid. Next he caught rainwater in a bowl, and chanted over it his own modification of the spell usually reserved to tie magic into ink. Then he used his rainwater-ink to draw symbols of preparation and containment all over the jug and the lid.

They would not be visible, but for Larek's purposes that did not matter.

Once the jug was prepared, Larek sealed it, tied a strand of his own red hair around the spout, and left it in his master's study while Larek hiked along the River Guill to its source, a waterfall halfway up the third of the Seven Peaks, the one commonly known as the Bastard for its steep angles and sharp rocks.

The journey to the mouth of that river took more than a week. Every night he had cast anchoring spells on small rocks and embedded them as deeply into the riverbed as he could. The chances were strong that the anchors would not be needed to support the jug enchantment, but Larek considered the effort a small investment compared to the hike itself.

At the mouth of the waterfall, in the pouring rain, Larek completed the enchantment. A set of seven spells, bindings and connections and transferences in ways that no wizard had ever managed to translate to larger scale work, despite the begging of kings and generals for ever more powerful siege engines.

And so now, sitting in his front room, hundreds of miles away from that waterfall, Larek could sip from his jug and drink from the waterfall: the freshest, cleanest water he had ever tasted.

Dyrra and Sindra had worried about water on the road, but Larek had smiled when he assured them that if they would handle the food, he would handle the water.

From his bedroom, Larek collected only a blue woolen blanket, his clothes, and his travel boots, hard leather beasts that reached halfway to his knees. A little heavy, yes, but they had handled even the sharp rocks of the Bastard without ruining his feet.

Nothing else in that room he would need on the road. It wasn't as though he would bring his small bed or his huge cedar armoire. He paused to look over the latter. Taller than he was, and twice as wide as even his current girth. He had paid for it from his first professional commission, one of the few non-magical objects that held pleasant nostalgia for him.

The armoire Larek would miss. But if a horse would draw too much notice on the road, an overweight wizard with a huge armoire strapped to his back would not exactly prove inconspicuous.

Perhaps he could send for it, once he established himself in Velstadt...

But the time for such thoughts was later.

Larek snapped his fingers, keying the ceiling trap door to open and the knotted rope ladder to fall down. Larek gripped the knot that fell to shoulder height, then snapped his fingers again. The rope pulled him up into the attic, and the trap door closed behind him.

Larek looked around his workroom and smiled.

If a passerby looked at Larek's house from the outside, he might not have realized it contained an attic at all. It might have had high ceilings instead, which, the passerby would presume, would be more comfortable. Any attic in that house could be no taller than a crawl-space, perhaps with enough clearance for a small child to stand.

And yet Larek stood tall within his attic workroom, and smiled at the three fine, white oak worktables, the two tall, wide, white oak cabinets. The deep, comfortable chair for lounging or reading in front of the simple stone fireplace, and the smoothed, custom stool for sitting at the worktables.

And the bookshelves. Rows and rows of bookshelves, each filled with histories and stories and most of all, theories and experiments in the arts of magic. Larek's own research took up a shelf longer than his arms could span.

The whole room smelled like books, rich herbs, and old incense.

Larek smiled at all of it. Because it was all coming with him.

One of the great trade secrets of wizards was the workshop. Yes, the skalds' stories touched on it and hinted at it, in their tales of houses roomier on the inside than the outside, of cabinets that held entire castles, or even worlds unto themselves. They guessed at secret rooms and twisting hallways that kept thieves away from the secrets of a wizard's workshop, of spells that befuddled the mind, or twisted space or bent time or even teleported whole people, or some other nonsense that — even if it could be done — would have been far more effort than it was worth.

And none of them came close to the truth.

Every wizard worth his spells — or her spells — hid their workshop inside a pouch.

The spells were hideously complex and time consuming, and covered every bit of the workroom's frame and structure, be it made of brick and mortar or board and nail. Completing the workroom was always the last step of apprenticeship, and took at least a year, under the careful supervision of the master. Every spell had to be cast perfectly. If a single spell had an error, the whole project would be ruined in testing, and the apprentice would have to begin again from scratch.

Larek's master had beamed with pride that Larek had needed to go through the process only once.

But the memory of his master's pride did not broaden Larek's smile. Instead, his shoulders fell.

Spells when he had time and space to cast them were never his problem. He had long suspected this was the reason his master had emphasized that he work away from the action, never under duress. Larek had no talent for that.

As he had so admirably proven.

Larek shook his head. No time for that now. He had to get what he came up here for. He dug through one of the cabinets' higher shelves for a small assortment of phials and potions that he thought might be useful on the road, and stuffed them into a knapsack.

He looked around the room, blinking fast as he tried to think of anything else he might need, despite not quite knowing what to expect in his travels. He shook his head. No flashes of brilliance. What he had gathered would have to suffice, and if it didn't, he would have to figure things out as they walked.

At least the long walk would probably afford him the opportunity to gather some herbs that might be useful, without depleting his own stock.

Now, he just needed one more thing…

"Wake up, Chitter!" Larek looked over at the comfortable chair, then at the tops of the cabinets and bookshelves. "Where are you hiding?"

Suddenly a weight dropped on Larek's shoulder, and four tiny claws gripped his best blue tunic.

He laughed. "There you are!" and reached out with one finger to gently scratch the gray flying squirrel from forehead to the base of his bushy tail. The squirrel pressed against his fingertip the whole way, but said, "Is this important? I was sleeping."

Larek caught his small friend up on the events of the day and his plans for tomorrow, while the squirrel paced thoughtfully around his shoulders.

"So," said Chitter, "these two companions of yours…"

"Yes, those names were women's names. No, don't get any ideas."

"Can't help it. I'm an earth spirit. I get earthy thoughts."

"Don't you cause me trouble on this trip." Larek pointed his finger at the squirrel, as though ready to shake it and emphasize his point.

"I'm not going to cause you trouble." The squirrel waved his forepaws back and forth in a very human gesture. "I just wish I could get you to open your eyes once in a while. Like that wizard in the green robe. At the tourney."

"Yes?" Larek had the sudden wish he had left that encounter out of his description of the day.

"You went straight to assuming she was going to give you a hard time." The squirrel held up a forestalling paw. "Now most people do. I get that. None of them give you a harder time than you give yourself, but that's beside the point. You say she mentioned that you *survived* facing a dragon, not that you *failed* to kill one.

"Now I wasn't there. You were. But it seems to me you were looking for confrontation where you might have found respect."

"She wanted me to enter the tourney. Where I would have looked like a fool."

"Did she? Or did she only ask if you entered? As though — and this is just a thought — she wanted to begin a conversation."

Tiny black eyes gazed at Larek with an ageless weight.

"The point is meaningless. She's here because she hopes to face a dragon, and I am going south tomorrow."

"With two women."

"Stop it."

"Let's just say we'll discuss it again later." The squirrel twitched his tail. His voice grew thoughtful. "I should probably meet them first anyway."

Larek blew an irritated breath out his nostrils.

"Fine. For now you need to come downstairs with me. I have to close this place up for the road, then we'll have something to eat and I can get some sleep."

"Take it easy, Larek," said Chitter. "I'm on your side."

Larek drew a slower breath this time, and stroked the squirrel's forehead as an apology.

He stepped up to the worktable in the center of the room, and dug into the center drawer, then into a secret drawer concealed within it. He pulled out a small pouch that had been turned inside out.

Larek took one last look around his workroom. "I wish I could have gotten the armoire up here. I hate leaving it behind."

"No! I love that armoire! Can you send for it later?"

"I hope to."

"I'll have a talk with the local animals before we leave in the morning." Chitter nodded, certain. "Most of them owe me for one thing or another. I'll have them keep an eye on the place. Discourage unwanted guests." The squirrel tilted its head as it regarded Larek. "And you *are* leaving wards behind."

"I don't plan on—"

"It's not about whether you plan to come back. It's about whether you can if you want to. You never know what will happen."

"I'll set wards before we go."

"And I'll talk to the animals." Chitter settled down on Larek's right shoulder. "We're set."

Larek stood above the trap door, took the rope ladder in hand, and snapped his fingers. The door sprung open and the rope ladder lowered Larek gently to the floor of his bedroom. He snapped his fingers again, and the rope ladder whooshed up into the workroom. The trap door closed after it, leaving not a trace that it was ever there.

Larek reached into the inside-out pouch and pulled it right-side out, quickly tying the drawstring tight. When he finished he appeared to be holding a stuffed-full red pouch, barely smaller than his hand, and covered in gold inlay sigils.

Larek's most important packing was finished.

3

———————

Wʜᴇɴ ᴛʜᴇ ᴄɪᴛʏ ᴡᴀᴛᴄʜ ʙᴇʟʟs ᴄʟᴀᴍᴏʀᴇᴅ ᴍɪᴅɴɪɢʜᴛ, Dʏʀʀᴀ ᴡᴀsᴛᴇᴅ ɴᴏ time leaving the market area. Useless evening, full of useless walking past laughing and drinking muttonheads. And not the quality muttonheads, like nobles and knights. Oh, no. The quality mutton-heads did their drinking and laughing within the city walls — likely within the palace walls — among their own kind.

No, the muttonheads Dyrra had to deal with all night were common folk who had come to gawk at the warriors and wizards. Or, worse, had come to make such money as they could from the spectacle.

Either way, they spent each evening pissing away whatever they earned during the day.

Twice as many tonight as last night, as though the cool evening air and the sight of fresh stars blowing out from behind the clouds had called them out from whatever holes they called their own.

And Dyrra had to babysit them.

"Don't let them fight, but don't hurt them if you don't have to." Stupid rule. Most of the troublemakers took one look at Dyrra's size, or her scar, and all the fight went out of them. Probably running down their legs.

Oh, thieves were different. "Thievery will not be tolerated. Make that clear. Without *killing* anyone." A more flexible limit. If Dyrra had gotten her hands on a thief, no one would have complained if she ... accomplished her mandate with enthusiasm.

Still, she'd have left them alive. She was sure of it.

But no thieves tonight. Not even a decent fight to break up, just the occasional pair of muttonheads puffing themselves up and yowling at each other like cats.

And they always stank like beer sweat and the cheapest pisswater they could throw coins at. Even the ones Dyrra had to kick awake from their hidey holes next to stalls they didn't own, so they could take their coming hangovers elsewhere.

As though the quantity they could consume was far more important than the quality.

Completely useless evening.

Dyrra shouldn't have gone on duty tonight anyway. When Larek had mentioned needing a little time to gather things, she thought he'd need an hour. Two at most. They could have been on the road by dusk, as was proper for all good journeys.

But for all her years here in the east, Dyrra could never quite adjust to their strange fixation with the dawn. She had yet to hear about a sun god important enough for them to build their whole society around, and yet everywhere she went it was morning, morning, morning. Each new job expected her to report in the morning. All their events. All their celebrations. All obsessively commencing with the first rays of sunlight.

She could understand that they did not feel the call of Lucala, the Moon, as her people did, despite the way their skin mirrored Lucala's pallor. But the way they huddled indoors and carried fire everywhere they went, as though needing tokens of their precious sun to ward off the big, bad darkness.

An entire society unknowingly held in thrall by Lucala's Jealous Sister.

Or perhaps their eyes were simply inferior to proper Karwalish eyes.

And it wasn't Larek's fault anyway. It was Sindra's. Larek had mentioned needing time to gather possessions, and that made sense. He was a wizard, after all. He probably felt stark naked without a book in one hand and a potion in the other. He would probably show up in the morning carrying his bodyweight in apparatus.

And if he did, he had better be prepared to carry it himself.

But Sindra. Sindra needed the whole night. Sindra, who should not even be coming along on this journey.

Any warrior can be defeated, even humiliated. Any wizard can fall to a dragon's fire. But a failed Healer? Why not just give care of their nightly meals to a failed cook? Either way, they were likely to end up poisoned. Or worse.

But Larek seemed insistent on bringing her. Probably smitten by her pretty face and inviting form. All these eastern men seemed to like their women soft.

Not that Larek was to Dyrra's taste. Pudgy, and all brains. Not like Dyrra's Ommure. Now there was a man. Huge and strong and swift ... except when swiftness was a liability. If only he...

Dyrra stopped there in the center of jewelers' row, where the party raged around her despite the lack of nearby food or drink. She slammed her fist into her hand to bring her attention back to the here-and-now.

No good dwelling on Ommure. He was dead. And their child...

Dyrra slammed her fist into her palm again, hard enough to scare some muttonhead into stumbling to the dirt and scrabbling backwards while his "friends" laughed at even that.

She resumed her quick pace and her irritation with Sindra. Sindra, who wanted a "good night's sleep" before they started south. Sindra who thought she knew better than Dyrra about horses. Sindra, who would probably carry more than Larek, and slow them down with her tears when she had to slowly abandon possessions she could not bear to part with.

Dyrra finally reached the small canvas tent provided for her by the captain of the tourney guard. A muttonhead himself, who had emphasized over and over his *commission* in the *actual* city watch.

But proud and self-important as the captain might have been, perhaps muttonhead was too strong a term for him. He had, after all, done three things right. He had hired Dyrra. He had been smart enough to give her the evening shift without her needing to ask for it. And he had given her a respectable tent, instead of forcing her to make do with her own bedroll.

Dyrra threw back the undyed cotton flap and looked upon everything in the world that she owned and needed to carry. The sword of war that was her only token of Ommure — apart from the gold necklace she wore under her armor, wrapped around her left wrist. Its pendant was a three-quarter-moon symbol of Lucala, from the story of her journey into the underworld to save the greatest of us to serve as stars in the sky.

Stacked neatly beside her bedroll was the chain and leather armor that Dyrra had dyed deep green herself. That was her concession to life in the east. Everywhere she went, the trees were green, the plants were green, even the hills themselves were green.

She sometimes marveled that the flowers themselves did not grow green, and that the sky above had escaped the spreading color.

But if everything here was green, Dyrra decided that her armor might as well be too.

Beyond that, Dyrra had only some clothing, her pouch full of coins, and a scattering of things she had found handy on the road. With the armor on her back and the sword at her side, everything she owned fit comfortably in the rucksack she had also dyed green, with room to spare and little weight added to her shoulders.

Dyrra imagined her two companions, casting hopeful looks at her from beneath their own mounds of luggage. The thought made her smile.

And with that, Dyrra lay down and attempted to sleep. It would not be easy, as she had wakened only a few hours before her shift began, but she needed to acclimate again to the schedule of easterners and their obsession with the rising sun.

The last thing Dyrra did before she slept was peer up at the night sky, searching for the star that Lucala must have made from

Ommure. There, at the vertex of the Great Cross, in the middle of things, as always.

She blew the star a kiss, apologized again for her great failure, and closed her tent flap.

4

After Larek and Dyrra left the three oak bench tables to go see about their own preparations for the road, Sindra went back inside her parents' food tent, where the smell of good roasted chickens could make even her sated stomach growl.

Her father plucked dead chickens with sure, strong hands and her mother cut those chickens apart with the swift expertise of a thousand thousand repetitions.

"Been out there jawing long enough," said her father, though not as though he were angry. "Those rooters won't prep themselves."

Sindra heard the question in his tone, saw a glint of hope in his eyes, still so green and like her own, however much his once golden hair had grown storm cloud gray. And he stood a little shorter these days, his back bowed from his years of hard work, and his left ankle weak from the time it got twisted in a furrow when the plough horse spooked.

Her mother added a hum of agreement that edged closer to the irritation she pretended to. Her cutting and carving movements as quick and sure as the dancing steps Sindra remembered marveling over at celebrations, when she was a girl. Her mother seemed the epitome of beauty then, and even today Sindra made a game of noting how many customers' eyes followed her mother as they ordered.

Too many over the years had been distracted by the beauty of Sindra's mother and failed to recognize the skill and intelligence beneath the surface. It was she who had developed the feed combination that made their chickens grow both stronger and tastier than anyone else's. She who organized a militia to keep watch over the town market days.

"The rooters don't need as much roasting as the chickens anyway," said Sindra, picking up pails of carrots and potatoes her father had brought in for the dinner crowd and carrying them over to the scrub bucket. "And I wasn't just gossiping out there."

"We heard," said her mother, tone just shy of accusation. "Running away south with a couple of strangers."

"At least she's not whoring," said her father, but that was what he said about anyone who made life choices he didn't agree with. Sindra had heard him use the phrase three times in the past week, and twice about his best friend.

It did make Sindra wonder sometimes. She had heard her mother once refer to her father as though he had a sister, but he had never mentioned a sister around Sindra.

"Not whoring now," said her mother, tone edging ever closer to accusation, "but in Velstadt? What other work could she find? She claims she's no farmer. She's proven she's no Healer—"

Sindra dropped the carrot she had scrubbed halfway to her father's specifications. "Any more of that and these rooters can clean themselves."

Both parents stared at her, eyes wide. Sindra flushed, and looked down.

Their scrutiny continued. She reached for the carrot, then stopped herself.

Sindra raised her jaw and stared them both down.

"No. You two weren't there, and neither one of you ever asked me what happened. You don't get to wave my failings in my face."

"Who was here to take you back in and put a roof over your head?" said her mother.

"You were, and I will always be grateful. But that doesn't mean you get to marry me off to that wheelwright." Their eyebrows managed somehow to climb even higher. "That's right. I know."

"The boy has a gentle nature," said her father, "and he makes a good living. And we wouldn't say no to a few grandchildren..."

"And just how much higher is my dowry than it should be?" That got them to look away. Even Sindra's mother would not meet her eyes. "Tell me I'm wrong then. Tell me that the rumors don't follow me like the train on a lady's dress. Tell me that you didn't have to sell your wheelwright on my looks and beg him to forget my past? *And* offer him more of our livestock than you can afford to get him to take me."

"We want what's best for you," said her mother, and her father nodded agreement, though neither one could yet meet her eye. "And after—"

"I told you," Sindra said, but softer now. "You never asked what really happened, so don't you dare use the rumors against me." She picked up the dropped carrot, looked at it instead of her parents. "And I know that what you offer me is security."

Sindra drew a deep breath.

"But I need more than that. I need purpose. There's something more for me out there. Despite ... that day, I feel that Nilasah is not done with me yet. Or maybe it's not Nilasah's call I feel, but something else. Either way, I won't find it here in Aeralfast. But maybe down in Velstadt, I will."

"And if you don't?" said her mother, finally looking up at Sindra. "We won't be there to help you. We'll be all the way up here on the other side of those tall mountains."

"Not that we wouldn't welcome you back," said her father.

"In my short time as a Healer, I asked strangers to put their lives in my hands." Sindra looked up at her parents. "How can I ask any less of myself?"

And with that, Sindra turned back to the carrots and potatoes and began to scrub them clean. And as she cleaned, she planned out her packing, what she could take and what she would leave behind.

And she prayed to any gods who would listen to look after her parents while she was gone. And that she wasn't making an even bigger mistake than the one that for far too long had hidden on the lips and tongue of every person she spoke with.

5

BEFORE THE FIRST RAYS OF DAWN BEGAN TO CREST THE HIGHEST OF THE Seven Peaks, far to the east beyond the forest Vala — which was still recovering from the devastation of Blackflame's last rampage — the purple sky of near-dawn began to fade to a deep rose that many found cheerful.

Larek would have chosen another color for it, if he could have. Though the lingering night chill felt pleasant enough.

He stood far to the south of the tournament grounds themselves, at the very edge of the cheapest of the encampments. He wore his brown shirt with wooden toggles, and his darker brown pants, with a wide-brimmed floppy undyed cotton hat — what he though of as his walking clothes. He had chosen a spot to stand on a small rise, where he decided he would be most easily spotted by his companions.

And where he would stay upwind of the largely agreed upon midden, though the odor was still strong enough to sour Larek's recollection of his fresh chicken eggs and apples breakfast.

Chitter had already complained three times of the smell, and they had only just arrived. But any spot where he would find fresher air either might have concealed him from the eyes of Dyrra and Sindra, or was already occupied by several of the countless peasants sleeping without the benefit of a tent.

This far out, most of those here for the tournament slept where they could find a soft enough patch of high yellow grass. Or at least smooth dirt. Others had bedrolls of their own, but nothing more than they could tuck into a knapsack alongside whatever else they needed for such work as they could find here.

Many of them clustered around communal fire pits, all of which had been banked or extinguished for the night, providing no more light than the gray of the fading night sky.

And as the crowd around Larek rose, and complained, and glared (some at one another, but all of them, it seemed, at Larek), and stomped about before going off to begin their days, they made certain to take with them any possessions they ever wanted to see again.

The tourney guard would not venture this far out. Only so many were hired for the patrols, so they stayed where the money was: closer to the palace. Larek wondered whether the tournament organizers had meant to leave the poor to fend for themselves, or whether they simply had not expected the crowd for this tournament to swell to the size it had.

But then, if they had not expected it, they should have. While tournaments in the kingdom of Aeralfast could be found at least once a season, this tournament was special. Would-be heroes from all walks of life had come to the capitol to try their skills and prove to the world that they would be chosen among the six deemed worthy to hunt and slay the great dragon Blackflame.

And six would be chosen, though Larek wondered how the king had settled on six as the appropriate number of heroes. Was he really trusting to the histories? Was it as simple as counting the rubies on his golden crown? Or did the court wizard involve himself in some days' worth of deep meditations and divinations to determine the most cosmically fortuitous combination?

Larek could only guess, for he had never met the court wizard. Nor even seen him. But his reputation said that his spells were more than worthy of his post. If his divinations had chosen the number of heroes for the quest, the chances were strong that it was the right number for reasons Larek could not guess.

Either way, selecting those heroes by means of so extravagant a tournament meant that most the noble families in the kingdom had either come to the capitol in force or sent emissaries, depending on who was in favor and who wanted to make a statement by their absence.

Such an influx of powerful nobility meant that the most important of them were housed in the palace, while the next most important were housed by the rich and locally powerful citizens who lacked noble titles, yet were eager for the honor of hosting their social betters.

Larek thought of those locally powerful citizens as the aspiring nobles. Most of them either wanted titles themselves, or to find their way into positions of influence with those who held the titles.

The least important nobles and their retainers had to make do with the various inns within the walls of the capitol city, no doubt lamenting that they slept outside the walls of the palace itself, and the image their accommodations presented to others.

Once outside the city grounds, the quality and proximity of one's sleeping arrangements to the tournament field varied directly with one's wealth and "importance." Guilds first, with their great pavilions, and the mercenary army they called their guards.

Then came the independent merchants — some with pavilions, but most with tents — who had shops and warehouses and more back where they came from, but who lacked the political connections to enter a guild.

After the merchants came those who had the means to maintain tents and stalls to hawk the wares and crafts they would normally bring to their own town centers on market day. Those who ran the little businesses that catered to the multitudes of others who slept under the sky and who had come hoping to find work, or luck, or destiny, or even just a sight to tell their children of someday.

Dawn finally found its way over the high peak of the Giant —

tallest of the Seven Peaks — and golden sunshine began to brighten the day.

"It's a wonder they don't all get sick, living this way," said Sindra, coming up to Larek from his left and looking over the poorest of the tournament crowd. She shook her head. She wore a yellow kirtle again, but Larek noticed this one had no trace of the embroidery above her heart. She carried a travel knapsack even larger than Larek's, and a pot and a frying pan dangled from it.

"Perhaps they're used to it," Larek said, while from his shoulder, Chitter looked her over.

"Nilasah teaches us that they should not have to get used to it." She closed her eyes for a breath, then said, "If I were still of Her order, I would try to organize them. If they worked together, they could have more livable conditions while they're here."

Unspoken and hanging in the air, Larek heard that if she were still of Nilasah's order, she would not be traveling south.

"You're telling me," said Chitter, "this beauty will be traveling south with you and you won't even *consider* asking her to share your bedroll? What's wrong with you?"

"Stop it," said Larek, and the same moment Sindra noticed the squirrel on Larek's shoulder and said, "Oh!"

She smiled brightly and looked closer. Chitter waved, but instead of waving back she stood straighter, a puzzled look coming over her face.

"Did it just ... wave at me?"

"Yes, *he* did," said Larek, not to chide her but to correct her. "This is Charespecusis, but he answers to Chitter."

Chitter bowed, one paw on his stomach and the other up touching the tip of his bushy tail.

"Well, hello, Chitter. And you are a handsome squirrel, if I may say so."

"Thank you," said Chitter, "and if *I* may say so, you are gorgeous. And if you have the brains to match your beauty—"

Larek cleared his throat.

"Was he ... speaking?"

"Yes. He thanked you, and he said that he thinks you are very pretty."

"That's not what I said."

Sindra had that look — lips pulled in and eyebrows slightly lowered — that told Larek questions would follow, so he decided to answer them first.

"Charespecusis isn't actually a squirrel. He's an earth spirit in the shape of a flying squirrel. And before you ask, he is not some sort of bound faerie or demon-granted slave. He's my friend."

Sindra tilted her head, considering. "Then why are you scratching him behind the ears?"

"Because he likes it," said Larek, with a shrug.

That got an approving nod from Sindra, but she quickly narrowed her eyes and said, "Speaking of friends..."

Larek looked where she pointed and saw Dyrra, eyes half-closed, hair unbound and savage, wearing full green armor with a huge sword at her belt, but dragging a pack on the ground behind her.

Neither Larek nor Sindra spoke as she plodded her way up their slight rise until she stood before them. Dyrra then yawned louder than the coughing roar of a forest cat, slung her pack on her shoulders, and said, "I'm here. Let's go already."

Larek devoutly hoped Chitter stopped laughing before Dyrra decided she needed more breakfast.

South of the capitol of the kingdom of Aeralfast ran a road that would take the three travelers all the way across the mountains and into Velstadt, though where it would run from there they could only guess. They did assume that the road would eventually reach Velstadt's capitol, but what it was called, and how much further they would have to travel once they cleared the mountain border, these things not one of them knew.

But around that table the day before they had all three agreed that they had plenty of time to find out.

In the meantime, they had a long, wide road ahead of them of smooth, packed dirt and clay. This close to the capitol it was maintained often, to avoid runnels forming from the many carts and wagons that traveled up and down it.

Farms to both sides all day as they walked, great expanses on either side of wheat, and corn, and barley and more, with occasion groves of fruit trees for variety, much to the delight of the songbirds.

But bird songs were not the only sounds, nor did the grains and trees alone dominate the air with their scents. Broad fields of cattle and pigs, sheep and goats and more provided variety to both, watched over by farmhands who glared at Larek, Dyrra and Sindra as though they had been the ones to keep those farmhands on duty and not off reveling at the tournament.

Larek mused that at least it was a different sort of disrespect than he usually got, though he could not decide if that should have made it better or worse.

He considered discussing the issue with Chitter, but would have had to speak in Aarkadian to avoid irritating his traveling companions with the subject. And he doubted that conversing in a language they did not understand with an earth spirit they did not know well enough to understand would improve the situation.

Especially given Dyrra's ... current disposition.

Dyrra seemed disinclined to talk at all. Larek had hoped that traveling would improve the foul mood she had arrived with at dawn, but as the sun rose higher in what looked to be a cloudless late spring sky he saw no signs of improvement.

And she certainly could not have an issue with the weather. The chill air of dawn had burned away, but slowly enough to promise a pleasantly warm day. Not cool, but not hot enough to tug at Larek's scars. Certainly the kind of day he preferred, and Sindra's light step and mood seemed to agree.

As the rising sun and the open road lifted their spirits, Larek and Sindra both attempted sallies to drag Dyrra out of her sullen silence.

Both had been rebuffed by impatient, half-closed eyes that

suggested they should consider it enough that she was both present and walking under her own power.

Larek was dying to ask if it were the sunrise/sunset issue and her Karwalish upbringing, or perhaps that the day was not hot enough for her liking, but he dreaded that she might call him a muttonhead and admit that she'd been up too late carousing.

Larek did not consider that possibility likely, given that she was as close to an outcast as he was, but this would not have been the time to be proven wrong.

Nor did Dyrra show much tolerance for the conversation of others. No sooner had Sindra had asked about Larek's parents than Dyrra stopped them both right there in the middle of the road, and said, "No."

Larek and Sindra had stared at each other for a moment while Chitter chuckled.

"No what?" asked Sindra.

"No chatter. No questions. Talk later. Walk now." And then Dyrra turned and started that plodding pace that seemed slower than it had to be, for someone with such long legs.

Sindra gave Larek a puzzled look. Larek shrugged. They turned to follow along beside her.

Chitter chuckled again, and when Larek tried to hush him, the squirrel said, "She doesn't want you two flirting. Doesn't want to risk the inevitable consequences."

"Enough," mumbled Larek.

"You two should invite her to join in. Sure, she's big, but—"

"Stop that thing from nattering on," said Dyrra, "or squirrel or spirit I'll feast on it for an early lunch."

Larek turned to attempt just that, but Chitter held up his paws in surrender and mimed tying his lips shut.

Larek smiled, despite himself.

***

LATER INTO THE AFTERNOON, LAREK'S OWN MOOD DARKENED. THE SUN had decided that the afternoon was the perfect time to heat up, and his many scars didn't like it. His floppy hat kept them from the worst of the direct sunshine, but he could not cover them entirely. Not even close. His hands, arms, chest, throat, and all of his face below the eyebrows were mottled in varying shades of red, from deep and dark to bright and shiny. And when the day grew warmer, as it did that day, then every dragonburnt inch let him know of its displeasure.

Worse, his legs and lower back reminded Larek that a great many months had passed since he had walked anywhere more than a day distant, and that a quarter to half-day's foot travel had more than met his needs for the past season.

Soreness and aches through much of his body. Even his feet got around to lodging a few complaints of their own.

Chitter would at least be able to ease these issues once the trio decided they were done walking for the day. But that knowledge did Larek little good when each step irritated him.

And then there was his sweating. Much as he would like to have blamed the dampness infesting his brown shirt and darker brown pants on the heat of the afternoon sun, he knew better. His faster breathing, and the increasing frequency of his wiping his forehead had helped. The latter might have even meant less sweat-staining in his hat, but he would not know without looking.

Not that the stains would last. Larek had a simple spell for them as well. Just a little something to maintain a good, wizardly appearance. But in his current frame of mind, the sweat stains represented just another irritation of the road.

At this rate, he feared that the journey south would seem endless.

All in all, he began to think that Sindra had been right about them needing horses.

Or perhaps, only Larek needed a horse. If Sindra were having any of Larek's problems with the road so far, he could not tell. Her yellow kirtle showed no signs of staining, and her steps looked just as light and effortless as they had at dawn. Her own forehead had developed a sheen of perspiration, but in her case that might have been from the heat.

At least, as the afternoon came on, Dyrra seemed to finally awaken. Her back straightened. Her steps lightened. She bound her hair back with that long leather thong that ended in a small blade. She even looked about from time to time. Oh, she had no interest in conversation — either having it or hearing it — but at least she appeared to be finished with her day's grousing.

Dyrra even smiled at her first drink from Larek's everfull water jug, as amazed as Sindra had been by both its cleverness and the wonderful taste of the water.

If anything, their nonstop walking seemed to have invigorated Dyrra.

And so it went as they passed more farms, neared and parted from a small river, and adapted to slight rolls and curves the land added to the road. The road's condition had yet to waver from its perfect maintenance, but Larek could gauge some of their progress by the changing farms on either side of them as they went. He had figured out early on that the farms could be told apart by the differences in fencing. Pine rail fences for some, oak slat fences for others.

Toward the end of their day's walk, the trio had a huge cattle range fenced in by pine rails on the left and right. So far as Larek had been able to tell, either the neighbors had the same sensibilities and trusted to the road to mark their border, or a single immense farm stretched out on both sides of them. He had spotted no markers on the fences to designate any difference between the two.

It was between these fences, at a spot where the grass grew lush on either side of them and sloped down from the road, that Dyrra stopped walking. She looked at the setting sun, then looked at her companions, and broke the long silence.

"I imagine you two aren't as comfortable walking at night."

Larek all but bit his tongue to avoid blurting out, "Yes! By all the gods above and below let's stop for the day! My legs are ready to fall off!"

In his silence, Sindra said, "Nilasah teaches us that every ray of sunshine is a blessing. To travel at night is to travel unblessed."

Dyrra's mouth drew to the side. She blew out a breath as though swallowing her first words, then said, "By night Lucala the Moon shines her love down upon us all. We will have plenty of blessings if we continue."

"Or," said Larek, trying to keep desperation out of his voice, "we could have dinner and rest because some of us are sore and exhausted and would dearly love to eat."

Chitter started to say something to that, but cut himself off when Dyrra started laughing, a loud, echoing sound that Larek would have sworn could have reached the Seven Peaks from where they stood.

Surprise widened Sindra's eyes and dropped her jaw. Larek was lost for words.

"We have many days to walk ahead of us, wizard." She clapped Larek on the shoulder hard enough to stagger him a step. "Speak up when you need a rest. So far as I know, we race only the snows of winter, and we have a considerable lead on them."

"Where are you sore?" said Sindra. "Do you need my help? Some liniment perhaps?"

"Chitter can take care of it for me," said Larek with a dismissive wave. Chitter smacked himself in the forehead and mumbled something about foolish wizards. Larek, speaking louder, continued, "In fact, if either of you have aches, he can help you too."

Dyrra laughed again, but Sindra thanked Chitter as she declined.

"Still plenty of farms about us," said Sindra. "Shall we ask if any of them will put us up for the night?"

"No!" said Larek and Dyrra together.

Sindra blinked in puzzlement, so Larek explained.

"In case you hadn't noticed, Dyrra and I do not blend in among a normal crowd. One look at either of us, and if you've heard our songs or stories you know exactly whom you're dealing with. I've gone a whole day now in the company of others without hearing a single insulting word. It's a luxury I'm rather enjoying."

Dyrra nodded agreement.

"Well, fine," said Sindra. "I suppose we can sleep out here along the road. But will you let me at least buy food from the locals? I'd rather not deplete our packs faster than we have to, and it isn't as though we could hunt any game out here."

That, Dyrra and Larek could agree with, and as Sindra wandered off Dyrra began telling Larek how the only advantage to the eastern insistence of traveling by day was that when they stopped for the evening, she would have time to hunt up dinner for them.

Once they reached the outlying areas, of course, and were sure they weren't poaching on some noble's private reserve.

As she continued into a story about the tricks of hunting rabbits without a bow in the scrub lands to the north, Larek gratefully eased himself supine against a pine rail post. Chitter began walking down Larek's torso, and each small step spread comforting warmth that eased and soothed sore muscles. By the time he reach the soles of Larek's feet, the wizard felt comfortably tired instead of exhausted and on the brink of collapse.

Dyrra broke off from her where she had gotten into the differences between hunting in the east versus the west and said, "Truth. I was unsure you were hard enough for so long a walk as this. Softness covers you all over."

"The hike will do me good," said Larek, resting back with his eyes closed.

"Truth from you now," said Dyrra. She waited until Larek opened his eyes and looked at her in the graying twilight. "Do you desire Sindra?"

Larek stared, considering what Dyrra might have meant by that question. Not directly — her meaning was clear enough — but why the question mattered to her. And it did matter. There was something intent in her eyes. Not romantic — though it had been so long since he had seen a romantic look he might not have recognized one — but assessing.

Larek's answer to this question would change how Dyrra thought about him. Would he give her the truth she asked for or a lie? Would he hide behind a single syllable or lay the truth bare before a woman he hardly knew?

Even Chitter stared at him, head tilted and waiting.

"No," Larek said with so slight a shake of his head it might not have been visible in the growing twilight. "I won't deny she has the kind of beauty that drives men to write songs. And despite what some say, the dragon did not leave me ... incapable." Larek looked down at the burns covering his hands. "But between my scars and my guilt ... I have not entertained such thoughts about any woman in a long, long time."

Dyrra nodded, then looked up toward the moon, which had only just crested the horizon.

"I have not even looked at men since my Ommure died. That would not please him, but..." She looked back at Larek. "If you find yourself 'entertaining such thoughts' about Sindra on our journey, do not hide it from me. Perhaps she'd share your bedroll and perhaps she wouldn't. I don't object either way. But loyalty and desire have many facets and demands. Best if we all know where we stand."

Larek and Dyrra both looked away then. He did not know where her thoughts went. Perhaps to her Ommure. But for his part, he could not imagine any woman desiring a body as mottled as his, or a man who let so many die.

Chitter strode back up Larek's torso until the tiny earth spirit could look him in the eye. In the softest tones Larek had ever heard him use, he said, "I like her. You need more people like her around."

6

Sindra was glad that neither Dyrra nor Larek had offered to
come with her to get them food. Let Larek have his rest and Dyrra her
silence. Neither one of them understood farms or farmers anyway.
They wouldn't have known what to say.

Not that she blamed them for that. Larek, no doubt, had spent his
life studying magic, not plants and animals, and Dyrra? Not only had
Dyrra grown up in the deserts, but with her green armor and her
huge sword — to say nothing of her *own* size — she would have had
the farmers thinking of their defenses, not what food they could
spare.

While Sindra herself knew she was no farmer — she had told her
parents the truth about that — her calling did not change her
upbringing.

For example, she knew that she and her companions had stopped
between fields belonging to the same family. Cattle on the west side
and sheep and grains on the east, to please Halstaffur the Green Lord.
No markings on the pine rail fence, which meant that the land
belonged to a noble, not a merchant. The nobles had all owned their
land so long they had their own ways of designating their territories,

while the merchants who had expanded into farm ownership all kept their lands clearly marked.

A noble family meant that the main house would be somewhere north in the property, closer to the capitol, and on the west side, closer to the river.

That meant that Sindra left the road to the east when she went looking for food. The nobles might not help common travelers, but the folks working their farm would. And if the nobles lived on the west side, then Sindra would find some small houses for the working folk on the east side, just past the fields of grains. Out of casual sight of the nobles, which worked better for both sides of the arrangement.

An evening breeze rustled the growing wheat around her as she walked. The wheat stood tall — some of it taller than she was — and was starting to head. That was Sindra's favorite time to walk along a wheat field. The breeze might have been cool, but the smell it carried was warm, earthy. It made her crave the taste of fresh baked bread.

Past the second field she saw lights from a row of four houses, heard the call-and-response shouts organizing the end of a work day. Sindra stopped walking where she was.

"Hello, the farm!" she shouted.

She waited, but heard no break in the end-of-day activities. As she waited for the shouts to die down, she could see the moon begin to rise from the north, above where the castle would be, if she could still see it in the dying light.

She turned back to where she could just make out movement near the houses. She tried again.

"Hello, the farm!"

She held her breath, waiting. Wondering if she should come closer. Wondering if she misread the situation. Though she had grown up on her parents' farm and seen farms like this through most of her childhood, from the time she had first bled she dedicated herself to Nilasah and taken up the path of the Healer.

Would they welcome her as Sindra remembered her own family greeting travelers when she was just a girl? Or were the old ways dying, as some of her parents' elder customers had lamented during the tournament?

"Who calls?" came a response at last. A high, unsure voice. A boy, who sounded on the verge of becoming a man.

"A traveler from the road, seeking food for three."

"Why—" started the boy, ready for the old give-and-take, the way it always went in the old stories. But another voice interrupted him, a mature woman's voice, older than Sindra. "No time for that. Come on then, or you won't make it back to your companions by full dark."

Sindra sighed. While the older woman had a point, she would have relished actually going through the formal words of travelers in the old stories. She trotted forward and found herself facing a woman her mother's age, with a severe face and straight, graying black hair. The boy stood beside her. Tall already, and skinny as a wheat stalk, with a chagrined look.

Sindra expected the woman to lead her to a house straight away, but the woman stood firm.

"Left it to the last moment, didn't you?"

"First day out together." Sindra smiled. "Weren't sure how far we could get. Plus one of us is Karwalish. Might have kept us walking all night if we hadn't stopped her."

The woman didn't budge. "Leaving the tournament in a big hurry, are you?"

Sindra looked as deeply into the woman's eyes as she could in the growing darkness.

"Nothing there for us anymore."

At that, the woman nodded. "Three, you said?" Sindra nodded. "And you can pay, or do you need the Green Lord's bounty?"

Sindra relaxed, for the first time since the woman took that challenging tone. If farmers were still offering the Green Lord's bounty to travelers, they should be able to find food all the way to the mountains, even if Dyrra proved to overstate her hunting skills.

"We can pay," she said, "but may the Green Lord smile on you for keeping the old ways."

The woman smiled, then said to the boy in a softer tone, "Eggs and cheese for them, and bread, and if there's any of last night's corn left, throw it in. And a bottle of Aric's latest."

The boy turned and ran off to fetch the food.

"Thank you," said Sindra, offering four iron stalls from her purse.

The woman took the coins, then pursed her lips and gave half of them back to Sindra. "If you're heading south, you'll need these more than we will."

7

Dyrra watched the moon rise in silence, listening to the slow, steady breaths of Larek. Fallen asleep already, and Sindra not even back with dinner yet. Wouldn't be much good for a shift standing watch, but she supposed that the roads were safe enough for another day or two yet.

Just as well that he was asleep anyway. Wizards lived by their questions, and Dyrra wasn't ready to answer any about what she was about to do.

That squirrel of his was awake enough though. It sat atop a post in the pine rail fence and watched her. Disturbing, to see a squirrel with such focus. Yes, Larek said it was a spirit in the shape of a squirrel, but that might have been a lie to make his pet sound more impressive.

The way it watched her, though, Dyrra began to believe it was what he said it was. Though why he called it an earth spirit instead of a nature spirit, she could not have guessed.

She let one hand drop to the hilt of her sword of war as she looked at the squirrel.

"Not one word to your master about this now. He'll see it soon enough — or something like it anyway — and he can pester me with his questions then. But for now, you hold that little tongue or I'll cut it out."

The squirrel chittered and waved its hands back and forth. Dyrra took that to mean it wouldn't say a word. She nodded.

She turned to face the rising moon and drew her sword. She held it up to the moon, point down, then lowered it to touch the guard to her forehead without ever taking her eyes from the sliver of the crescent, waxing moon.

"Great Lucala," Dyrra whispered, "Mother of all who walk by night, it is your eye that watches over us. Your blessings are our bounty, and Your smile lights our way where the eyes of others cannot follow. It is in Your honor that I dance, and I ask that You bless me and my companions on our journey even though I travel with those who were not blessed to be born beneath Your smile, and who will make me tread beneath the unforgiving rays of Your Jealous Sister."

Dyrra tossed her sword, twirling, into the air. She spun in a tight circle, then jumped, still spinning. In mid-air she caught the sword by the pommel and whirled it about her.

She landed, dropping to one knee in the lush grass, facing the moon. She pressed the tip of her sword into the earth before her then, without turning, swung it over her head to do the same behind her.

Dyrra released the handle with her left hand, spun the sword in the air with her right, then pressed the tip into the ground on her left, switched hands, and repeated the movement, poking the sword into the ground on her right.

Dyrra brought the handle to her lips, blade once more point down, and kissed the handle again, then flipped the sword point up and kissed the handle one more time.

She sprang to her feet and carved the sixteen shapes of the moon into the air above her, pausing between each shape for the twisting, rhythmic steps, spin, and leap her people used to celebrate that shape.

When she finished the last shape, she shoved her sword of war back into her scabbard with a solid click and cried out the salutation of the crescent waxing moon, "*Zugath!*"

"*Zugath?*" said Larek waking up. His words were groggy, but clear enough as he sat up. "*Nik talava djai zugath?*"

"The old language is dead," said Dyrra. "I'll thank you not to speak it."

"But—"

"The old words are not yours for the taking. We keep them only in praise of Lucala."

"I didn't mean any offense."

Dyrra shrugged. "Offense doesn't come from ignorance. It comes from ignoring a fair and proper request."

"I won't speak that language around you again. In fact, I'll try to avoid Karwalish at all. My grasp of the modern form is ... rudimentary at best."

"Good enough," she said, digging into her pack for a flint stone. "Speaking of offense." She lifted her flint and looked at him in the rising gray. Poor easterner probably couldn't even see her beyond a vague shadow. Might not even realize what she had in her hand. "Got some flint, but I didn't want to set a fire without checking with you first."

The squirrel chittered something, and Larek chuckled. "Be a hard way to live, without fire."

"You're a wizard. Figured you might have an alternative."

"Haven't found one yet," he admitted, and Dyrra heard truth in his words. He had looked.

Dyrra raided the shrubs and bushes on the other side of the fence for enough twigs and branches to make a small fire, but set it near the road, as far as she could comfortably set it from Larek.

"Was that a blessing dance?" he asked, once she got the fire going.

"Tell that squirrel of yours he's the appetizer while we wait for Sindra."

"He didn't tell me," said Larek, over the anxious chattering of his little earth spirit. "It was your cry of ... that word. I've read about it."

Dyrra smiled that he didn't say *zugath*. She crouched beside the fire and warmed her hands. "There are many blessing dances. That was the dance to begin a new journey."

"Good people here," said Sindra, slipping between rails of the fence without pausing in her approach. "They gave us enough food for dinner and breakfast, and look at this!" She held up a green, unlabeled bottle. "Mead!"

Now that was the best thing Dyrra had heard all day.

8

———

After dinner, they passed around the bottle of good, strong mead. Dyrra drank the best share, but that was fine with Larek. He had no interested in getting drunk, and he wanted the other two feeling relaxed and happy when he brought up the subject none of them would want to discuss, but they all had to.

He waited until all three of them seemed comfortable in their own spots on the lush, fresh-smelling grass, their bellies pleasantly full of eggs and cheese and bread.

And then, when speculations about the road ahead and what they might find in Velstadt died down, Larek said, "There is a serious matter we must discuss."

Dyrra gave him a suspicious look, while Sindra looked only puzzled. He wondered where their thoughts had run that they failed to see what the obvious subject was.

"Dyrra mentioned to me earlier that travelers must have clarity among them. That—"

"Not quite what I said."

"Then it was close enough, and a point that stands. Right now, each of us knows only the rumors, stories and songs about the other two. But if we are to trust each other, we must have the truth."

"No," said Dyrra, lying down, her head on her pack.

"That is a topic for another time," said Sindra, taking a long pull off of the mead bottle before handing it back to Dyrra without offering it to Larek.

"Maybe," said Chitter, "you should hold off on this one…"

"No," said Larek to Chitter. To the others he said, "A journey is a time of new beginnings. Let us—"

"No," said Dyrra again.

"I like you both well enough," said Sindra, "for two people I've known about a day." She looked off into the distance. "But I don't know you *that* well."

"Exactly," said Dyrra, still flat on her back and shaking the bottle to dribble the last drops of mead into her mouth. "Talk to me again when I can call you friend, and not just companion."

"Very well," said Larek, standing up.

"This is a bad idea," said Chitter.

Larek waited until both women were looking at him, then said, "Then I will tell you my story, because we will be traveling far together, and I want you to know the sort of man you have walking beside you."

And with that, Larek told them the tale, beginning with the end of his apprenticeship, the journey that led him past those farms when Blackflame decided to attack there instead of fighting the regiment of knights and wizards sent by the king. He told of Inga, and Taran, and their decision to fight the dragon rather than see it destroy the farms and eat the livestock.

And he told of his failure, and his burning, and the death that surrounded him for miles in every direction.

The crickets and bats seemed to still their cries and chirps as he spoke.

And when he finished, he stood there in the silence for a moment. Tears ran down Larek's face on cheeks that could never flush to show the pain and humiliation he felt. He concluded, "So in a way, all the stories about me are true. Two hundred forty-seven dead, and all because my nerve broke when I needed it most."

Neither woman spoke.

"And even now, my fear haunts me. I told you I'm going to Velstadt to flee the endless taunts and jibes. And it's true. It's a factor. But that's not the whole truth.

"I'm fleeing to Velstadt because that damned dragon is back. I want to put mountains and miles between me and it."

Larek slumped back down onto the grass, which felt significantly less comfortable than it had even a few minutes before.

"And even then, I know I'll watch the skies for the rest of my life, spending my days in dread that I will again see that winged shape. That widening mouth. That fire, blacker than the pits of the Underworld itself."

Larek wept quietly in his shame. Chitter trotted onto his chest and nuzzled his chin, but even that could do little to ease his pain.

"My story," said Sindra in a quiet voice, "isn't quite so elaborate. I had been a full Healer of Nilasah for eight months, after spending half my life in study and training. I loved my work. I loved my calling. Tending the sick and wounded. I could think of no better life.

"There was a squabble between those eastern barons, the ones whose lands touch the Seven Peaks. Gold, I think, had been discovered close to a border, and one thing led to another, and soon their people were killing each other.

"The first time I was working alone. Eight or nine of us had come in answer to the call for succor, but there were so many wounded we each set up our own tents and ran our own treatments.

"Dozens, scores, perhaps hundreds of soldiers came through my tent. More than I ever treated before. And they came so fast. In the time it took me to set a limb or apply a poultice a half-dozen more patients showed up.

"My hands kept up the pace. I ground all the right powders and oils and liniments. I applied the right cures to every wound.

"But I lost my focus. The wounded and dying just kept coming." Sindra's voice took on a haunted quality that Larek knew all too well. "I applied all the cures, but my prayers..."

Her voice broke, and only the crickets kept the silence from growing oppressive before she continued, voice unsteady.

"My prayers grew rushed. Became just words. Then by the end, I barely said them at all.

"On their own, the herbs and poultices help, but without the blessing of Nisalah, they're just plants. Soldiers on the brink of death? Dead. Soldiers who might have recovered? Dead. Wounds festered. Invited in sickness.

"It was as though I did the work of Kulath, The Pestilence. Dozens dead who should have lived. Scores of men and women maimed for life, when they should have recovered. All by my hand. All because of my panic."

She lapsed into silence then, and Larek could see tears trickling down her face, as they had down his before she spoke.

Dyrra inhaled loudly, then said "We need sleep if you early risers intend to get me up at dawn. Still many miles to go before we reach Velstadt."

Larek and Sindra glanced at each other from where they lay, but neither could find the nerve to press Dyrra for her story. Not with their own failures so fresh in their minds. And so the three of them lay back and tried to let sleep take them.

And in the near-silence of his own breathing, Larek thought he heard Dyrra mutter a prayer to her moon goddess.

9
———

THAT NEXT MORNING THEY ESTABLISHED A PATTERN THAT THEY expected would continue for several days, if not all the way to the southern border. Sindra awoke first, and put breakfast together from what remained of the previous night's dinner. Larek arose not much later, wakened by Chitter, who helped him reassemble the packs for the day's travel.

Either Sindra had changed yellow kirtles before Larek awakened, or Nilasah had shown her some method of reducing travel grit, because her clothes looked as fresh as his own brown tunic, darker brown pants, and undyed cotton floppy travel hat. And Larek had freshened his own clothes and person with magic. His old master had insisted that Larek perfect the spells of cleanliness early on in his apprenticeship.

Larek had been told that part of a wizard's mystique was to seem unaffected by effort and the elements. But Larek suspected that his master simply did not want a smelly apprentice sleeping under his roof or greeting his petitioners.

The other two may have been working, but Dyrra refused to open her eyes until the last possible moment, which included the first hundred or so steps down the road. She slept in her armor, and tying on her sword belt seemed to be reflex, so as far as Larek could tell, she would be ready if a fight came.

But he was not at all certain she would be able to see if it did. In her walking sleep state, her hair remained a wild mass of black wool. And the long leather thong he had seen her use to tie it back? That dangled from her fingers, its blade ready to whip at any onrushing foes.

Or perhaps at any talkative wizards? Larek decided against finding out.

Once Dyrra finally started blinking against the harsh morning light, she accepted her share of breakfast from Sindra, and speculated loudly that perhaps she ought to have a larger share of the food, given that she was bigger and heavier than Sindra would ever be or Larek *should* ever be.

But there was no real force behind the complaint, so Larek and Sindra wrote it off to the price of making the huge warrior woman travel by day. And apart from their own dark morning cloud, the day promised to be pleasant. The bright sun in its cloudless royal blue sky brought a gentle heat to the morning — too mild for even Larek to complain — the road remained smooth and well-tended underfoot. And the horizon promised rolling hills that meant an end to farms and a change of view.

By the sun's apex, Sindra had purchased their dinner early from the last of the farms near the road. This one specialized in peas, but also raised chickens and pigs in large quantities. Thoughts of the dinner ahead of her seemed to help revive Dyrra, and soon her hair was tied back in its deadly whip, and her step had lightened from its morning tromp.

Conversation was still not an option, but on the whole Larek considered the situation an improvement. The rolling hills ahead of them thrilled him less. Sindra had hinted that any change to the environment was a sign of progress and a treat for the eyes.

But it wasn't his eyes Larek was worried about. It was his legs.

Chitter's soothing magic, applied at the end of each day's travel, would help him recover endurance and strength more quickly than he would otherwise, without nearly so much suffering. But the fact remained that rebuilding muscle was a slow, sweaty, uncomfortable process. And the mere prospect of going up and down those hills brought warning twitches from his shins and calves.

Still, Sindra had a point about the positive aspects of the changing environment. The hills ahead promised shade from oak and alder trees, growing in copses and groves, as well as points with long, unobstructed views of where they had been and where they were going.

And the smells! As the trio left behind the last farm and began passing wild meadows of green and gold grasses on either side, Larek's nose thrilled to be free of the manure smell that had become the undercurrent of their travel without his even realizing it. Instead the wild grass smelled sweet enough that he plucked a long blade and sucked on the tip as they walked.

When they reached the bottom of that first hill in the mid-afternoon, Dyrra held up one hand and said, "Hold."

Her eyes narrowed as she inspected their surroundings, but Larek could not guess what she saw that he did not. The grass was just grass, rustling and waving in the same cool breeze that gently tickled his face, not even strong enough to move the wide brim of his hat.

The pile of stones off to their left was a cairn. Four sides sloping to a single point, nearly as tall as Dyrra, meaning four buried beneath it. A white rock at the top, meaning warriors dead in service to the king. Looked as though marks had been left along the bottom row, if she wanted more information than that, but she stared instead as though wondering if another cairn were set behind it.

On their right, some berry bushes among the grass, but out of season. The greenish-red gemberries would not be fit for eating until late summer when they resembled rubies. Everyone knew when and when not to eat gemberries, but Dyrra stared with such intensity, Larek wondered if she were trying to ripen them by desire alone.

And then she looked up at the road ahead, and the copse of alders halfway up, growing high and straight with their bark as white as bone. More trees awaited at the hilltop, but she stared at that one copse, and spoke without moving her eyes, or even blinking that Larek could see.

"Here we leave the road," she said.

"What?" said Larek.

"But the road is still smooth," complained Sindra.

"I smell an ambush." Dyrra shook her head. "Not sure exactly where, but it's up there. So we need to be elsewhere."

"Something is definitely upsetting the animals among those alders," said Chitter.

"If an ambush is waiting," said Larek, "then they can see us already, yes?"

Dyrra nodded, eyes still fixed on that copse.

"Then aren't they already worried at the way we've stopped and you've stared with such suspicion? Won't they attack the moment they see us leave the road?"

"Yes."

Larek gave her a moment to elaborate, but Dyrra seemed to consider her answer sufficient.

Sindra tried her luck. "So why invite the attack?"

"The attack will come either way." Dyrra drew her sword of war, both hands on the pommel. "Doesn't mean we should let them pick the battleground."

———

Dyrra turned ran toward the cairn, crouched low, but her long legs moving swiftly. Her sword held in both hands, but its blade over her shoulder along the strap of her rucksack like a fishing pole. Her heavy boots hushed through the thick grass.

She was ten strides out before Larek pushed his legs to follow, but though Dyrra's responded as though fresh, Larek's legs already burned from more than half a day's hike. His pack felt as though it doubled in weight, and his feet seemed to stick in the grass like mud with each step. A fresh round of sweat broke out all over his body.

Sindra overtook him quickly, her strides lithe and rapid.

Dyrra and Sindra were already waiting for Larek at the cairn when a frustrated cry came from the copse of alders halfway up the hill. Larek declined to look at his oncoming death and instead pressed for more speed.

"A dozen," said Chitter, from his shoulder. "Spears and swords and bows."

"Slow them down," panted Larek.

Chitter nodded and bobbed his tail.

From behind him Larek could hear swearing and crashing and tumbling and knew what Chitter had done. He had grabbed their ankles with the grass. Not a strong grip, not when the earth spirit had to act fast and at such distance, but enough.

"Two out, six more down and sorting themselves," said Chitter as Larek arrived at the cairn and leaned forward, hands on his knees and breath gusting in and out. "Four still coming. Two spears, a bow, and a swordsman."

"Well done," said Dyrra, turning back to fight. "Four, I can handle, but I'd not say no to more help."

Larek's exhaustion might have been tricking him, but did she say that before looking up at the unrushing foes? Did she understand Chitter?

Sindra pulled a small bundle out of her pack, wrapped in a square of oil-stained, soft cotton. She pulled out one of several long needles by its bulbous end, and Larek noted that the points of the needles were darkened and dripping.

Larek turned to see how he could contribute. The ambushers all looked like Aeralfasti mercenaries to him: big, bearded and mean. Which meant keeping their numbers down was the first order of business. "Keep ... those six..."

"Understood," said Chitter, and the apparent flying squirrel dove straight into the dry earth at Larek's feet without raising so much as a cloud of dust.

"KEENARACH!" screamed Dyrra, running to meet the charge of the remaining four, sword of war whirling twin circles before her. She met one of the spearmen first, splitting his weapon at the haft then driving her shoulder into his jaw with all of her momentum. Larek could hear teeth breaking from the impact.

The bowman stopped running and knocked an arrow, raising his aim not at Dyrra, but at Larek. Sindra's wrist flicked, and a needle sank into his cheek. His eyes rolled back and he fell to the ground, limp.

In the background Larek could see the wild grass stretch and twist, wrapping tight around the six downed ambushers.

The swordsman and other spearman moved to flank Dyrra.

"Drop the sword, Dyrra," said the swordsman. "You're outnumbered."

Dyrra spun, swirling her sword to knock both menacing sword and spear out of line, whipping her head as she went. The blade tied at the end of her hair slashed the swordsman across the face, drawing blood.

That same moment, one of Sindra's needles caught the spearman on the hand, collapsing him to the ground.

"Count again," said Dyrra, her threatening smile made ghastly by her long, white scar.

"Perhaps *you* should count again," called a voice.

Larek, much of his breath recovered, saw another dozen mercenaries approaching, but not quite the same crowd. Ten of them held crossbows with blunted hammer-bolts. The eleventh was a man in a yellow kirtle that matched Sindra's, but unlike hers, his still had the soothing hand insignia of Nilasah over his heart. A Healer, pale as his hair and almost as thin.

And then there was the speaker. He wore a fine red tunic with the buttons of a noble over pants that looked softer than anything Larek owned. But this man was no noble. At his cuffs and collar, Larek saw not lace, but hints of steel chain armor. Tall, he was, with the swarthy look to his skin that spoke of either a good deal of time at sea or a family background that included ancestors in far western Karwale or Boll as well as the pale east. His dark hair and beard had begun to gray, but his bearing made his wiry build look vital. Strong. The sword of war at his side was sheathed.

"Keon," said Dyrra, all but spitting the name at him.

"You have named me," Keon said. "But I am more. I am the past returned to claim you."

"Bounty hunter," she said to Larek and Sindra.

Chitter returned, swimming up out of the ground to climb his way back onto Larek's shoulder. With each step Chitter fed soothing restoration into Larek, making him feel ready to fight, if needed.

"Bounty hunter? I am justice," Keon said, "and I have a writ of arrest for you Dyrra, widow of Ommure, called Dyrra Slow Sword, called Dyrra the Tall." He looked to Larek and Sindra. "You may examine it if you wish. I assure you I have a legal right to claim her."

"Issued by the Duchy of Flanair," said Dyrra. "And assuring me what would happen if I returned there. Flanair is well to the north and west." She tapped the ground with the tip of her sword. "This is the king's land. And that is not a royal warrant."

"The Duchess is at court. Do you doubt that she will persuade the king to honor it when I shove you before her in chains?"

"Why does a Healer ride with a bounty hunter?" asked Sindra, and Larek wondered if she meant to break the tension in the air, or add to it.

"Why does a faithless question me?" sneered the Healer.

Sindra drew back as though slapped, then said in an angrier tone, "Failed. Not faithless. And at least I went where I was needed. I did not ride for *money* nor to ease the *brutal excesses* of others."

The Healer only looked at her as though she were beneath contempt.

"Enough," said Larek.

"The Burned One speaks?" said Keon. "Stay your tongue before one of us—"

"ENOUGH!" and this time Larek lent his word the power of the storm, making it clap like thunder. The one word jarred everyone around him and raised the hairs all over their bodies.

All eyes were on him now. Most amazed, but Keon's narrowed. Shrewd.

"Seek another bounty, hunter," said Larek. "We stand beside her, and you are not numerous enough or powerful enough to take her. You claim the right of law, but no soldiers ride with you, nor the king's Collectors. You are a bandit, hoping to find a market for a prize you cannot steal.

"Leave now with your lives. Or stay, and find out just how much the Burned One has learned about fire."

Keon tried to stare Larek down, but Larek had faced accusing glares for the past decade, and no one yet had even matched the one he saw in his own mirror. Much less exceeded it.

"Your final warning," said Larek.

"Very well," said Keon. To his men he said, "Lower your weapons, collect the fallen. You" — he addressed the spearman — "fetch our horses from the trees."

Then Keon turned to Dyrra and said, "You, I will see again."

"Then I shall look forward to killing you."

ONCE KEON AND HIS MEN WERE GONE, DYRRA SHEATHED HER SWORD OF war, then turned to continue around the hills and back to the road south. They still had a few hours of sunlight left, and Larek expected that she wanted to put as many of the hills and trees between herself and Keon as she could.

But before Dyrra had taken two steps, Sindra said, "No."

Dyrra ignored the word and took another step. Sindra rushed forward and grabbed her by the shoulder. Dyrra spun away from her into a low crouch, one hand on the grip of her sword.

"You're quick with those needles of yours, I'll grant you," said Dyrra. "But if you think a sleeping draught like Nilasah's Tears can put me down before I cut you in half—"

"Threats?" said Larek. "Has it come to threats so soon? Only moments ago we stood united against those who wanted to take you."

Dyrra lowered her eyes. Eased her hand away from her sword.

"We have smoked pig and green beans for our dinner," said Sindra. "Let us go make camp among the alders. We already know what threat was waiting there, and the chances are good that no other threat waits nearby."

Dyrra nodded.

"And while we eat," said Sindra, "you can return the courtesy that Larek and I have already paid you. You can tell us the truth behind your story and songs."

Dyrra nodded again, and she did not look up the whole way up the hill. Though she did at least clear space for the fire while Larek gathered the wood and Sindra organized their dinner. The undergrowth was lush and green, but recently cut away and gathered at the north end, where it concealed Keon's ambush.

Once the fire was going, Dyrra went out to gather yet more wood, claiming the alder would burn too fast, however sweet it smelled.

Larek took that opportunity to arrange sections of the cut-away undergrowth to serve as bedding beneath their blankets, and Chitter waved his paws over each arrangement, adding to the comfort.

Whatever else came of their night on the hill, at least they would have another good night's sleep.

The trio held their silence through dinner, the tensest silence among them during the short time they had known one another.

But Dyrra waited until they had finished their meal, and Sindra had wrapped away the remaining food for the morning, and Chitter had set it free from pests or threat of local animals.

Then, and only then, did Dyrra stare into the fire and begin to speak.

"Your stories sound so simple to me. You each faced a trial and fell short. Understandable. Not one of us is a hero out of the stories told by our wanderers or your skalds. We're people. And people fail. If we didn't, we wouldn't need the gods to help us. Neither of you deserves the scorn heaped on you.

"But me, I deserve it. Every word, every look."

She lapsed into silence then, staring at the fire. Larek opened his mouth to speak, but Chitter shook his head frantically, so Larek waited. Finally, she continued.

"It started with Ommure. Big, beautiful Ommure." Her voice grew misty. "Never did Lucala grace our world with a finer, stronger man. He was a warrior without peer. His honor above reproach. And his smile outshined the jealous sun.

"At my best, I'm not sure I ever deserved his love, but he gave it to me anyway."

"Love is never deserved," said Sindra. "Only given and received."

"Perhaps," said Dyrra. "But he loved me." Her voice grew faraway. "And he gave me a child. A strong, healthy girl. We gave her to the temple to raise, of course. We were warriors, we both, and needed on the lines.

"Keon was our commander then. Ruthless. As any half-blood had to be to rise in rank. He sometimes split Ommure and me among different volleys because he realized we fought harder to get back to each other.

"We were apart that day, me in Keon's volley and Ommure off in another. Both volleys fighting in a border skirmish with Mem over river rights, among the sandy rocks and foothills of the north. My volley got caught in a trap — the sandy rocks gave way and left all dozen of us outnumbered and cut off from reinforcements.

"It was the bloodiest, evilest battle I've ever seen. Dead all around us. Our own comrades falling like pebbles before an avalanche. But Keon was slippery, and a hard man, and one of the two finest warriors I've ever known. We fought our way through that trap side by side. And then we flipped the trap on them.

"I don't know how many we killed that day. I only remember the battle haze. The screaming, much of it mine. And, when it ended, the need-fire."

Dyrra looked up at Larek and Sindra. "You aren't warriors. Do you know the need-fire?"

Sindra nodded. "Never felt it. But I've ... seen it in action."

Larek shook his head.

"Battle is death, wizard. And the end of a battle is rebirth. Both are painful." Dyrra looked back into the fire. "And they burn through you with the need to live. To feel alive. To fuck."

The word hung in the air. Larek could still hear the popping of the alder wood logs as they burnt, and the songs of the birds in the trees, but still the world felt paused by her word. As though nothing could breathe until she continued.

"Never have I faced a worse battle. And never have I felt a worse need-fire. Keon felt it too. And he was there. And we were alone. And Ommure so distant he might have died in the battle."

Dyrra's voice grew more disgusted. "And so Keon and I were together. Right there. Among the blood and bodies of fallen friends and foes alike."

She fell silent again, and squeezed her eyes tight against the memory. When she opened her eyes they shone with unshed tears.

"Only the once. A frantic expression of need that lasted less time than I've taken to tell it. But it happened.

"I lacked the nerve to tell my sweet, perfect Ommure. But I didn't need to. Because only three days later Keon bragged of it in a drunken revel.

"I ... could not face my crime. I claimed that I had been dazed by a mace, too insensible to even remember. Ommure took it as rape, and I didn't correct him. He accused Keon. Keon demanded Lucala's Justice, a fight under the full moon where each man is bound to the other at one wrist and one ankle. They share a grip on a double-bladed crescent knife.

"And then Keon won and Ommure was dead. I was shamed, but no more than I deserved for all I had done. I fled east, where I hoped to leave the past behind me. And every night I prayed that Lucala would forgive me, and that Ommure's shade would forgive me.

"I still do."

This had nothing to do with any songs Larek had heard, but as Dyrra clutched her knees to her face and wept, he did not have the heart to ask for more.

"You can stop there, Dyrra," he said, looking at Sindra for confirmation, but Sindra looked uncertain. He pushed ahead. "I think we both understand—"

"No," said Dyrra. She looked up, red-rimmed eyes shining in the firelight with much of the late afternoon sun shaded out by the trees around them.

"That is just what you needed to know to understand the rest."

THERE HALFWAY UP THE HILL, WITH A COPSE OF ALDERS SHELTERING them from the afternoon sun, the remains of their smoked pig and peas dinner safely packed away to share as breakfast in the morning, Larek and Sindra sat watching Dyrra as she continued her story.

Even Chitter seemed fascinated, though Larek wondered if the earth spirit shaped like a gray flying squirrel truly understood the social significance of Dyrra's words, or simply read their emotions plainly enough to make up the difference.

Either way, Dyrra continued.

"When I came east, I knew leaving Karwale was not enough. I rode through the peaks and valleys of tiny Boll and across the vast plains of Yunt until I stopped in a tavern here in Aeralfast and people seemed amazed by the color of my skin alone." She shrugged. "I figured that if you folks see so few Karwalish, there was little chance of my name or my shame reaching you.

"All the same, I was a warrior with no one to fight. And I wasn't sure what to do about that. Didn't want to serve in the duchess' forces. Word about me would spread too quickly. I'd stand out for my height and my skill. And my skin, of course.

"But mercenaries weren't any better a choice. Mercenaries live on the road, and the further west a mercenary company is willing to go, the more battles and the more money they'll find." She shook her head. "No. Mercenary work would have meant risking discovery."

"Why didn't you try some other line of work?" asked Sindra.

"Why do you still carrying your herbs? Why does he still cast his spells? It's who we are. Giving that up is worse than failing."

Dyrra looked back into the fire as she continued. "But one thing I hadn't counted on. The very qualities that made me stand out made me fashionable. The locals didn't even know my reputation, had never seen me fight, but in no time at all I had merchant families offering me positions as a bodyguard or a house guard.

"Bodyguard work was too risky. That meant travel. But house guard? Not much of a challenge for a warrior, but I didn't think much of myself in those days."

Sindra met Larek's eye, and he knew what she was thinking. Nothing had changed on that front. Which meant she was in the right company.

"So there in Fent, in the Duchy of Flanair, I took work as a merchant's house guard. Watched over his pretty little wife and his darling little children as they went about their days untouched by horrors like those I had seen. But I wasn't jealous. I got more protective of them. Thought that maybe, just maybe, if I could preserve such innocence, that I might have done one right thing before I died."

Dyrra looked off in the direction the moon would later rise.

"They weren't from Mem, and they weren't banished. The bandits that came that night. That's must have been for a rhyme or something. Make a better song. No. It was Keon again.

"I had been working for the merchant for more than a year. And though the song likes to claim that I failed the first time I was tested, that's not the case. Must have been four, five attempts to rob the place that first year. Killed them when I had to. Left them for the local justice when I could. I was just thinking that I would serve the family better if people knew not to try. Knew that house was guarded and they should test their luck elsewhere.

"Wasn't how it worked out. Word didn't spread about the safety of the house. Word spread about me. Merchant was bragging on his long treks west about the Karwalish giant woman protecting his family. Didn't take long for word to reach Keon. He had a mercenary company by then. His own man. But he still felt he owed me for the accusation.

"Keon didn't come alone in the night to fight me one-on-one. He hit the house with his whole company, a volley from each side. Laid a trap for me when I came running downstairs at the start of the assault. I froze when I saw him. His grin. And he damn near cut me in half."

Dyrra gestured to her scar, that white line against her dark skin, running all the way from high on her cheek down across her chin, her throat, her collarbone, and disappearing into her armor.

"It goes all the way down my ribs.

"He plundered the place and made me watch." Dyrra turned her eyes back to the fire. "Made me watch everything he did there. Then he stabbed me in the belly and left me for dead.

"I woke up three days later in a Nilasah tent, alive and recovering."

"You couldn't have fought off a mercenary company," said Larek. "Not alone."

"You shouldn't blame yourself for that," added Sindra, tears in her own eyes to match Dyrra's.

"No?" said Dyrra, looking up. "Keon hit that place because of me. It was my fault. Everything he did to them. What he did to Ommure too. I've caused pain and misery everywhere I've gone, and it's all my fault."

Dyrra put her head down on her knees, but spoke loud enough to be heard.

"The smartest thing the two of you can do is leave me before I get you killed. Or worse."

"No," said Larek, sharp enough that Chitter, Sindra, and even Dyrra stared at him. But under their scrutiny his words failed him. He wanted to say something about shared misery, or perhaps friendship. Something to the only two people he had met in years who hadn't either wanted to mock him or wanted something from him besides his company. So he settled on the only thing he could think to say.

"We each have things we're running from. The least we can do is run together."

It wasn't much. But it got him a couple of smiles.

10

————

THE FIRST RAYS OF DAWN HAD NOT YET PASSED THE SEVEN PEAKS TO shine through the copse of alders halfway up the first true hill south of the capitol when Chitter eased Larek awake. Larek was surprised the pleasant smell of breakfast had not woken him. He looked over to see that Sindra had revived the fire and warmed the leftover smoked pig and green beans, along with some bread from the day before.

"Good morning," he said, his voice hushed, and the smile he received from Sindra looked knowing.

"Good morning," said Dyrra loudly, from three paces to Larek's right.

He cricked his neck, whipping his head around while Sindra laughed at his shock. Even Chitter chuckled, before easing peace into the aggravated muscles.

But Larek's eyes did not deceive him. Not only was Dyrra already awake, she had packed everything for the road except his own bedroll.

"I meant to ask you..." said Dyrra, her words rising and falling in the familiar manner of her accent. That at least reassured Larek. If she had sounded bright and cheery he might have suspected interference from the spirit realm.

Dyrra continued, "That threat you made yesterday. Just how much fire magic do you know?"

"Fire magic?" Larek shuddered at the thought. "More than I like, and as little as I can get away with. But it sounded impressive, didn't it?"

"True..." Dyrra lowered one eyebrow and looked at him out of the other eye. "Do you know *any* battle spells?"

Larek could see Sindra paying closer attention out of the corner of his eye.

"Yes," he admitted, "but I wouldn't call it my strength. Too difficult to calibrate power under that kind of pressure. Too often I use too little and accomplish almost nothing. But that's better than using too much..."

Larek let the words hang, not ready to discuss the bandits who haunted his dreams sometimes. The ones he tried to shove back with a spell, but hit with the force of an avalanche.

Better he had given them his money pouch.

But he may not have needed to say a word. The way Dyrra nodded, then gave excess attention to tying a strap suggested that she understood.

"Breakfast," called Sindra. "Many miles to go before moonrise."

As they ate, Larek was certain he saw Dyrra stifle at least three yawns, but he said nothing. He appreciated her attempt at early rising, but feared that it would only delay her intolerant mood until later in the day.

"By the way," said Sindra. Timed, perhaps, to cover one of those stifled yawns. She held up a pair of her throwing needles. "Which of you recovered these for me from those mercenaries? I thought they were lost."

Larek looked at Dyrra, who looked at him expectantly. Chitter cleared his throat.

Sindra's eyes widened with something like joy.

"By Lucala's light," said Dyrra, brow furrowed and voice thoughtful, "that may be the most adorable sound I've ever heard."

"Me too," said Sindra, amazed. "Thank you, Chitter."

"Thought you might have trouble replacing those on the road," said Chitter, who looked entirely too pleased with himself. At puzzled looks from Dyrra and Sindra, Larek translated. The words, at least.

Sindra thanked the earth spirit again, and Dyrra said, "Reminds me, Chitter. I guess I should stop threatening to eat you. You did us more good against that ambush than your floppy-hatted friend did."

Larek opened his mouth to object, but Dyrra smiled and his words lost their way. Was that ... *gentle* teasing? Like he remembered vaguely from his own youth?

From the days when he had *friends*?

Larek was afraid to speak and risk ruining the moment, but he did smile as he finished eating his breakfast. The prospect of the day's travel looked brighter to him than it had a few minutes ago.

Friends. Perhaps, since they shared their pains, before long he, Dyrra and Sindra might be able to call each other friends, and mean it.

To have friends again. After so many years with only Chitter for company.

Larek could only hope he would not let them down.

When Dyrra imagined the eventual punishment she would face in the Underworld for her many failures and crimes against others, she pictured something very much like what she did that day: awoke too early and faced a long march under the direct heat of Lucala's Jealous Sister, without even the promise of clouds to offer respite.

Glare everywhere her night-preferring eyes looked. Even watching her own feet made her squint.

And the heat. Even the air smelled warm. Dry grass, dry dirt ... ever since they had left that bank of hills, the world had turned parched, baked by too much direct heat. No trees along the road to add shade, though Dyrra could see the occasional stump where a tree had been felled without any sisters or children to grow up and replace it.

Even the songbirds barely bothered to open their beaks as they flew past, hunting for lusher climes.

The sun hadn't helped the road, either. Not so flat and smooth now as it had been on the other side of those hills. More wagon breaks in the dirt, more rocks. Not enough to be trouble while walking, but if they had cause to run, they would have to watch their steps. Wouldn't do to twist or snap an ankle.

At least Dyrra felt that she *could* run if she had to. Sleep had helped. She felt human. Hair bound and limbs capable. For the first time since they'd started this journey she did not feel as though the least sound of joy or interest from her companions might send her into a murderous rage.

Well, not a *murderous* rage. Not over speaking on the road. But perhaps an unwelcomed fit of punches.

Dyrra had to hand it to the ex-Healer. Sindra had been right to stop them early for the day. It gave Dyrra time to think, to see the logic of forcing herself to rest earlier than came naturally. To lie there and rest and pray until Lucala blessed her with the early sleep that life in the east required. It meant that she would be awake and aware if that *daywalker* Keon came back for her before peak sun.

And when Keon returned, that would be the time of day he came. When the glare did its best to obscure the world around her. When he expected Dyrra to be least capable of defending herself.

No. When Keon returned, Dyrra would be ready. After Flanair, Keon had lost his righteous high ground. Dyrra would be of a single mind when the time came to spill his blood.

Dyrra glanced over at Sindra, who gave her a guileless smile. Dyrra tried to return it. Hoped it came across right. How could Sindra look as content as the birds that had serenaded them over breakfast? Was it some Healer's trick? Some gift of her goddess that she managed to retain, even though banished from her order?

Larek had the right of it, however much his sweat soaked through his clothes. No doubt that floppy hat of his saved his eyes from this cursed glare. Not to mention keeping him cooler as it protected at least some of his many, many scars.

So many scars.

Dyrra could not understand these eastern women. In Karwale a man's battle scars made him desirable. A survivor with a tale to tell, not a coward. And a man who could feed himself as well as Larek plainly did, who also had most of his body scarred by *dragonfire*? And those red eyes. Obviously a side-effect from some spell or other.

In Karwale Larek could have had his pick of women, for a night or a wife. Even among the nobles. He could have had anyone but a warrior.

No warrior would ever find a wizard desirable, however great his scarring. Wizards lived in their heads, while warriors lived in their guts. Both could find love among common folk and nobles alike, but together? Disaster.

And yet even Sindra, who had heard the tale behind those scars, did not look at Larek as desirable. She looked on him with trust. She looked on him with friendship. But not with fire.

But Dyrra had no worries about finding someone for Sindra. With her face and form, no doubt men would make fools of themselves for her. Even though her failure was worse than Larek's — in Dyrra's eyes — Sindra would find love and a family while Larek went ignored. Punished for standing up against a dragon and daring to live.

Ridiculous, these easterners.

And the source of a touch of nagging guilt in Dyrra, for taking Larek down to Velstadt, where likely the women will pay him no more attention than they did in Aeralfast. Dyrra could have suggested he travel west. Told him of the welcome he would get in Karwale. Even in Boll, or Mem.

But the truth was, Dyrra could never head that way again, and she needed him to travel with her. Especially with Keon lurking about. Dyrra was happy to test her skill against Keon, but he would not come alone.

Perhaps she would find Larek a woman once they reached Velstadt. They couldn't all be muttonheaded about men. Surely one of them would see his value.

No man should face a dragon and die without knowing a woman's embrace.

Dyrra's mind played with that thought for a time. Wondering what sort of woman Larek would want for himself, and how she could help him find her. She even wondered if she should enlist Sindra in the search. If Sindra had no interest, she would likely be glad to help. And if she *concealed* an interest, Dyrra might make her face it.

Such thoughts were pleasant ways for Dyrra to pass the time as they walked beneath the damned sun. It had been a long time since she had considered anyone friend enough to wish to help them, and it felt good.

And it was much better than thinking about her own abstinence since the day Ommure died. Even if Keon's return had begun to waken the banked coals of her own guilt about betraying the only man she ever loved.

Thinking about Larek and Sindra helped Dyrra pretend she wasn't thinking about Ommure at all.

WHILE SINDRA TRIED TO APPRECIATE ALL THE SIGHTS AND SOUNDS THE world had to offer, by mid-afternoon she was ready for variety. The stretching fields that had looked golden by the early morning light now seemed dingy yellow to her, even blowing in the breeze.

And the breeze should have been pleasant. A touch of cool air on the face under the heat of the late spring sun. Except that the smells it carried were dry. Desiccated. The hills this morning must have been full of water, with their soft green grass and alder trees. But whatever water may have lain below them did not extend south along the road.

And the road. Still decent. Still better than the cracked ground beside it. Even if she did have to watch for rocks, and the occasional crevice large enough to snatch an unwary foot.

She knew there was a river somewhere ahead of them. She

remembered that much from her training. Nilasah required all of her Healers to know the main features of the land they served. It meant that they could never be lost for long, and would always know which direction to find life and people.

Sindra knew some Healers who had memorized the kingdom's official map, down to the meanest towns and baronies. But Sindra had considered the meaning behind the mandate, and focused on the land's features. A Healer always needed to know where to find water, where to hunt for herbs.

Politics did not matter. Supplies did.

But even then, Sindra had to admit she had not given the lesson enough attention. Properly speaking, she should have known how far the river was from the hills, both by foot and by horse.

But this was no test, and she had no wounded to heal just now. If any would even accept the prayers and poultices of a failed Healer. If Sindra were willing to risk offering up those prayers.

And if she thirsted, for water they had Larek's wonderful jug, which brought every sip to them pure and clean and tasty.

Oh, what Sindra would have given for such a jug when she was a Healer of Nilasah. Water was more precious than gold in a healing tent, and too often spent as fast as blood.

Would Larek be able to make more such jugs? Would he be willing? Sindra wondered what such an enchantment must cost. She knew the spells had to be tricky, or demanding, or the fact that one wizard had created such a jug would have meant that every noble in Aeralfast...

Or would they?

Sindra glanced at Dyrra, in case sleep did not help the warrior's disposition toward conversation. But Dyrra seemed lost within her own thoughts, though she did glance toward Larek on occasion, speculation in her eye.

Speculation?

Sindra shook off her curiosity — though that was no easy feat — and spoke to Larek.

"Was it difficult? Making your water jug?"

Larek shook himself loose from his own thoughts, and he looked at Sindra without understanding, as though the sound of her words had reached him, but not their meaning.

She was about to repeat herself when he said, slowly, "Difficult? Yes. Time consuming, and the spells are ... precise. Err in one calculation and the jug will likely shatter. Err in two and you could drown in your folly."

"So it would be expensive to commission?"

"Definitely." He blinked. "But as long as we are traveling together—"

Chitter said something, and though Sindra thought she could hear the shape of words hidden in the sounds of a natural squirrel, she could not interpret them.

"Do you think so?" said Larek, hesitation all over his face. "That would require a series of anchors that depended on each other. Risky. Much easier to do what most wizards do — find water in the ground like everyone else."

Chitter had a response ready for that.

"Have you ever sold one to a noble?" Sindra pushed the words out quickly, before Larek and Chitter got involved in a discussion that she had no hope of following.

"Sell my everfull jug?" Larek shook his head. "I've only made the one. Never even shown it to anyone except you two."

"You undervalue yourself," said Dyrra, sudden but certain. "Even here where water regularly falls from the sky such a thing is precious. In Karwale, people would overthrow rulers and put a crown on your head for giving them such free access to water."

Chitter said something else, but Larek shook his head, firm.

"It's not that simple."

Dyrra huffed and returned to her silent contemplation.

Sindra decided to let the subject go for now. It was more conversation while walking than Dyrra had yet tolerated, and Sindra did not want to push her back into demanding travel without speech.

They walked in silence for a time, and Larek's words echoed in her thoughts.

Not that simple.

Sindra remembered. When she had been cast out of her order she had knelt there on the cobbled street of the capitol's Gods District, a thunderstorm of tears flowing down her face and shaking her whole body. She begged to make amends. To prove her fidelity to Nilasah.

No fewer than three elders had stood before her and scoffed, and the High Healer Alain most of all. He had stood tall and thin as the rope around his waist, his aged skin soft and weak, but free of blemish or wrinkle.

"It is not that simple," he said. "Broken faith can be found again. Proving regained faith means nothing. Can you heal the maimings made permanent through your failure, Sindra? Can you raise the dead men and women you should have saved?"

He stood there, while all about them passing tradesmen stared, and the penitents and acolytes of other faiths watched and listened. High Healer Alain stood there and he waited for her to answer, even though he knew well the only answer he could possibly receive.

"No."

A sob wracked Sindra's body, the flush of shame burning through her.

"No." He shook his head, as slow and certain as the rocking of a hanged man. "You cannot undo the harm you have caused. And we cannot trust that your *restored* faith will last. That it will not fail you again when the sick and dying need you most."

And then he crouched down and wiped the tears from her cheeks. Sindra heard sympathy in his voice when he spoke again.

"I understand the pain you feel. But though much of the Healer's craft involves lessening and mending pain, there are some pains we must sharpen, because the lessons they teach must be allowed to take hold."

His hazel eyes met hers, and she wondered how such sympathy could show so little mercy. "You will again be tempted to use the skills we have taught you. But you are not a Healer. Sincere failure is no crime, nor shame, but it must be remembered so that others will not suffer under your good intentions.

"You are not a Healer, Sindra. You must find another path."

"WE MAY HAVE TO FIND ANOTHER PATH," SAID LAREK, STOPPING IN THE middle of the road.

Dyrra nodded wary agreement, but Sindra gave him a horrified look that made him wonder where her thoughts had run off to. They had all three of them been drifting in their own minds throughout the day's hike, and if Sindra were anything like Larek, the dry, nearly dead land around them had sparked unpleasant memories to focus on.

Larek doubted her own were worse than his. Dry land and hot late afternoon sun like this made him think of the dragon and the dead, yes, but worst of all they made him think of the living he had to face on that fateful day. The few maimed survivors, weeping over all they lost and blaming Larek for his failure. Accusing Larek of angering the dragon, of driving it to greater acts of destruction...

But if Sindra's trembling chin and worried eyebrows were any indication, wherever her mind had run, the memories had not been much happier than his own.

Larek chose not to ask about so private a pain. If she wanted to discuss it, she would. Instead he reminded her of the present. He pointed down the road at the sight that had spurred his pause. A town. Perhaps an hour down the road ahead of them, but plenty visible without trees or hills in the way.

And they were not looking at just some little village or hamlet, either. Even from where he stood Larek could see that the town had a wall, with towers, and at least three buildings that must have stood thirty or forty feet tall. A place like that housed hundreds of people. Perhaps more.

The town could only be Lillikan. If Larek remembered right, the site was once a spring-fed pool that served as a meeting place used by traders until they had found that feeding that spring were wells that ran deep and wide.

Larek never understood how the wells could have proven so impressive when close to such dry land as he saw and smelled around him right now. Perhaps it was the depth of the spring's source.

"This is the only road that leads all the way from the capitol to Velstadt," said Sindra. "Of course there will be towns."

"That doesn't mean we have to walk through them," said Dyrra. "They don't have anything we need, and Keon might be there."

"We saw him ride north," said Sindra.

"And he knew we were traveling south. He laid one trap for us. Easy to lay another here. Especially if he can persuade the locals to support his writ."

"Why would the Duchess of Flanair issue a writ for you?" said Larek. "If losing a fight were a crime, I'd be in the king's dungeons right now."

"There's a reason my employer gets referred to as *the* merchant of Fent. He has quite a bit of influence, or did back when I was working for him. And since Keon is half-Karwalish, the merchant accused me of working with him to plan the raid. Of never really fighting back."

"Even with that scar," said Sindra, her words angrier than Larek expected. "And the small fact that he *stabbed you and left you for dead*."

"I could never explain how I got to that Healer's tent. And the merchant was a grieving man and I was a convenient target." Dyrra shrugged. "It wasn't as though I intended to stay in Flanair anyway."

"This had to have been years ago," said Larek. "I first heard the *song* on the king's forty-fifth nameday."

"Six years ago. Keon's probably the only hunter who still cares about it," said Dyrra. "Doesn't mean he won't get paid if he brings me in. Writs don't spoil like fruit."

Sindra sighed. "We won't have many chances to sleep in an actual bed on this journey. How likely do you think..."

Larek had been staring at the town, but when Sindra trailed off he turned to look at her. As did Dyrra. The rest of the question seemed obvious enough, but Sindra was smiling.

"Keon won't be there," she said.

"You can't know that," said Dyrra.

"It's a copse of trees in the hills ahead."

Larek joined her smile. "Of course. He knows you too well. He knew you would spot that ambush among the alders, so—"

"So he used it as a feint to drive me into the real ambush, where he was waiting. Because he knew I would go left, keeping the enemy on my sword side." Dyrra shook her head, unconvinced. "It's a good point. Except that he had troops at the copse too. Suggests he'll have troops in town."

Chitter started to speak, but Larek was way ahead of him this time.

"He might have spies there. *Probably* has spies there. But a foreigner with no patron? He won't be working with the town watch."

Dyrra narrowed her eyes at that, until the pieces clicked in her head and she smiled.

"Because here in Aeralfast, the king has his Collectors, but bounty hunters are *independent*."

"Exactly." Larek thumped his fist into his hand. "Why risk the mayor — or the captain of the guard — stealing his bounty by virtue of authority?"

"Or to curry political favor," added Sindra, who then frowned. "Although that would depend on how much the duchess still cares—"

"You don't want to go into town either," said Dyrra, to Larek.

"True. I didn't. Mostly I didn't want to see the *look* I get when people recognize me. Or get questions about my eyes. Or hear stories and songs of Larek the Burned." Larek exhaled sharply. "But Sindra has a point about sleeping in beds when we can. And I like the idea of not breaking open our trail rations until we absolutely have to."

Larek made a show of studying the vast fields of near-dead wild grass, the stunted skeletons of the occasional shrub.

"Unless you think you can hunt us up some rabbits worth eating."

Dyrra laughed, an explosive sound that continued until she

pounded Larek hard on the shoulder. Painful, but at least this time she didn't stagger him a step.

"True. Around here, even if I caught us a dozen rabbits they would be too scrawny to fill our bellies. And the longer my jaw can wait before it has to gnaw its way through those dried meats and fruits, the better."

"And the bread," said Sindra. "Don't forget the road bread."

"I've eaten road bread before," said Dyrra. "I think my guts are still trying to get rid of it."

"Have you ever tried wizard bread?" said Larek, and he could tell by the raised eyebrows that neither Sindra nor Dyrra had heard of it. He chuckled. "I thought not. There's a reason for that. I still think it's a joke they play on apprentices…"

And the three of them shared tales of the worst foods they'd eaten as they made their way to the town of Lillikan.

11

———————

The sinking sun was just beginning to kiss the sky with orange when the trio reached the Lillikin. They stood before a wall of shaved tree trunks, the top of each sharpened to a point, but they all looked to Larek as though they had dulled with age and disuse.

Still, the trunks were cut from a hard-looking wood, and thick enough. And the wall they formed was solid. Larek guessed that each trunk had been sliced twice into perhaps a rhombus shape, allowing the trunks to overlap and fit together into an almost seamless unit. The total structure stood at least five times as tall as Larek, and had been arranged in a rough rectangle, with wooden towers at the corners rising a good ten feet higher.

He could see a few guards with crossbows keeping an eye on them, but more as though they were curious than threatening.

But the guards on the walls were not Larek's concern. It was the two pike wielders standing before the closed gate, which stood just as tall as the walls around it, and had been visibly reinforced with iron bands.

The pike wielders lowered the points of their weapons the moment they caught sight of Dyrra.

"We want to trouble here," said the one on the right. He was older, perhaps half-again Larek's age, with a weathered look to his skin and graying hair under his steel cap. "If you're looking for work, go to the tournament. We don't need mercenaries."

"We're not mercenaries," said Sindra. They had all agreed that she should do the talking, and worked out their lie in advance, so they did not have to answer questions about their journey.

"We're simple travelers. I'm on my way to visit family in Velstadt, and these two are keeping me safe on the road. We only wish to stay a night in your town. Sleep on beds softer than dirt. Give our jaws a break from travel fare and remember what flavorful food tastes like. We'll be on our way again at dawn."

"Will the three of you swear peace?"

"Yes," said Larek and Sindra without hesitation.

"What does that mean?" asked Dyrra.

That got a chuckle out of the old pikeman, though the younger one tightened his grip on his weapon.

"Thought you had the look of a career mercenary. Swearing peace is what it sounds like. You have to swear you will not cause trouble or start a fight while you are within our walls. And you'll have to surrender that sword until you leave. No weapons."

"What if someone attacks me?"

"Hasn't happened in a year or more." The old pikeman tilted the point of his weapon to the sky and gestured for his partner to do the same. "No travelers here right now. Them that came through are already off at the tournament. And the townsfolk are a peaceful lot. No one's going to attack you here."

Dyrra furrowed her brow. "*What if someone attacks me?*"

"Never known other work, have you?" said the older pikeman with some sympathy. He sighed. "If someone attacks you, you can stop them. But if you fight back or stop them ... let's just say too hard, you'll be up before the magistrate pleading your case alongside your attacker. And then you'll probably spend the next year digging, or carrying, or whatever else the town needs but no one wants to do."

"No travelers here," muttered Larek. "Keon can't be here."

"No travelers *right now*," answered Dyrra at the same level of volume.

"I think you'll be safe enough," said Sindra. "Let's not insult our hosts' hospitality."

Dyrra looked unconvinced.

"Have any clothes but that armor?" asked the older pikeman.

"No," she said, but Larek thought she had changed the shirt beneath it at least once since they left.

"Thought not." He shook his head, but Larek thought the man shook it at a memory and not at Dyrra.

The pikeman continued, "Then if you swear peace, I'll let you keep your armor."

"What?" said the younger pikeman. "But the law—"

"The law doesn't say I have to make a woman walk around naked, and I don't intend to do it." To Dyrra he said, "You tell anyone who asks that Barth said you could keep the armor. And I'll make sure the whole watch knows."

"Thank you," said Sindra.

"So will you swear peace and enter?"

"I will," said Dyrra with a solemn nod.

Together the three of them said the words, following Barth's lead: "I swear that I will cause no trouble, nor raise arms, while within the walls of Lillikan on this visit."

"That is all?" asked Dyrra.

"That and your sword."

She exhaled slowly, flaring her nostrils, but removed her sword belt. She handed it to Barth.

"To you I will entrust this. It was my husband's before his death. I will look for you to reclaim it at the southern gate at dawn. And if any try to keep it from me—"

"I'll make sure you get it."

"Thank you," said Dyrra, clasping arms with him.

"You are welcome, Dyrra the Tall."

The old pikeman also recognized Larek — and raised an eyebrow at Chitter — but Sindra had to name herself to enter. When she did, the older pikeman's eyebrows all but disappeared under his steel cap, and he took a closer look at her yellow kirtle. But he said nothing.

The first two names, once spoken aloud, distressed the younger pikeman. He began thumping the handle of his pike on the ground. But when Sindra was named as the third member of their party, he started lowering his pike and said, "Wait, Barth. We can't let—"

"You folks enjoy your stay tonight," said Barth loudly and shoving the younger man's pike aside. "You might try the Springwater. Folks who come through here a few times a year all seem to like their beds and meals the best. It's just shy of the town center from here. Sign makes it plain enough."

Dyrra turned as though she might say something to the younger pikeman, but Chitter jumped onto her shoulder and said, "Barth is taking a chance, letting you keep your armor. Going to break your oath?"

She pulled her lips way to one side, and blew a deep breath out of her nose. Then she turned and fell into place beside Larek, two steps behind Sindra to maintain their story. Chitter jumped back onto Larek's shoulder.

"Can you understand Chitter?" Larek said to Dyrra, voice just above a whisper.

Dyrra didn't hush her reply.

"Don't have to speak the language to know sense when you hear it."

"Open!" yelled Barth to the crossbowmen atop the high, wooden walls. They relayed the call, and Larek heard one more echo of the order. Then he heard clunks as the support braces were removed, and more muted, fussed orders from beyond the walls.

Finally, pulleys began to squeak as ropes pulled the great, iron-banded gate wide, raising dust from ground that had faced the same hot sun that the trio had dealt with all afternoon. Larek wondered if the ground were as eager for the sun to finish setting as he was. He liked sunsets no better than sunrises.

Ahead, Larek got his first glimpse of Lillikin.

Strong wood buildings with stone and mortar foundations. Most a single story, but he saw many two-story structures off of the main street. And it did look as though the buildings had been arranged in streets along straight lines, leaving enough space between the outer-most and the wall that as Larek passed the gate he was not sure he could have hit the closest building with a thrown rock.

And that rock would have stood out where it landed. Lillikin kept its streets clean and in good repair.

Three buildings down near the town center clearly towered above the others. One of them was likely the town hall, or perhaps the mayor's residence. The second, Larek guessed, was likely some kind of merchants hall, since the town had started as a meeting place for traveling merchants.

But what the third was, of that Larek could not feel certain. None of the temples he knew of needed more than one level. Perhaps it was the home of a prominent family. The founder, maybe.

Not much activity about the town though, at least not this close to sundown. Larek couldn't see anyone on the street ahead of him, and he could hear only the sound of the guards around him, shouting to each other and re-closing the gate with Barth and his junior inside.

"Must be closing for the night," he remarked to Chitter.

"Sensible," said Dyrra, as she looked around at the walls, which from the inside all appeared to be reinforced with iron. "At some point this place must have been a haven for gangs of bandits."

"I'm going to guess that it isn't anymore," said Larek.

Sindra gave them both an exasperated look. "We're someplace safe. I can smell three kinds of roast meat *from here*. And you two want to discuss their fortifications?"

"No one builds like this without a reason," said Dyrra.

"I'm mostly wondering where they got all the wood," said Larek. "I mean, we know it didn't come from those fields we walked through today."

Sindra sighed hard enough to drop her shoulders, and let her head fall forward. Larek heard her mutter something, but the only word he could make out was Nilasah.

When she raised her head again, she said, "There's a river south of here. The Quar. It's about three hours from this town on foot, much less than that on horseback. Used to have a small forest of oaks on the north bank. It was a great place to harvest mistletoe, holly, elleray, and more."

Sindra shook her head. "But it's no good for those plants anymore, because almost all the oaks are gone. Have been for years. A few have started growing back, but not like it was." She waved her hands to gesture at the walls and the buildings. "I'm guessing those oaks are here all around us."

Sindra cupped her hands into a pleading gesture.

"Now can we please, *please*, go find a place to sit and eat food that I didn't cook?"

Dyrra laughed loud enough to make some of the guards turn and stare, though Larek noted with some chagrin that she didn't clap Sindra on the shoulder.

"Larek," she said, "I believe our lady is hungry."

Her humor infected him, and Larek grinned. "By all means, then, we should find her something to eat."

"*Thank* you," said Sindra, who turned and started to walk before either of them could distract her with another observation.

Larek and Dyrra fell into step behind her. He let them take five steps before saying, "Of course, her noble family has enemies. As her guards we must be sure her food is safe before we can let her eat any of it."

"Good point," said Dyrra. "What kind of guards would risk letting their employer get poisoned?"

"The testing might take a while."

"I never thought," said Sindra, "that I would yearn for Dyrra's insistence on walking in silence."

Three steps later, Dyrra said, "That was while Lucala's Jealous Sister was trying to blind and cook us with each step. Now that evening is coming on, I feel positively ... what's the word you used, Sindra? Chatty?"

Even Sindra started laughing at that.

As they made their way through town — Larek and Dyrra continuing to tease Sindra, but Sindra taking humor in it now — Larek began to at least see signs of life. A boy leading a horse to a stable, which needed to be cleaned, if the smell was any indication. A handful of men and women talking with the vigor of a long day's work as they pushed their way into a tavern bearing the sign of a brown dog, sitting.

The men and women looked over the trio with interested eyes, but made no move to intercept. They instead seemed pleased to have gained a fresh subject to discuss over their night's drinking.

"So much for anonymity," said Sindra.

"We gave that up when we gave up our names," said Larek.

"Barth already knew mine," said Dyrra, wonder in her voice. "And still he treated me with respect. I will drink to his health."

"As long as the drinks come with food," said Sindra.

"I'm sure they will," said Larek, pointing to a wide, two-story building with a sign overhead that depicted a bubbling pool of water. "That must be the Springwater."

Perhaps there were no other travelers in Lillikan that night, but that fact did not seem to hurt business at the Springwater. The main room was at least half-full when Larek, Dyrra and Sindra entered, and Larek's stomach rumbled at the smells of rich food. Two or three kinds of roast meats, stews, vegetables — some roasted and others boiled — and breads that smelled as though they would melt in his mouth.

The room had no central hearth. Instead, it was arranged around three raised concentric rings in the stone floor. Each ring comprised an armspan of burning coals, surrounded on each side an armspan of flowing water and separated by perhaps a foot of stone. Each ring was crossed by six stone bridges spaced evenly around the ring. Each bridge wide enough for only one person to cross at a time.

Between the rings were round wooden tables surrounded by groups of eight diners. One table inside the center ring, a dozen inside the second ring, two dozen inside the third, and a few odd tables outside the third ring, at each of the corners of the room.

Larek wondered about the arrangement. He supposed it *could* have been done for effect. It certainly kept the room pleasantly warm. But given the utility of circles in certain types of magic...

Larek wanted a closer look at the stones that bordered those rings.

"Welcome to the Springwater," said a young woman in a soft blue kirtle, whose eyes and skin hinted at western ancestors, despite her blond hair. She looked twice at Larek's eyes and Dyrra's armor, but hid any questions or comments she held behind a smile. She said, "You're our only travelers tonight. May I give you the seat of honor?"

Dyrra started to shake her head, but Sindra said, "I would be delighted."

The seat of honor was the central table, and Larek immediately felt the uncomfortable scrutiny of the entire room. From the apparent itch between Dyrra's shoulders, she must have felt the same way.

As they crossed the bridges going deeper into the room, the silence all about him weighed on Larek. Made him want to hide Chitter before someone complained about a "wild animal."

Sindra, however, reached the table and took her chair with simple pride, as though she actually believed herself to be a noble traveling home to Velstadt.

No. Not quite. Most nobles Larek knew would have made the guards sit at another table.

"You've come on a good night," said their hostess, once all three had been seated. Larek so he could see the front door. Dyrra so she could see the kitchen door and pass-through. Sindra in whatever chair the hostess offered. The hostess continued, "Only once in a month do we offer lamb and veal, and that night is tonight. We also have fresh, river-caught salmon, but that you can enjoy here on any night from the spring through the summer."

She focused on Dyrra and said, "We even have..." She took a closer look at Dyrra, perhaps studying her scar, then said something in Karwalish. It might have been a question, but from the dips and rises in the speech pattern, Larek couldn't be certain.

Dyrra answered with a quick sentence that seemed to slam the subject closed with finality.

The hostess' smile faltered for a moment, but then returned.

"I recommend getting the lamb and veal together. We serve it with carrots, broccoli and potatoes. You won't be sorry."

"Enough of that for three then," said Sindra, "Beer for her, a Terhold white for him, and a Terhold red for me. We will also need a room with two beds for the night."

"Of course. Shall I send a boy to stable your horses?"

"No horses."

That got a strange look from the hostess, and another glance at Dyrra's scar, but she covered it behind her bright smile before returning to the kitchen.

"I'm having second thoughts about this cover story," said Dyrra.

"What did she say to you?" said Larek.

"She asked if I knew Keon. She's spying for him, as sure as Lucala will rise tonight."

"What did you say?"

"I said I didn't know her name. Why should I know his?"

"It sounds better in Karwalish," whispered Chitter in Larek's ear. "It's idiomatic. Doesn't translate right."

"You speak Karwalish?" said Larek, drawing amused looks from Dyrra and Sindra.

"You aren't the first wizard I've met, you know."

The food and drinks followed shortly, and Barth did not mislead them about its quality. The meats all but fell apart on the tongue, and the vegetables retained enough of their crunch to delight the mouth with the contrast. And all of the food was spiced so that some bites came out sweeter and others more savory.

Larek could not remember when he had eaten better food.

All three of them drank toasts to their trip, and their friendship, and to Barth. But once the toasts were done and their cups empty, they refused all attempts by the serving boys and girls to refill them with alcohol. They opted instead to drink water.

In Larek's case, he knew the switch was habit. But even had it not been his custom, he would have made the switch tonight for the same reason he suspected the other two made it: the scrutiny of the room. Sindra and Dyrra had to feel it as acutely as he did. Surely not one of them doubted they were the subject of discussion at every table. And many of the locals did not mind staring openly.

"Well," said Larek, "whether our hostess is an informant or not, if Keon has any spies in this town he'll hear about us soon enough."

"It would have been worse if we sat in the corner," said Sindra. "We would have looked like we were up to something."

"Or that we just didn't want to be the night's show," said Dyrra.

"To most people, that's the same thing."

"Well, if you did not want to be part of the night's show," said a man crossing the bridge toward them. "Then you should not have dined with Red-Eyed Larek the Burned."

* * *

From her seat watching the kitchen door and pass though, Dyrra had a clear view of the man approaching across the stone bridges to where the trio sat inside the innermost ring of fire and water. He had come from the back, so he either worked here in the Springwater, or he owned it.

By the steady confidence in his step, and the excited murmuring that sprang up at every other table in the half-full inn, Dyrra guess that he owned it. All the other diners seemed to recognize him.

And the man was no warrior. His rotund frame had the loose fat of a man who gained most of his weight in a short period of time. Perhaps when he acquired the inn. He knew how to wear his finery though. Dyrra had to give him that. The reds and yellows in his shirt and vest — both with actual buttons instead of toggles — breathed life into the light tan of his breeches. Yellow stockings and soft leather shoes completed the look, accented further by the gold and gems glittering from his finger rings and earrings.

More gray in his beard than black, and he grew it long as though to make up for his bald head. His weathered skin might have been called dark by an easterner, but to Dyrra the deep tan still looked pale, and faded over what it must have once been.

Though Sindra turned to look at the speaker immediately, Dyrra was pleased to note that Larek first checked the door and the corners of the room that Dyrra couldn't see. And even when he did turn, Chitter stayed watchful of those areas from Larek's shoulder.

Larek's slumping shoulder. And even from the corner of her eye, Dyrra could see the weary sigh he heaved.

Recognition.

She was about to ask Larek about the interloper when Larek sat up straight and spoke.

"We've enjoyed the meal. Both the lamb and the veal were exquisite. The vegetables were spiced a little more than I would have asked for, but I imagine it's a local choice, and I can't deny that they tasted good."

"As master of the house," said the spangled man with a slight bow that Dyrra thought contained more than a trace of mockery, "I thank you for the compliments."

"And we brought coins enough to pay for our meal, our night's lodging, and breakfast to take on the road with us. So I hope these good people will forgive me if I have been mistaken for a skald. I never intended to perform for my meal."

The spangled man smiled.

"I could no more mistake you for a skald than you could mistake me for a common innkeeper."

That stilled the excited chattering at the other tables. Dyrra decided that the spangled man needed a reminder that Larek did not sit alone. She toyed with her dinner knife.

"In all my years as a mercenary," she said, "I've never once seen an innkeeper who wore so many jewels."

"He's a wizard," said Larek.

The spangled man bowed again, and this time Dyrra was certain it was intended to mock.

"That I am. And since it seems I have our burned friend here at a disadvantage, I'll name myself. I am Sebas."

"We appreciate your hospitality, Sebas," said Sindra, "but we've had a long day on the road and several more ahead of us. Please forgive us if we forgo any performances tonight."

"But I'm afraid I must insist," said Sebas.

"Such an insistence could prove hazardous," said Dyrra.

That made Sebas look at her.

"I can see Barth is slipping in his duties if he allowed a mercenary to keep her armor. He'll have to be censured for that. But certainly his incompetence did not extend to allowing you into town without first swearing peace?"

Dyrra smiled and spun the knife in her hand.

"We swore peace," said Larek, refusing to take his eyes from Sebas to meet Dyrra's warning glare. "And we were assured that the locals were peaceable folk who would offer us no threat."

"And none of these good people around you would. Nor would our hostess here sell your presence to Keon, however much he might pay for information about Dyrra Slow Sword."

Dyrra growled, but that only broadened Sebas' smile.

"We get too many travelers through town to worry about the writs of every little country noble. Now if Keon gets his hands on a *royal* writ..."

"I note you did not include yourself among those who would offer us no threat," said Sindra.

"I assure you Sindra — whom I assume to be Sindra the Poisonous — that I would never offer harm to you nor your tall friend."

"I note you—"

"Larek the Burned is another story," said Sebas, and as he said the name this time all joviality fled from his voice. The appellation came out hard and cold as a mountain peak in winter. "I was away in Boll when Blackflame last struck, but my house was among those destroyed by Larek's failure.

"*As were my wife and child.*"

The silence was so acute that Dyrra could hear only the burning coals in the stone rings, and the muffled clink of cooking pots in the kitchen.

Chitter said something, and from the tone Dyrra thought it sounded like a question. That little sound seemed to bring the other tables back to life, and the harsh hushing of dozens of whisperers sounded as though someone had stoked a fire.

Sebas' expression darkened.

"It doesn't matter," said Larek, softly, to the spirit-squirrel. Louder he said, "Very well. You claim loss to the dragon. But certainly you could not have been staying in Lillikan, stewing in your vengeance, in hopes that I would one day visit your inn. Why are you not at the tournament, fighting for your chance to slay the beast that killed your family? Why hide here in your inn?"

"HIDE?"

The roar stilled the whisperers again, and Dyrra felt disgusted to see such excitement in the eyes of the locals. But Sebas' rage gave him away. She could read it plainly in his red face, his trembling jowls.

Fear.

Larek was right. Sebas was hiding.

"I can see that you do not want us here," said Larek. "So let us pay for our meal and we will seek our accommodations elsewhere."

"No!" Sebas' arms came up, fingers twitching as though they ached to throttle Larek. "No, Larek, who burned the names of all wizards with his failure. I will have my revenge and I will have it now."

"WAIT," SAID SINDRA, HOLDING UP HER HANDS AND RISING TO HER feet. She turned in place, claiming the eye of every other diner in the main room of the Springwater Inn, not that any were paying attention to their meals or their wine. Sindra did not speak until she again faced the colorful innkeeper wizard, Sebas.

"Nilasah teaches us that vengeance serves no one. It masters them and works them to death.

"Even now we see Nilasah's truth played out before us. If you would seek vengeance, Sebas, you must offer us violence, here in front of some sixty witnesses by my count. If you act on this it will be you the watch imprisons for it. Even if we must defend ourselves.

"Spare yourself the risk. Spare yourself the embarrassment. Let us leave in peace."

"Odd," said Sebas turning his weight to face her. "The words of Nilasah from the lips of one who forgot how to pray. Well, content yourself, *Healer*. I will offer no violence to you or your armored friend."

He turned back to face Larek. "And to you, Burned One, I do not merely offer violence. If I only sought your death I could have poisoned your meal and no one would argued for your name. I seek your defeat. I seek your humiliation. I—"

"Oh, say the words already," said Larek. "Listening to you talk is more tiring than hiking in the mid-day heat."

"*Skara brach.*"

Sindra had heard her share of the ancient tongues that wizards used. She had even managed to pick up a word or two of Aarkadian, though nothing suitable for polite company. But those were words Sindra did not know.

Dyrra either seemed to recognize them or pick something out of their tone, because she tightened her grip on that carving knife.

"No," said Dyrra, making both Sebas and Larek blink at her in surprise. "I'm no wizard, but I know a duel challenge when I hear one. And Larek is not free to fight a duel. He has a commitment to me and a commitment to Sindra to see us through the mountains, safe from magical threats. He can't do that if he's dead."

"I doubt he can do it at all," said Sebas, spiteful. He turned back to Larek. "Well, Burned One? You accused me of hiding, but who is hiding now?"

"I'm not hiding, Sebas." Sindra heard resignation in Larek's voice. He shook his head as he said, "*Skara na, fil pirek.*"

"Larek," said Sindra, waiting until he met her eye before she finished. "You don't need to do this. You have nothing to prove. Let him seek his vengeance against the true guilty party. The dragon."

"He has already accepted," said Sebas, his voice almost gleeful now. "And a duel confirmed in front of witnesses is perfectly legal." He clapped his hands and rubbed them together. "Now, if the two of you will cross a bridge to another table, we can have our duel right here without endangering—"

"No," said Larek, his voice quiet, but loud enough to stop Sebas' rubbing hands.

"You have already accepted—"

"A duel. I did not concede the choice of location, which is mine as challenged."

"I have no intention of accompanying you to Velstadt. I have a business to run."

That made Larek smile.

"I considered it, but I have no desire to listen to your complaints the whole way." Larek looked over the excessively heavy man in his expensive finery. "And you look even less accustomed to such travel on foot than I am."

"Very well then. Where?"

"On the banks of the Quar."

"That's half a day from here!"

"No more than three hours," said Sindra. "At a *reasonable* walking pace."

"You're trying to get me to back out."

"No," said Larek. "This whole duel is about your pride, so I know you won't do that—"

"*It's about—*"

"Yes, yes, your family. So you said. Loudly." Larek shook his head, without ever taking his eyes off Sebas. "And you hoped you could goad me into dueling you here and now, in front of your regular customers while I am weary from the road. A quick victory with an excellent view for all those who would carry the tale with them.

"But while I may have failed to slay a dragon, I am still a wizard, not a fool. You have fed us, and your hostess already agreed to find us rooms for the night, so even though you have challenged me to a duel, you remain our acknowledged host. You will uphold your duties tonight, *innkeeper*, and see us provisioned for the road before we leave, knowing well that if anything happens to any of us in the night the blame and the inquiry will fall on your head." Larek smiled. "For all you denigrate Barth, it seems to me that he would happily lead that inquiry himself.

"And tomorrow, when you and I are equally rested, Sebas, we will travel to the Quar and have our duel without putting my companions and me too far behind schedule."

"You sound confident of victory," said Sebas with a sneer twisting within the folds of his face.

"What is the first rule all apprentices are taught?"

For the first time, Sindra thought she heard a taunting tone in Larek's voice.

Sebas' face darkened its red to a shade deeper than his vest. So deep Sindra felt a fleeting worry about the heavy man's heart. When he spoke his words came out little more than a growl.

"Ilarra will see to your needs. Until tomorrow, dead man."

Sebas turned and stalked off, and conversation in the room exploded the moment the kitchen door swung shut behind him. Chitter was talking fast to Larek, who had his head bent, listening.

Dyrra was smiling as though Larek had already won the duel. She reached out and thumped him on the shoulder.

"You must have fought many duels to understand the preliminaries so well."

Larek was speaking fast Aarkadian to the earth spirit, but looked up at Dyrra as though he missed what she said.

"Wait," said Sindra, but Chitter said something more and Larek's focus was back on a conversation in a dead tongue.

"Was your master an accomplished duelist?" said Dyrra, her eyes almost as excited as the diners in the other rings of tables.

"What is the first rule all apprentices are taught?" said Sindra.

That seemed to catch Larek's attention. He looked up.

"What? Oh. The first rule every apprentice is taught is always know more than your enemy."

"Perfect!" said Dyrra, slamming her fist down on the table. "You're in his head, and that's half the duel! Come on, tell us. How many duels have you won?"

Larek blinked, eyes flicking to Chitter over something quick the spirit-squirrel said. Larek looked back at Dyrra, and did not look nearly as confident as he had a moment before.

"None. I've never fought a duel before."

12

———

Larek had to give Sebas his due. The man may have been a coward and a bully, but he did know how to run an inn.

The upstairs room the Springwater's hostess led them to was as fine as Larek had been expecting during that delicious lamb and veal dinner, not the near-stable he assumed he'd be given after Sebas challenged him to a duel.

Two beds, feather stuffed mattresses so long and wide that even Dyrra could lay across them any direction and not have her feet or head hanging off the side. Not that she was willing to test this theory. The beds sat on wide, thick carpets of red and brown, and beside each a large oak armoire that made Larek miss the one he had left behind.

The beds pointed at each other across the long section of the room, and between them was a stone fire pit, circular and surrounded by an armspan of water, continuing the theme from the dining room downstairs. It was a testimony to the size of the room that the fire pit did not seem to dominate it, nor did the moat impede crossing the room. Brass oil lamps in the corners of the room supplemented the light from the fire pit so Larek could read in comfort if he chose.

Along the long, outer wall were no fewer than four shuttered windows, and in the space between the center two, sat a marble pedestal with a great copper bowl filled with bubbling water. An enchanted spring for a room in the Springwater Inn. The pedestal also held a copper pitcher and a few towels, and a rack of four leather flagons hung from the wall above it.

The spring was a nice touch, and even at a glance Larek could tell that the water refreshed itself constantly. True, the process would not leave the bowl's water as fresh and clean as Larek's jug, but the effect was impressive nonetheless, and probably took a lot less work.

Larek wanted to find some fault in the room. Something he could complain about. But he could think of nothing. The door even had its own lock.

The truth was, Larek had to admit it was the finest room he had ever stayed in.

"How much did we pay for this?" said Dyrra, poking around an armoire as though expecting it to conceal soldiers.

"A silver flat," said Sindra, patting down the mattress next to Dyrra with an expression of near bliss.

"Only one?" said Larek, still standing near the closed door. He had guessed a silver round, which would have been five times as much.

"I reminded dear Ilarra that her employer had interrupted our dinner and challenged one of us to a duel in front of the whole crowd." Sindra looked up at Larek with a smile. "She agreed that it showed appalling manners."

"I should think so," said Dyrra, who now looked under the bedding. Perhaps checking for snakes. "He took us in and fed us. Even offered us his roof, through Ilarra. In Karwale, if he had done all that and then challenged one of us to a duel—"

"We're not in Karwale," said Larek. Chitter finally got tired of waiting for Larek to step further into the room and leapt all the way to the top of the untouched armoire.

"No," said Dyrra, looking up. "But Ilarra must feel just as ashamed of Sebas as I am disgusted by him."

Dyrra shoved her mouth to one side, tilted her head, then said, "On second thought, she couldn't match my disgust with any emotion she could conjure. Between the three of us, the reason I didn't shove that knife into him was that I didn't want to ruin the knife."

Larek and Sindra stared at her. Even Chitter joined the stare.

"What?" said Dyrra. "A fine eating knife is not a thing to be taken lightly. I remember one time—"

"Did you steal that knife?" said Sindra.

"If he isn't going to hold with proper host rules," said Dyrra, turning back to her check of the mattress, "I'm not bound by proper guest rules. And trust me. Somewhere on the road you'll be grateful we have that knife."

"I should get some sleep," said Larek, and something in his tone made both women look him over.

"You don't have to fight him," said Dyrra, which startled Sindra out of whatever she was going to say.

"I do," said Larek, moving toward the unoccupied mattress with heavy steps.

"You don't," insisted Dyrra. "This is no duel of honor. You are not responsible for what the dragon cost him, and—"

"He lost nothing to the dragon," said Larek.

"What?" said Dyrra and Sindra together.

Larek dropped his pack next to the bed and yawned into a stretch of many tired muscles and joints accompanied by a symphony of small pops and cracks. Chitter jumped down onto the bed, clearly impatient to provide another round of healing waves.

"He was playing to the crowd." Larek stretched again, both arms high and wide, and this time the accompanying yawn infected Sindra. "He just wanted an excuse."

"Then you definitely don't need to do this," said Dyrra as though the matter was now closed.

"How do you know?" asked Sindra, sitting on the edge of the mattress.

"I looked over every inch of Blackflame's devastation. I spoke to every survivor. Did everything I could to help, and listened to every round of blame."

Larek shook his head.

"No wizard made his home there, much less one with a family. I would have found evidence. Some survivor would have thrown the other wizard's name in my face. Something."

"Then we're agreed," said Dyrra, sitting across the mattress from Sindra.

"No," said Larek. "I need to do this."

"Why?"

No frustration in Dyrra's voice as she asked. The word came out simple and direct. But her gray eyes bore into Larek with intensity that would have done a wizard proud. Not the time to play games with words or ideas.

"Sebas is a bully. You heard the way he wants to go after poor Barth. He probably intimidates a lot of the townsfolk. Someone needs to bring him down." Larek looked over at the copper fountain, which he had to admit was a nifty bit of work. "I just hope I can do it."

"Can you?" asked Sindra.

"Tough to say." Larek shrugged. "He may not be that good. He probably thinks I'm an easy target. No doubt he's heard the way the tales have ... exaggerated my failure. As though the truth weren't bad enough."

Larek shook off the dark direction his thoughts began to turn. There would be time enough for that when he tried to sleep.

"Guess we'll find out tomorrow."

"You will beat him," said Dyrra.

"Wish I had your confidence."

"You misunderstand me." Dyrra reached for where her sword should have been, then frowned. Instead, she raised her stolen dinner knife. "You will beat him or I will kill him."

"What?" said Sindra.

"Simple," said Dyrra. "If our Larek here doesn't wish to see me become a murderer and a fugitive, he must win." Dyrra smiled at

Larek. "Now you have something urgent to fight for instead of nebulous ideals."

Larek looked at Chitter. Chitter shrugged.

"Dyrra," said Larek, "you don't really mean that. Do you?"

Dyrra twirled the dinner knife in her fingers.

"I guess we'll find out tomorrow."

13

Dawn at the Springwater Inn came sooner than any of them wanted. Sindra had been enjoying the most marvelous dream. She was a full Healer again, and had discovered the secret to some foul plague. Through her Nilasah had healed multitudes, not merely saving lives, but restoring full health and faculties.

But a knock on the door to their room chased the dream away and bid her groggy eyes to open.

Sindra did not want to get up. She could not remember the last time she had seen a feather bed, much less slept on one. This one was every bit as comfortable as she could have hoped for, and with the coals of the banked fire keeping away any morning chill and adding a sweet cherry scent to the air she could have happily passed the day away in bed. Even the dimness of the room encouraged Sindra to return to sleep.

Dyrra, sleeping next to her, seemed to agree. Dyrra had not so much as stirred at the knock.

And why should she be stirring? It wasn't as though they had to keep to a timetable. No. Meals could be sent for. The road to Velstadt would still be waiting tomorrow. Surely no one would deny her a few more hours of blissful…

There was that knock again. Worse, Sindra could hear rustling across the room.

Larek! The duel!

So much for sleep.

The door opened, but Larek spoke only in whispers with whatever servant came to waken them. The warm, comfortable mattress called to Sindra. Surely they had some time yet. Surely...

The door closed. Not loud, but something about the finality of that closing door sank into Sindra's stomach. There would be no day of indolent rest.

She sat up, adjusting the strap of her nightdress where it had fallen past her shoulder. The nightdress was half the reason she yearned for more sleep. Soft, delicate silk, Sindra had never expected to find a reason to wear it this side of their destination. She had packed and unpacked it a dozen times before she left her parents' tent.

In the end, she had kept it as her one civilized thing, a touchstone for her on the hard days and nights she knew she would face crossing the mountains near the Velstadt border.

And now that she wore it, she didn't want to take it off. Didn't want to don one of her yellow kirtles of failure. But she had to. Sindra had sworn to herself that she would wear the trappings of her failure every day until she found some way to atone.

At least her clothes were clean again. She and Dyrra had been ready to put that magic copper spring to good use before they turned in last night, but Larek had cleaned all their clothes with a quick chant and a wave of his hands.

No wonder he carried so little clothing.

Fortunately his spell cleaned Dyrra's armor as well. Sindra had not wanted to mention to the huge warrior that she had begun to smell of travel and effort. Fortunately no longer true. They had each even bathed in the dark last night.

Sindra had noticed, during her turn, that the bowl's water had a distinctly tepid and earthy flavor, compared to Larek's wonderful jug.

At least, Sindra assumed Larek had bathed at the copper bowl after Sindra and Dyrra had their turn. Perhaps he knew a spell for bodily cleanliness as well.

Larek began rustling packs again, and Sindra realized she was delaying. No more time for that. Time to rise and see Larek to his duel.

"Dyrra," she said, and though she held no hope that the simple use of the woman's name would wake her, Dyrra's eyes snapped open.

"Awake," she said. "Is there trouble?"

"Well, it's almost time to leave, and you're still naked..."

"Bah," Dyrra said, throwing off the covers and standing tall without the slightest hesitation. "If Larek wants to see what a woman *should* look like, he's free to feast his eyes. But *only* his eyes." She looked around. "Not that his eastern eyes could see much in this gloom."

Sindra had to admit that Dyrra's hard life had kept her fit, though the roughness and scarring of her skin had not given her womanly curves their proper due.

Dyrra began throwing on the linens she wore beneath her armor, and Sindra had no more choice. She had to slip out of her nightshirt and into her kirtle once more. Though as she did, she envied Dyrra her brazen confidence. Sindra's teachers had emphasized that Healers on the battlefield — whether women or men — should not taunt warriors with their flesh for fear of igniting the need-fire. Dressing or undressing in front of another was simply not something she did.

Still, soon enough all three were clad, and the shutters thrown open to let in fresher, if cooler air.

"That was Ilarra at the door," said Larek. "Sebas is gone."

"Ha!" said Dyrra.

"Nothing like that." Larek shook his head. "He's gone ahead to 'prepare.'"

Dyrra nodded as though that made sense to her and adjusted something on her pack. Sindra had no idea what it meant.

"Anyway," Larek continued, "it seems that Ilarra is trying to make up for her employer's rudeness with food." He hefted a sack, and it seemed to take some effort. "Fruits, vegetables, meats, breads, cheeses. Three sacks worth. We'll eat for days on Sebas' lack of manners."

Something about that last sentence must have troubled Larek, because his brow furrowed. Probably worry over the duel. Sindra wished she could think of something reassuring to say that wouldn't sound ... inane. Dueling was a world she didn't know or understand.

Chitter must have known the right thing to say — or at least something to say — because he began chattering at Larek.

Dyrra appeared to miss the change in Larek.

"Well handled," she muttered. Louder she said, "I'll need to speak with her before we leave."

"She said she would be in the kitchen if we need anything," said Larek. "We'll be waiting outside. Please don't take long."

"I won't need long. Last night I told her I didn't know her name." Dyrra tied one of the sacks to her pack. Donned it. "I want her to know that now I do."

Dyrra left the room, and Sindra marveled at how little she understood of Karwalish culture. She turned to remark about that to Larek, but he had a grim cast as he tied a sack to his own pack.

Sindra inhaled deeply. She still didn't know what to say, but she needed to say something.

"You can beat him, Larek."

"I hope so. I think Dyrra's serious about killing him."

"Oh, I know she is. But that isn't why you'll beat him."

Larek looked at her, curiosity rather than trepidation raising his eyebrows now.

"You said it yourself. He's a coward. He wants to fight you because he thinks you're weak. But you were brave enough to challenge a dragon.

"And bravery beats cowardice. Every time."

Dyrra was in a foul mood. And this time the early hour was not to blame.

Yes, Lucala's Jealous Sister shone brightly as She rose this morning. But She held back the heat of Her jealousy, and allowed the white puffs of Drandle's smoke to spread through the sky, even covering Her at times.

Nor could Dyrra blame her mood on the land around her. The road still suffered from its lack of proper maintenance, but not so dangerously as they had faced north of town. What was more, it seemed that they had left the dry fields and cracked earth of yesterday behind, and their road south of Lillikan was surrounded by small farms and green wild grasses, even the occasional copse of trees. It all smelled fresh enough to be almost rejuvenating.

No, these were nearly perfect conditions for Dyrra to be traveling with Sindra and Larek. That they were traveling to a duel was not ideal, but Larek seemed to know what he was about with his magic. Dyrra felt some concern that he doubted his ability to think under pressure, but the practical life of a mercenary had taught Dyrra that such doubts were better tested alone than when the whole volley depended on him.

All of those things she could handle. Especially bolstered by the smile Barth gave her when he returned her sword. It was the smile of a comrade-in-arms, not a stranger. A smile Dyrra had known all too rarely for the last several years.

But Dyrra could not abide the crowd.

It seemed that the whole of Lillikan knew about the duel, and since the current populace had been unable or unwilling to travel to the tournament, they, and every one of them, intended to have a picnic down by the river and enjoy a mini-tournament of their own.

Horses and riders. Mules pulling carts full of families and friends. And multitudes with no better transportation than Dyrra herself had, forcing the three of them to walk as though surrounded by a swarming crowd of gnats.

At first the gnats seemed bent on pestering Larek with their pointless questions. *Are you good enough to put up a fight? Did you really get those scars from a dragon? Do you have any next of kin we should notify?*

Each time laughter followed. Never from the speaker. Always from the safety of the crowd.

Sindra stared straight ahead, pretending not to hear the questions. That was bad enough. But Larek seemed to feel it was somehow his duty to take all of it. Every bit. Not a single question went by that he did not turn and listen to.

He never answered, but they didn't need answers. They didn't want answers. They just wanted their friends to think them clever for asking the questions.

Chitter was going crazy, chattering and barking, but that only seemed to enflame the crowd's humor further.

Dyrra hated it. She tried to dissuade them with her scowl, and though that had slowed things down in the beginning, when they decided she wasn't going to kill them, they ignored her.

What they didn't realize was that Dyrra *wanted* to kill them.

She would have been only too happy to draw her sword and spill the blood of some laughing jackal. It would drive back the pack, that was certain. It might even have driven them off.

But Larek kept giving them his attention. Listening as though any one of them had value. As though they had somehow earned the right to their questions.

Dyrra didn't feel it was her place to stop them if Larek considered this some sort of personal penance.

And so she scowled, and she hated it, and her mood darkened further and further as they walked, surrounded by the laughter of muttonheads.

But then it started.

That two note, drawn out first syllable Dyrra had heard often in the taverns and ale tents around the capitol. She knew all too well the words that followed...

Blackflame
A dragon of fame
Was raiding the countryside...

"KEENARACH!" screamed Dyrra, whipping her sword out of its scabbard and bringing everything around her to a grinding halt. She held the sword high in a two hand grip, and turned slowly to take in the whole of the crowd.

Every one of the townsfolk fell back at least one step when they saw her eyes. Most fell back two or three. One skinny little man fell down.

"Begone. All of you."

"Dyrra," began Larek, but she did not let him finish.

"NO!" She twirled her blade to make sure every eye was on her. "Go to the river if you wish. Go to town if you prefer. Go to the deepest pits of the Underworld for all I care.

"But I swear, on the eye of Lucala, on the blood in my veins, and on the memory of my beloved Ommure — I will count to ten. And when I reach ten I will kill everyone within an arrow's flight of me and my companions."

No one around her so much as breathed.

"One," she said, and there were screams and a mad scramble.

"Two," she said, and men and women dragged their crying children.

"Three," she said, and the crowd of townsfolk fell over each other in their haste to flee.

Dyrra continued to count aloud, a slow, steady pace. When she reached ten she was alone once more with Larek and Sindra.

And Chitter, who, Dyrra decided, deserved to be counted as a full companion.

"Well," said Sindra, looking at the nearest townsfolk, who were largely still putting more distance between themselves and Dyrra, "that was something they won't likely forget soon."

"Good," said Dyrra.

Larek said nothing. He only looked at her, with that slightly puzzled furrow his brow got sometimes that drew down the wide brim of his floppy hat.

"I won't pretend to understand why you would tolerate their questions. But we have all three of us suffered the taunting songs of muttonheads for years." Dyrra thrust her sword back into its scab-bard. "I say *no more*."

Larek smiled and thumped her on the shoulder. She barely noticed the friendly strike, but Dyrra let herself match his smile nonetheless.

* * *

THE RIVER QUAR WAS WIDE AND SLOW, AT LEAST WHERE IT PASSED THE road south of Lillikan. The bank here on the north side was an even lusher green than Larek had seen in the wild grass and farms he had passed through the early morning sunlight.

It really was a lovely spot by the river. The perfect place to rest his weary, sweaty body from the morning's hike.

Less appealing to Larek's eye was the forest of stumps. Sindra must have been right about how the people of Lillikan razed a small forest for the wood they needed.

Shortsighted. The act of merchants looking for profit, but that suited a town that grew out of a meeting place.

Even less appealing to Larek was the encampment of those townsfolk, all spread about to watch the show. Some had even kindled small cooking fires, and the smells of roasting chicken and heating stew reminded Larek that he had not eaten much since the few apples and cut of cheese Sindra had forced on him around dawn.

"Listen to your stomach if you won't listen to me," said Chitter. "Eat something."

"I couldn't keep it down if I tried."

Larek kept his words in Aarkadian, to avoid worrying his other two companions. But Sindra looked worried nonetheless. Dyrra kept confidence in her smile, but Larek doubted she would have glanced at him as often as she did had she not felt a need to check on him.

Of course, right now Dyrra was sneering at the crowd, who kept well back from her. Apparently they did not feel that numbers gave them enough safety. After that display on the road, Larek didn't blame them. Still, he was half-surprised that none of them carried weapons themselves.

Perhaps only members of the watch armed themselves, and the watch had been required to stay behind and keep an eye on the town.

Or perhaps none of them were willing to display a weapon and risk Dyrra taking it as a challenge. If so, Larek would not blame them for that either.

Chitter scurried across Larek's shoulder and into the sack Ilarra had provided. He could feel the earth spirit rummaging, and was about to ask why when Dyrra spoke.

"There," she said, pointing to a red pavilion down by the river.

"I don't see him," said Sindra, slowly, "but I think you're right. The crowd's attention is focused there."

Larek sighed.

"Figures that he would want me to approach like a petitioner."

"Then don't," said Dyrra, one hand on Larek's chest to stop him from stepping forward. "I'll be your guard. She'll be your herald."

Sindra smiled. "I know just what I'll say."

"Here," said Chitter, back on Larek's shoulder and offering a single strawberry. "Eat this, stem to seed. But do it standing still."

Larek could feel the magic flowing out of the strawberry.

"What did you—"

"You've been walking for hours. You've barely eaten. And Sebas doesn't strike me as the sort to let you rest before—"

The sound of trumpets blowing fanfare echoed all around them.

Chitter gestured with one paw, as though to say, "See what I mean?"

Larek popped the strawberry in his mouth, and as he chewed he felt stiff, sore muscles ease. Strength, vigor flowed through him spreading from his mouth down his throat, and then from there through every part of his body, from the tip of his red hair to the soles of his feet. Even his mind grew clearer, as though awakening from the most refreshing night's sleep of his life.

"Thank you, Charespecusis."

Chitter managed a lop-sided smile and said, "Now go stomp that arrogant bully."

A SECOND BLAST OF TRUMPET FANFARE ISSUED FROM THE AREA OF THE tent, and the crowd fell still and silent on the northern bank of the Quar.

As Larek walked down the incline toward the red pavilion near the river itself — a bounce in his step thanks to the power Chitter had infused into that strawberry — he noted that many of the spectators from Lillikan were using the stumps of old trees like seats in the tournament grandstands.

Dyrra and Sindra paced him on either side, following two steps behind. Chitter rode high and proud on Larek's right shoulder.

The silence of the crowd felt almost oppressive in its anticipation, and though the strawberry had settled Larek's nerves as well as his fatigue and hunger, he found himself paying attention to whatever sounds he could. His boots hushing through the thick grass. The cries of hunting river birds in the distance. The thump of his own heartbeat.

When Larek closed to within a hundred paces of the pavilion, a gust of wind from within blew its cloth doors open, carrying the smell of sulfur and yaro.

Billows of smoke followed, first black, then gray, then white, red, orange, yellow. It held yellow until the smoke faded, faded, vanished.

Standing at the entrance was Sebas in a formal robe of red that matched his pavilion, trimmed and embroidered with gold thread. His bald head gleamed as though freshly polished, and his long, gray-and-black beard wound into a single braid that glittered with gold and gems from its ties. More gold and gems on his fingers and ears, and in his hand he held his staff, a branch of shining black oak that stood tall and thick.

"It's all just distraction," muttered Chitter.

Larek nodded, but wished he shared the earth spirit's certainty.

Sebas seemed a bully, and he had taken hours to prepare for this, but Larek could not afford to underestimate him.

"Before you stands Sebas the Mighty," boomed a voice from his staff. "Once court wizard to the Duke of Pleyst. He who rained stones at the Battle of Seven Peaks. Master of fire and water, and binder of spirits."

The crowd applauded enthusiastically. Sindra might have said something, but Larek couldn't hear it and he refused to look away from Sebas.

When the applause at last began to falter Larek drew breath to speak, but Sindra stepped forward. Her words could not match the volume of the booming staff, but they rang out nonetheless.

"Before you stands Larek Firetested. Ally and friend of warriors and spirits alike. The only man to face the dragon Blackflame ... *and live.*"

Those last words stunned the crowd into silence. Larek could understand why. Put that way it sounded impressive. Why mention that Larek was the only *wizard* to face Blackflame at all? That Blackflame had struck several times where he wasn't expected, then vanished for years without a trace throughout the kingdom?

Those were the points the songs emphasized. The skalds portrayed the dragon as a coward, fit to destroy those who could not resist, but fleeing from any real opposition. Larek was a wizard. He was supposed to be real opposition...

But in the moments after Sindra's new kenning, the crowd forgot their humor at Larek's failure. Instead, they murmured. Softly, and to each other, but so many of them speaking at once carried a volume of its own.

Sebas certainly had an irritated wrinkle to his nose as he looked about at the crowd's reaction. Perhaps they did not break into derisive song fast enough to suit him.

And they would. Larek had no doubt of that. If he gave them enough time.

"Very well, Sebas," said Larek. "You have issued the formal challenge, and given as your reason that I am responsible for the death of your family when I failed to slay the dragon Blackflame."

Larek projected his next words as loudly as he could without a spell.

"I deny your claim and give you the lie. No wizard lived in the area devastated by Blackflame that day, nor did any wizard lose his family. I know because I walked every inch of it before I slept that night."

"You dare say such things to me? You, a wizard barred from wearing the robes and carrying the staff? *I saw their burned bodies myself!*"

Larek shook his head.

"Dragonfire leaves no burnt bodies. It leaves no bones to bury. It devours as surely as the dragon's gullet."

"Enough of your lies!"

"You will not withdraw your claim and with it your challenge?"

"*Skara brach!*"

"Shall we at least prepare the area—"

A spear of green flame leapt from the tip of Sebas' staff, soaring at Larek and growing wider as it flew.

And just like that, the duel began.

DYRRA DOVE TO THE RIGHT AND ROLLED DOWN THE SLOPE OF WET, thick grass, away from the spear of green flame. She came up in a crouch facing the duel, her sword naked in her hands by reflex.

The fire burnt the grass below Larek to bare, scorched earth. It left the very air singed and smelling volcanic. But Larek stood untouched, calm as Chitter on his shoulder. The only difference that Dyrra could see was that his hands were raised.

Must have had a counterspell ready.

On the other side of Larek, just up the slope, Dyrra could see Sindra, sprawled in the grass from her own dive for safety. She slapped at fingers of flame along the bottom of her kirtle.

Larek made no move to counterattack. He seemed content to wait. He looked almost picturesque, there under the deep blue sky of the east, with Lucala's Jealous Sister obscured by fluffy white puffs from Drandle's pipe.

Almost. Dyrra could spot nervousness in the rapid rise and fall of his shallow breaths.

Dyrra boomed out the loudest laugh she could, which she knew from experience could carry across a wide tavern in the middle of a full scale brawl. She let the laugh continue while she tried to remember Sindra's brilliant new kenning for Larek.

"He throws fire at Larek *Firetested*? Does he wish to duel him or kiss him?"

Excited burbling through the crowd now, but Larek only stood and waited, his eyes never leaving Sebas.

Sebas thumped his staff into the wild grass, and a crack spread in the ground.

The crack raced toward Larek, widening into a massive fissure more than thirty feet across, centered on Larek.

Dyrra stepped back, sword raised in a guard position. Sindra hustled backward up the hill.

But Larek shook his head and waited.

Just before the fissure reached him, Chitter jumped to the ground.

The fissure halted, perhaps a stride from Larek's toes, as still as though it had not spread a hand's breadth since it formed in ancient times, when the rise they stood on first swelled up.

What remained of Sebas' spell looked as though some god, Drandle perhaps, had taken the head of a giant arrow and pushed it into the ground in front of Larek, so that it pointed at Sebas.

"Hiding behind spirits?" sneered Sebas.

"You took the morning to prepare while I spent it walking. You chose the battleground despite being the challenger. You—"

"You chose by the banks of the Quar! We stand near that river right now."

"You quibble over semantics. You placed your pavilion and

summoned me like a noble to court. And you did not set the space for the duel. You endanger the very spectators you all but invited."

Dyrra wondered how fast she could close the distance to Sebas if Larek fell. She began edging that direction, a bare fraction of a step at a time. Not enough to notice, she hoped, if Sebas kept his attention on Larek.

Of course, it would help if Larek would actually *attack*. What did he plan to do? Tire Sebas out?

Sebas twirled his staff over his head, shouting syllables in some twisted wizard tongue, then pointed his staff at Larek. Three whirling blades of steel flew from the end of the staff. Each as long as a short sword, and spinning so fast they looked like solid discs.

From the corner of her eye, Dyrra could see Larek's mouth moving as he raised his hands high.

The blades flew closer.

Larek dropped to one knee and slammed his hands down. The blades banked sharply down into the fissure, sticking into the torn-up earth below.

But Larek wasn't done this time.

He shouted some harsh word and pulled, straining as with all his inconsiderable physical might and somewhat more impressive weight. His arms came in and his back levered like a fisherman pulling his net.

Sebas was jerked forward off his feet, falling into the fissure.

The crowd oohed in surprise.

But instead of tumbling down into the broken earth below, Sebas thrust his staff high and *stopped falling in mid-air*.

Dyrra stopped her edging forward.

Sebas simply floated there, unsupported by anything but his magic. Dyrra had never seen such a thing. She had never even heard of such a thing. Not without some enchanted object to ride.

Larek paled. Apparently he had never seen such a thing before either. Or worse, he had, and the skill intimidated him.

And that troubled Dyrra more than the sight of a floating wizard.

Chitter was saying something, his arms waving to get Larek's attention, but to no avail.

"Perhaps you *are* Larek Firetested," said Sebas. "But I am Sebas, the Flying Wizard."

SINDRA DID NOT LIKE THE PALLOR SHE SAW ON LAREK'S FACE. THE FRESH beads of sweat beneath the brim of his hat. She knew that look. She had seen it on battlefields. Talked to its victims as part of their treatment.

It was the look of a man who expected to die.

Right now Larek probably fixated on the details of what he thought of as his death tableau. He probably didn't hear the scattered applause and excited babbling of the crowd or the urgent words of Chitter. He more likely heard only the sweet songs of the hunting river birds. Perhaps the loud, rapid beating of his own heart.

The green of the grass probably looked emerald to him and smelled pure and fresh. The red of Sebas' robe and pavilion must have looked a deep scarlet. The blue of the sky, sapphire. The white of the clouds, pearl. The lingering taste of that final strawberry sweet and sharp on his tongue.

She could imagine all Larek went through in that frozen moment, but she could think of no way to help him.

Then she saw Dyrra begin edging her slow way toward where Sebas floated above his spell-hewn rent in the sloping ground. Sebas who chanted rapid words and made passes with his free hand, his shaggy brow drawn down in deep concentration.

Then she knew what to say.

"Larek!" She shouted, as much force in her voice as she could muster. "Don't make Dyrra a fugitive from murder!"

Larek blinked, glanced toward Sindra.

Chitter ran up his front, frantically talking as fast as his squirrel mouth could move.

And out of the fissure came a hand. Giant, cragged and formed of rich, dark soil, that hand looked big enough to catch Larek's whole body in its fist.

And attached to that hand was a wrist.

Some of the crowd screamed. Others hooted and cheered.

Up came a human-shaped head made of long, narrow stone, with slits for eyes, but no nose or mouth.

Sindra could no longer see Dyrra on the other side of the earth giant.

"You want to play with spirits, Burned One?" taunted Sebas. "Try your squirrel against *that*! Let us see who is the true master of earth magic."

Chitter shook his head, then turned and braced against Larek's shoulder for a leap at the giant, which continued to pull its massive body out of the earth.

Larek steadied Chitter with a hand.

That hand should not have looked so steady. Larek's knees shook. Sweat had soaked through his brown travel shirt and more ran down his face. His nostrils flared like a panting horse.

"*Neja!*" yelled Larek.

At least that was what it sounded like. Whatever language he spoke, it was not one Sindra understood. But as he continued to speak, she would have sworn he was not casting a spell.

He looked as though he was *talking* to the earth giant.

Sebas laughed and flew a loop in the air, twirling his staff, but he kept his free hand forward in a steady fist.

Whatever Larek said to that giant, it didn't listen. It pulled the whole of its body out of that fissure in the earth and the banks of the Quar trembled as the earth giant steadied its feet.

Chitter was staring at Larek, but Sindra could not read his face. The much smaller earth spirit turned and began speaking to the earth giant, and for the first time his words did not sound to Sindra like a squirrel's barks. He sounded like a mortar grinding away at a pestle.

From the corner of her eye, Sindra saw Dyrra moving swiftly now, heading for Sebas' pavilion.

Larek brought his fists together, thumb to thumb, in the air before him. His hands and arms shook, though whether with fear or effort Sindra could not tell. Either way, he had his eyes closed and was chanting now, voice rising and falling in a singsong pattern.

With a deep sound of cracking stone, the earth giant raised its fists high.

Still Larek chanted.

The fists began to swing down.

"Never," laughed Sebas where he floated above the fissure, that single fist thrust forward as though in victory. "I had all morning to prepare that binding. But please, fool, try. Even if you succeed, you'll never manage to—"

"*Nejatask!*" shouted Larek, ripping his hands apart so hard he fell backward into the grass.

No chance to run. Nowhere to hide. Even his hat came free from his red hair and fell on the grass as though the final indignity.

Sindra closed her eyes. Waited for the crash.

And waited.

Then she opened her eyes. The giant had stopped with its fists no more than an arm's length above Larek. It stared at him, as though thinking.

Chitter continued to talk in that grinding sound, and the earth giant seemed to be listening.

The crowd's excitement flipped to fear. Spectators began running away, some even leaving picnic foods behind.

"No!" yelled Sebas, shaking his fist. "Crush him! It is *I* who commands you!"

Then Sebas looked at his fist.

His eyes grew wide, and for the first time sweat broke out on his face.

With the roar of a raging avalanche, the earth giant turned.

Sebas grasped at the air, chanting desperately.

The earth giant spread its arms, as though to clap Sebas between its hands like a mosquito.

Sebas flew straight up, chanting desperately and waving his free hand.

The earth giant slammed its hands down hard enough to send shock waves that tumbled every standing person as far as Sindra could see, including Sindra herself. But she kept her eyes on Sebas.

Sebas plummeted straight down into the fissure.

The earth giant fell into the fissure on top of him.

And then the fissure was no more, and the ground and grass where they had been, as solid and steady as ever.

And Sebas was gone, as though he'd never been there.

14

———————

LAREK LAY THERE IN THE THICK, COMFORTABLE GRASS, STARING UP AT the cloudy sky, and thinking about how his shirt would need that freshening spell to get the sweat stains out of it. His pants would need that spell too, but he could not pretend it was only to clean out sweat.

But another spell would be effort, and Larek was exhausted to his very bones. Not a single muscle even seemed interested in helping him sit up. So tired that the sky seemed to try to spin above him, but could not manage the effort. It would get perhaps a quarter turn before the clouds all snapped back into place.

Was it really only a short while ago that Chitter had given him that strawberry? It must have been. He could still taste it on his tongue.

Chitter. Chitter was saying something, and he sounded nearby. Turning to look was too much effort though. Larek settled for trying to tune into the earth spirit's words.

"Can you even hear me, Larek? Snap out of it! I know you're tired, but you know I can't help you with this. Come on, Larek!"

On his third try, Larek's lips responded and something like sound came out.

"Here." The word slurred, and took longer to say than it should have.

"Larek!" yelled Sindra, and he could hear her running down the slope to him. She sounded worried.

Larek didn't want to deal with that right now. He wanted to sleep. Sleep just sounded like the best idea he had heard in years. In fact, just thinking about it made him yawn, but yawning made all his muscles cramp.

Sharp pain through the spasms and Larek's body doubled forward.

Sindra reached his side, knelt next to him. He heard some voice shout in the background. That had to have been Dyrra, but he could make no sense of what she said.

Sindra's hand gentle on his forehead. Her fingers alighting his throat.

"Why so ragged?" she said, but not as though to Larek. To Chitter, maybe. He was responding about spell exhaustion, but Larek could have told him not to bother. Sindra wouldn't understand him.

Larek closed his eyes. Started to drift.

A tiny paw slapped his face with strength that would have done Dyrra proud.

Larek's eyes blinked open again, rapidly. Sindra gripped his face, stared down into his eyes. Dyrra was there now, kneeling on his other side and looking equally worried.

"What's wrong with him?" she asked.

"I think," Sindra said, "it's spell exhaustion." She shook her head. "But I've only read about it."

"Well, exhaustion needs rest," said Dyrra.

Chitter began lecturing about spell exhaustion, but Sindra, obviously not understanding, spoke over him.

"No. Sleep is bad for him right now. He needs to get ... balanced."

"What does that mean?"

"I'm not a wizard."

Sindra furrowed her brow, and Larek marveled that even that

made her look so pretty. Like the clever princess in a skald's tale. How did that tale go…

Dyrra shook Larek by the shoulders just as he began to nod off. Sindra wasn't there, but Larek thought he heard someone rummaging through a pack. His pack? It would have been the closest…

Water gushed over Larek's head, flowing like an icy waterfall that moved down his body, drenching every inch of him. Larek could hear the tiny clapping of Chitter's applause.

Larek blinked water out of his eyes. Could not rub them because Dyrra still held his shoulders. He saw Sindra re-capping his everfull jug.

Larek felt clearer now. Stronger, but still tired. He managed to sit up on his own.

"I…" he tried, and the word came out. "I think. Air next."

"How?" said Dyrra.

Chitter laughed.

Larek felt blood rush to his face in a flush that would never show past his scars.

"I'll … have to stand naked in the breeze for a while."

Dyrra laughed, but not as though mocking him. Sindra raised an eyebrow and quirked a smile.

"I hope you don't need us for that part," she said.

"No, no," he said quickly. "I just needed water to counter the fire magic I worked earlier, and air to counter the earth magic."

"Does this happen all the time?" asked Dyrra, as though considering the potential liabilities.

"No. I overreached to break that binding. It was too strong. That threw me off."

"Great work though," said Chitter.

"Thanks," said Larek, with an attempt at a smile. "Now if you two will excuse me…"

"Wait," said Dyrra. When Larek turned back, she said, "Exactly what did we just see? How did you beat him?"

"Oh," said Larek. "Of course." He rolled his neck to a chorus of pops and cracks that felt blissful. "That was the biggest earth spirit I've ever seen. If Sebas actually rained stones at the Battle of Seven Peaks, that must have been the spirit that helped him do it.

"Anyway, most spirits don't care much for being bound. And they like it even less when asked to do things against their natural inclinations. Ask that thing to throw a bunch of boulders and it would have done so all day without a second thought, not caring much where the wizard wanted them thrown.

"But ask it to deliberately snuff out a human life? That's not the earth's way." Larek shook his head. "He would have been smarter to have it throw a boulder at me."

"What's the difference between a boulder and its hand?" asked Sindra. "Its hand was bigger than some boulders."

"Made it personal. Deliberate." Larek shrugged. "I'd have to ask Chitter to give you the full explanation. Anyway, that was why Sebas was laughing. He knew the spirit would be angry about what he tasked it to do, and he figured that even if I broke the binding, the spirit would still crush me while I tried to re-bind it."

"But you re-bound it that fast?"

Dyrra and Sindra both looked impressed.

"No," said Larek, allowing himself a smile. "That was never my plan."

Chitter stood tall and proud, twitching his tail.

"Chitter," said Sindra, realization building in her voice. "You told me Chitter isn't some sort of bound faerie or demon-granted servant."

"Nope." Larek reached out and scratched Chitter's head. "He's my friend."

"And that's what Chitter was telling it while you worked to break the binding."

"He was telling the spirit about me and our friendship and everything he knew about Sebas."

"It cared that he was a bully?"

Chitter answered, and Larek translated.

"No, but the contrast between Sebas and me was important. And you saw what it did to him."

"I'm not sure what I saw," said Sindra.

"Yes you are," said Dyrra. "Admit it. The earth spirit broke Sebas' flight spell and crushed him like an avalanche.

"Well, while you two discuss the details, I need to go ... find balance."

Larek grimaced at the smirks that got him.

"Do something about those clothes while you're at it," said Dyrra. "You may be a great wizard, but you stink!"

LAREK CAME BACK DOWN THE SLOPE TOWARD THE RED PAVILION NEAR the river Quar, where Dyrra and Sindra had gathered a good deal of the picnic food left behind by fleeing townsfolk from Lillikan.

He felt balanced again, and the tiredness that pulled at his limbs felt more normal for the level of exertion he had put his body through with the urgency of his spellcasting.

And with clean clothes on his body and Chitter perched on his shoulder, Larek felt good again.

Well, almost.

He had put on a brave front for Dyrra and Sindra, but the truth was that he hadn't wanted to kill Sebas. Beat him, yes. Embarrass him in front of people he likely intimidated or bullied on a regular basis, definitely.

And Larek was certain of that part. Sebas might not have bullied every person in Lillikan, but Larek felt no doubt that Sebas was not above throwing his weight around to get what he wanted.

Otherwise there was no reason for such a show. No reason for a duel at all. Unless...

Unless Sebas truly had once had a family. And that this family had truly lived near the area devastated by Blackflame. It was possible. It was possible that bandits had used the dragon's strike as an excuse for looting, burning everything in their wake and hoping that no one would know the difference between dragonfire and regular fire.

It could have been that Sebas told the truth as he understood it. Yes, as a wizard he should have known the difference between dragonfire and normal fire, but grief can blind a man to facts. Especially if those facts would deter revenge.

But it was not so simple, and Larek knew it.

That confrontation in the dining room of the Springwater had been a performance. Sebas had been smiling and cocky, even threatening the job of Barth the guard over allowing Dyrra to keep her armor.

Sebas had not looked like a man twisted by revenge to the point of murder. Yet the spells he threw in that duel would have been fatal.

And a showman would have set the ground first, ensured the safety of his audience. For the length of a single duel, such a space setting would not have taken long or overmuch effort.

Larek stopped halfway down the slope, and pinched the bridge of his nose. Cycling around these thoughts would bring madness.

If only Sebas still lived, Larek could have asked him. But Sebas was dead. Slain by his own conjured spirit, freed and encouraged by Larek.

He would have to learn the truth, even if it meant returning to Aeralfast after seeing Dyrra and Sindra safely into Velstadt. Most of the families ruined by Blackflame's last attack had refused Larek's help, claiming that he'd already "done enough," and that the community didn't need him.

But Sebas might have family yet living. There might be a way for Larek to make amends.

"Sebas was a liar," said Chitter.

Larek narrowed his eyes at the tiny earth spirit.

"Since when can you read my mind?"

"I can't." The flying squirrel reached out and patted Larek's face with a gentle paw. "But I *have* been living with you for years now. I know a thing or two about the way your mind works, especially when there is an opportunity for blame."

"Then how do you know Sebas was a liar?"

"Hurry up, up there!" called Dyrra, poking her head out of the pavilion. "You need to have a look at this."

Larek waved a hand to acknowledge her, but kept his eyes on Chitter.

"I've known dozens of wizards over the course of centuries. I know the focus you folk require for your magic, and I know what that focus looks like when turned toward revenge. And though you were facing the door when he walked up to our table last night, I got a look at him the moment I felt Dyrra stiffen."

Chitter grabbed Larek's chin with both forepaws and looked him straight in the eye, and in that moment Larek could see the spirit's age in the squirrel's eyes.

"He was everything you thought he was. An arrogant bully, bent on impressing as many people as possible. You were a trophy to him, not a source of inner peace."

"But the fury in his voice when he spoke about his family. The urgency of his attacks. What if?"

"He may have had and lost a family. His pride may have been all he had left. But he did not look at you the way a man looks at his living vengeance. You'll have to trust me on that."

"I do." Larek looked down, and Chitter let go of his jaw to let him. "It's just—"

"You didn't want to kill him." Chitter's voice grew gentle as he continued. "I know. And that's a good thing. But trust me, you did the people of Lillikan a favor."

He patted Larek on the cheek. "Come on, let's see what Sebas had in his pavilion."

On the outside, the pavilion looked like a great red tent with gold embroidery around the edging. Easily six strides wide, it peaked in the middle, but the outer walls stood tall enough that even Dyrra likely did not have to duck to enter.

Larek knew that *he* did not need to duck when he finally entered.

The moment he passed the flap, he smelled bacon, and fried eggs, and toast with butter. His stomach immediately informed him that a single strawberry — even an enchanted strawberry — was not sufficient to the needs of his body, and that breakfast sounded wonderful.

And what he saw, well, was not the inside of a tent at all. And it was more than a little bigger.

It looked like the inside of a castle tower, large gray quarry stones mortared into place to form a round room at least ten strides across. More stone for both the ceiling and floor, although the latter was covered in vast, lavish rugs that continued the red-and-gold theme. Stairs around the outer edge led up to at least a second floor. Tapestries covered large portions of the walls, depicting great moments of wizards throughout history, from Filias discovering the orders of spirits, to the triumph of Gord the Maker.

The room itself was decorated as a living space. A thick bed, wide enough for four of Sebas, jutted out from near the stairs. Armoires and chests of drawers to both sides, enough to clothe a noble or two. Near the bed a huge hearth where flames burned without smoke or wood.

The chamber even had a garderobe, tucked away behind a curtain along one wall. Larek tried not to wonder how Sebas disposed of its contents.

Sindra was at the hearth, working diligently to prepare more breakfast with iron skillets from the rack beside her, which hung above a larder. A larder that Larek could tell was enchanted to preserve food stored within it.

Dyrra sat at a small, yet ornate table made from the purple hardwood that grew only in Boll.

If Larek had yet held any doubts about the wealth Sebas possessed in life, that table and chairs would have assuaged them. They had to have cost more than the armoires, chests of drawers, larder and bed combined.

The utensils in Dyrra's hands were wrought from silver fine enough for a duke, and her plate and goblet were both of crystal.

"Tell me you can unlock this magic, Larek," said Dyrra. "Tell me we can bring this pavilion with us. Free from sleeping in the rain and dining like queens every night? Now *that* would be the life."

"In terms of opulence, it's the most impressive workshop I've seen," said Larek. "Certainly fancier than my own. Although I must admit that my own hasn't been redesigned since I built it. It was never meant to serve as my home.

"Though clearly Sebas thought along different lines."

"The armoire you left behind is still finer than either of those," said Chitter. "Probably more comfortable too."

Larek chuckled.

"Does that mean we can't bring this with us?" asked Sindra, carrying a plate of bacon over to the table, which prompted Larek to grab a chair before Dyrra claimed it all.

But Dyrra seemed content to let Larek take a large portion of that plate's bacon. Perhaps she had already eaten her fill?

Larek doubted that, because he knew she held an enormous capacity for food and alcohol.

"I don't know yet," said Larek, handing one of the thick, crispy strips of bacon to Chitter. "Depends on whether or not I can find the key."

"We'll help you look," said Dyrra.

"I'm not sure you can. And even if we find it, we might not be able to use it while we travel. But I'll explain all that after we eat."

"Fine, but then at least tell us what you and Chitter were going on about on the hillside. For a moment I thought he was going to kiss you."

That got a laugh out of Larek and Chitter, but a raised eyebrow from Sindra.

"Nothing like that," said Larek, "I assure you." He shook his head. "I just ... realized that Sebas might have been telling the truth as he understood it. That bandits might have—"

"Crap," said Dyrra.

"No, really," insisted Larek. "Grief can—"

"Look around you." Dyrra held up her crystal goblet. She waved her free hand at the other finery. "Is this the work of a man living with grief? Ready to throw his life away for the chance to avenge his beloved?"

"Well," began Larek, but Sindra interrupted him.

"She has a point. Grief is one of the things we are taught to heal, and this is the home of a man who has made peace with his losses."

"That may be. But still, I—"

"If you lament killing that bastard," said Dyrra, her free hand raised, "I will reach across this table and slap the scars off your face."

Chitter jumped down onto the table and out of the possible slap zone.

"Do that and no one will recognize me," said Larek.

Dyrra laughed that booming laugh of hers, drawing Sindra and Chitter into it, until finally even Larek chuckled.

With that, the four of them focused on eating until sated, which took a considerable amount of food. Larek, after all, was truly eating for the first time that day, following more than a little exertion. Dyrra's appetite preceded her, as usual and even Sindra ate more than her standard portion.

When they finished, and Larek, Dyrra and even Chitter had presented their thanks to the cook, Sindra said, "Now what will this key look like? Is it actually a key?"

"No." Larek rubbed his bare chin. "I'll know it the moment I see it, but it's hard to say exactly what it will look like to your eyes. Something opened, like a box, or perhaps a pouch that's been turned inside out."

"And we close it?" said Sindra.

"No!" Larek snapped both hands up in a halting gesture. "If you find it before I do, come get me and let me look at it."

"Is this place safe for us?" said Dyrra.

"Seems to be, but it's tough to say for certain," said Larek. "At least, without proper study, which, depending, might take me weeks. If we find the key, though, we can at least take it with us."

"Then we better start looking," said Sindra, "Or we won't get any further today."

LAREK LEFT DYRRA AND SINDRA TO LOOK DOWNSTAIRS, WHERE CHITTER assured him that no magical traps lay in wait. Apparently Sebas was thoughtful enough to at least not kill any of the townsfolk who wandered into his pavilion. Or perhaps he simply used it to host meetings, or card games with his friends.

And surely he must have had friends.

But Sebas' lost social life was not what Larek thought about as he ascended the cold stone stairs around the inside wall of the tower. His focus was on the door at the top.

More of the fine, Bollish purple hardwood, engraved with tiny script and heavily enchanted to keep out any visitors.

No doubt all of Sebas' secrets were locked away in there. Whatever personal library he had managed to acquire. Whatever projects lay there yet unfinished. All his years of research.

That flying spell.

All of them, locked away behind that door and its layers and layers of enchantment.

Larek could not possibly puzzle his way through all his warding spells, not without weeks to devote to the effort. Perhaps months, depending on exactly how good Sebas was, and how much effort he truly put into it.

Considering the cost of the wood alone, Larek was inclined to believe he might need the better part of the year to—

"That is quite a piece of work," said Chitter, leaning forward to peer up and down the door.

"He spared no effort or expense on this place."

"So, the workshop key." Chitter drummed tiny fingers along his jawbone. "That will be in there, won't it?"

"That's where I'd put it. Wouldn't even need to hide it."

"That's what I thought."

Chitter ignored the door and plunged straight through the stone wall before Larek could utter a syllable.

Moments later Chitter returned to his shoulder, holding the

plainest, most ordinary little burlap bag Larek had ever seen. The sort that even the meanest grocer will include in the price of a scoop of walnuts.

The bag, of course, was inside out, because it was the key. And the last thing a normal thief would ever notice among all the rich trinkets Larek had seen so far.

"The wards extend through the wall," said Larek as he accepted the bag. "How did you manage to slip past them?"

"They're keyed for humans, not spirits." Chitter pointed to the outer wall. "That one's warded against spirits. I couldn't have entered at all if Dyrra and Sindra hadn't left the pavilion flap open. But I guess Sebas figured that any spirit that made it inside had to be his own."

"Sloppy," said Larek, with a slight shake of his head.

"Like sending an earth spirit to kill a wizard who travels with an *unbound* earth spirit?" Chitter twitched his tail. "He was clever, but his blind spots were *immense*."

"Doesn't matter anymore." Larek held up the pouch. "Dyrra? Sindra? Chitter found what we needed."

Larek hustled down the stairs to where the two of them waited.

"Doesn't look like much," said Sindra. "But I guess that's the point, isn't it?"

"It is." Larek gestured for them to follow. "Come on outside. I'll show you how it works."

"Does this mean we can sleep inside every night on the road?" said Dyrra. "Eat from his larder?"

"Maybe, depending on how he set it up. Trying to ward the key is tricky because the workshop spells require a good deal of precision. Any unrelated spells risk warping them and destroying everything inside." Larek looked at the eight tiny silver pitons woven into the pouch's drawstring. "We'd probably have to carry the pavilion too."

"For all this, I will carry it," said Dyrra as they stepped outside.

Where Keon and his mercenaries stood waiting.

15

The clouds had drifted off, and the early afternoon sun shone down bright and hot on the north bank of the river Quar. Sindra could not help thinking of it as a bad omen. Dyrra called the sun Lucala's Jealous Sister, and here it showed its face for the first time that day just as they stepped out of the workshop-pavilion.

Where Keon waited.

He sat astride a strong, white stallion. The smile on his face matched the arrogance of his noble clothes worn over steel chain mail. His Healer sat next to him aboard a piebald gelding, mocking Sindra with his sneer, chest thrust forward to proudly display the soothing hand of Nilasah, embroidered over the heart of his yellow kirtle. Telling everyone that he was a Healer in good standing.

Which she was not.

The two dozen men-at-arms around them looked like an afterthought, despite their array of weaponry. A quarter of them trained crossbows with blunted bolts on Dyrra. Another quarter aimed crossbows at Larek, and nothing about the tips of those bolts looked blunt. Another quarter were spearmen, their spears lowered and ready. The final six had swords and maces and shields raised. And all of them had hard, well-used looking leather armor.

The hints of bacon grease still in Sindra's mouth soured on her tongue.

"Have another threat ready for us, Burned One?" said Keon.

Dyrra snarled that he addressed Larek first, but after that duel, Sindra understood thinking of the wizard as the bigger threat.

"I've caused the earth to swallow one man already today," said Larek, and Sindra was impressed at the bored, matter-of-fact tone he affected as he reached back to close the tent flap behind him. "I'm not above doing it again."

The Healer muttered something, and Sindra smiled. She had the same training. She knew he could hear the truth in Larek's voice, and might not be able to tell that Larek had left a few key details out of his statement.

"Excellent!" Keon roared a laugh that reminded Sindra uncomfortably of Dyrra. She glanced at the woman reflexively and saw her tightened jaw, her grip on the hilt of her undrawn sword of war.

"Tell me, wizard," said Keon, and Sindra didn't like the humor in his tone, "can you do it again before my men shoot you down?"

"Perhaps not." Larek shrugged. "I might only kill half of you."

"Enough," said Dyrra, without budging her jaw.

"You surrender?" said Keon.

"Your writ is for me. Not them."

"I'm sure the duchess will..." started Keon at the same time Larek said, "You aren't..."

But neither got to finish his sentence.

"NO!" yelled Dyrra, and Sindra saw the crossbowmen shake just a little as her cry echoed into silence.

Into the stillness Dyrra said, "This isn't about gold, Keon, and you know it."

"The price on your head is—"

"Less than you could have earned fighting along the border of Boll and Yunt in the time it's taken to track me down."

Keon narrowed his eyes in thought, and Sindra noticed that more than a few of his men looked at him sideways. His Healer yawned into the back of his own hand.

"True," Keon said at last. "Of course, the risk here is significantly lower."

"So you're here because your men are cowards? Or because they aren't good enough to fight a war?"

Dyrra smiled wide and evil, while Keon suffered more sideways glances and a few men-at-arms even lowered their weapons, expressions angry.

"Or will you admit that you came here for more than just gold?"

"You know why I'm here," said Keon, and Sindra heard more simple truth in his flat tone than she had in anything else he had said so far.

"Then let's drop the pretense." Dyrra spat into her palms and rubbed them together while muttering something Sindra couldn't follow. Then she cupped her hands together to form the full moon of Lucala and held her hands high above her head.

"You wouldn't," said Keon, his eyebrows high.

"By Lucala I swear that I wronged you by telling Ommure that you took advantage of me when a mace blow left me insensible after a battle. Here and now, my hands in Hers, I swear that I suffered no such blow, and that I lay with you because the need-fire was upon me after we alone survived impossible odds. And the need-fire must be quenched."

"The need-fire must be quenched," echoed a number of the men-at-arms, all lowering their weapons now. Unless Sindra was mistaken, even Keon muttered the words, as though they were part of some soldier's code that she had never heard.

"But by Lucala I swear that you wronged me," continued Dyrra, hands still high. "You violated the code by telling Ommure what we did when the need-fire was upon us, boasting as though you had seduced me. And I cannot prove it but I believe you poisoned Ommure during Lucala's Test of Justice."

Sindra noted that more and more of Keon's men were giving him angry looks now. But Dyrra wasn't finished.

"I failed to stop you in Fent, and I confess before Lucala that I knew you to be in the area. I told myself it was coincidence. I told myself you would not come after what I protected just to get to me.

"But I knew you would. And it was my crime that I did not seek the help I needed because it would have exposed my shame.

"But your crime was greater. Acting as a raider and not a respectable mercenary, you violated and slaughtered innocents for the sole reason that I had sworn to guard them. Then robbed and ruined the man who dared to hire me. Then you spread your lies about what happened that night, to heap yet more blame upon me.

"With my hands in Lucala's, I swear all this to be true. May She judge and punish me as She sees fit if I have spoken a false word in my testimony."

Dyrra lowered her hands, but kept her eyes locked on Keon, whose wide nostrils flared in anger. He seemed to know what was coming next. But he made no move to stop Dyrra from speaking.

"And in full view of witnesses and he who wronged me, I call for *xincalu.*"

Sindra did not know that word, but it seemed that the men-at-arms all knew it. None of them were menacing with weapons anymore. They all looked up at Keon. Most angry, some curious, and all expectant. Even the Healer who rode with them seemed to know what was going on, his expression bored as he waited for Keon's answer.

Chitter said something to Larek, and she heard him whisper, "Lucala's Justice? But I didn't hear—"

As if in answer, Keon sighed, swung one leg over his horse, and jumped down. He looked around at his men.

"You don't have to confirm it, you know. She's worth a good deal less dead than alive."

All of them thumped something. Maces and swords struck shields, spear butts flattened small portions of lush river grass. Even the crossbowmen knocked their fists against their weapons.

"Very well." Keon sighed as he looked around at the expressions of his men. "Some of you look ready to walk away if I don't do this. Surely you can't all be unseasoned enough to still believe in honor."

They stared back at him, though a few looked uncomfortable about it. Sindra wondered whether it was honor that troubled them, or whatever code they followed that stood between them and chaos.

And was there a difference?

Keon shook his head and turned to face Dyrra. His eyes flicked to Larek and Sindra.

"What about your 'mighty wizard' and your expert needle thrower? What guarantees do I have that they will let me take your corpse with me?"

"I—" began Larek, but Dyrra cut him off.

"They will."

"Given that all of my men have lowered their weapons, I'll need more than your word on this."

Larek shook his head, but Dyrra said softly, "This is part of *xincalu*. The matter is now entirely between us. His men can't get involved, but neither can you. If I win, I have my vengeance. If he wins, he gets his bounty."

"And a reduced bounty at that," called Keon, showing that he heard.

Larek looked around at the Keon's men, and Sindra could see him calculating now. Figuring whether or not he could actually stop them if they all attacked.

Sindra knew she couldn't. At best she could hit two of them with needles before they took her down. She nodded quickly, saying, "I have no weapon to strike."

"Stamp your foot," said Dyrra.

Sindra stamped her foot.

Larek grimaced. He exhaled sharply through his nose and stomped his foot once.

Sindra noticed that Chitter did nothing, and wondered if Larek's acceptance included him. She had the feeling that it did not.

"I refuse to wait for the full moon," said Keon. "We're not in Karwale, and I doubt either of us has the proper double-crescent dagger anyway. The most I'll give you is a fair fight here and now, under the watchful eye of Lucala's Holy Sister Marpa."

Keon kissed his two small fingers and raised them to the sun.

Dyrra spat at the sun, but drew her sword of war. She held it before her in a two-hand grip.

Keon snorted and drew his own, holding it with one hand.

"The blame is with your precious Ommure, you know," he said. "Boasting of his brilliance in battle. Do you think I don't know he wanted my job? That he made that trap sound like my fault?"

"KEENARACH!" screamed Dyrra.

LUCALA'S JEALOUS SISTER BURNED HOT AND BRIGHT IN THE SKY, perfect for a *daywalker* like Keon. No doubt the real reason he refused to wait for the full moon.

The ground was good for a skirmish though. Soft, cushy river grass. A slight slope, but level enough. No breaks or rocks to ruin Dyrra's footing. She might have been able to use the stumps to her advantage, but they were a good dozen yards past the great, gaudy pavilion.

Sindra's bacon, eggs and toasted bread sat heavily in Dyrra's stomach. Great food for a long hike, but not what she would have chosen before a fight.

Sloppy. She had allowed herself to get caught up in the splendor of the dead wizard's portable house and not thought about the threats she would face on the road.

Now faced.

Keon. At last. Just the two of them.

He was stronger. More experienced. Had better armor. Steel under his frippery.

But their swords of war were a match. And he had no armor on his neck.

And he dared insult sweet Ommure one more time.

Dyrra screamed her battle cry and leapt forward, sword twirling high.

Go for the head. Control his balance.

But Keon countered low. Dropped to one knee. Two hand swing.

Dyrra was faster.

Her boots touched down ahead of his sword's arc. She dove into a roll over it. Came up three paces away. Twisting toward him, now on one knee. Guard high.

All around her Dyrra heard shouts and encouragement. Or maybe just men used to death enjoying the spectacle. But she at least heard Larek and Sindra on her side.

Keon already faced her. Must have used the swing's momentum to turn.

"Fancy," he said. "But not very effective."

Dyrra began to spin her sword through a double-loop in front of her. Teasing him. Trying to draw him in. Get him to attack one side while the other was guarded.

Oohs from the crowd. Never seen a sand dancer before?

Keon took one step. Lunged just below the join between the loops.

Dyrra whirled right with a closing step, but kept her sword spinning. Their blades rang out with the parry, but hers had momentum. Worked with her entrance. Dyrra's attack followed naturally. Downward at Keon's left shoulder.

Keon jumped forward. A one-foot spring.

Not fast enough.

Dyrra's sword ripped away the pretty red shirt along his left side and chinged against the chain mail guarding his ribs.

Bad angle. Not much more than a bruise. Yet Larek and Sindra's cheers made it sound like a death blow.

"Better?" said Dyrra, varying the rhythm of her sword's loops. Mixing in a high and low arc to keep him guessing.

"Do you see any blood?" Keon brushed his torn shirt as though sweeping away dirt. Drawing mocking laughter from his men. "I don't."

Dyrra spun to her left and came in low. She had the angle and distance to take out his knees, armor or no.

But Keon was ready.

Perfect timing on his jump. Her sword wooshed past beneath his feet.

All momentum on his side as he brought his sword down.

No chance to parry. Dyrra jumped away, but not far enough.

Worse. Keon anticipated the dodge.

No crouch as he landed. Caught his weight on bent knees. The downstroke was a feint. Rolled his wrists to keep momentum. Spun his blade into a torso strike while Dyrra was mid-jump.

Resounding pain across Dyrra's right hip, shocking up her torso and down her leg. Spinning her. Her feet out of control.

Urgent shouts around her. The cries of hard men eager to see blood.

Instinctive sweeping swing as she stumbled.

Her sword clashed metal. Didn't feel like another sword. Still, it foiled Keon's death stroke.

Dyrra's half-numb right leg gave out. She rolled in the grass, trying not to skewer herself. Desperate to raise her blade against the next blow.

It didn't come.

Where?

Whipped her head around. Keon, clutching his wrist. Scrambling for his dropped sword.

"DRAGON!" someone yelled.

Fear made both Keon and Dyrra look up.

A shadow passed over the sun. A shadow with great bat wings and a tail longer than its body.

The dragon.

Larek stared at the shadow of the great dragon, soaring high in the blue sky above. Sudden sweat drenched him. Why did the clouds have to burn away? A dragon's eyes could see for miles. Its ears...

It might have been able to hear Dyrra and Keon fighting.

Not here. Not now.

The char and charnel reek of dragonfire in Larek's nose was just memory. The world was not turning to ash all around him. No one was screaming and dying. Not now. That was then. No dragon here. Dragon high in the sky. Maybe not even a dragon. Maybe some long-tailed southern bird…

He did hear screams though.

No. Not screams. Shouts. Organized. Larek could make no sense of them over the high-pitched ringing, so loud in his ears. The white edging around everything he could see.

Not that he could focus on anything except that one shadow, passing the sun now.

And banking right. Was that this way?

Was it coming this way?

Someone screamed. Was it him? Sindra grabbed Larek's shaking shoulder. Why was his shoulder shaking?

Wait. Not just his shoulder. His whole body shook, his arms and legs locked tight.

She grabbed his jaw. Her face in front of his now. Sindra's mouth shaping words Larek couldn't hear. Only that ringing sound, and a rapid pounding. Faster than a skald's drum during a battle chant.

CRACK!

Sindra slapped Larek hard enough to stagger him back a step.

He was still standing by the river. He could see Keon and his men moving fast. Away. Heading for shelter from the…

CRACK!

Another slap, this time on the other cheek. Larek couldn't help rubbing the stinging pain, and realized that his hand wasn't shaking anymore. Neither were his legs.

"Larek! Can you hear me?" The words synchronized with Sindra's lips.

"Yes?"

"Good." Her eyes searched his, suspicious. Her words came slow, but forceful. "Dyrra is hurt. We have to get her into the pavilion."

"Yes."

Larek started to follow Sindra to where Dyrra lay in the grass.

Blood all over her right hip. Staining her green leather armor through a gash.

The shadow of the dragon shook him to a stop.

"No!" he said. "Not the pavilion."

Larek's fingers trembled as he dug at his pockets. Chitter scrambled around low on Larek's back.

"Yes!" insisted Sindra. "It's the safest place."

"Dragons smell magic." Larek surprised himself with the evenness of his tone, since he could not quite work the knot on a belt pouch. "The pavilion will—"

Chitter circled Larek's waist with Sebas' inside-out, cheap burlap pouch in his mouth. Larek took the pouch with a nod of thanks. He quickly pulled it right side in and knotted the tie while the pouch appeared to inflate as though blown into with a slow, steady breath.

Behind Larek, the pavilion vanished, leaving only a single silver piton. Chitter leapt down and skittered toward the piton.

"I'll get it," Chitter yelled. "You get Dyrra down to the river."

"He's right," said Larek turning to Sindra, who stared at Larek in a moment of confusion.

That's right. She couldn't understand the little earth spirit.

"The river," said Larek. "We have to get her down to the river."

"I can ... *get* myself..." said Dyrra, her jaw clamped, leaning forward and trying to get a foot underneath herself. She still had her sword in one hand, her grip as strained as her voice.

"But you shouldn't," said Sindra, kneeling beside her. She grabbed Dyrra's chin this time and forced the warrior to meet her eyes. "Keon is gone, but we all know he'll be back. If you make your wound worse, you're doing him a favor."

Larek looked up. The dragon continued its flight west. It had to be Blackflame. No other dragon had been seen in Aeralfast in hundreds of years, and Blackflame was known to be active. Dragons were not social creatures. If two of them came together, they would fight until only one remained. They stayed well out of each other's ways.

Besides, Larek know that shape well. He had spent hours following it with Inga and Taran all those years ago. He knew the wingspan, the length of the tail, the shape of the tip. What Larek saw in the sky could only be Blackflame.

But Blackflame shouldn't be here. *Couldn't* be here. He was known to be hundreds of miles to the north.

This wasn't like last time. There was no great army hunting him. Right now, *no one* was hunting him. The tournament wasn't over yet.

The king's best scouts had found Blackflame's lair. A dragon's lair is no easy thing to mistake. It's a burned, scarred thing, arranged in ways only they can understand, but that somehow make them more comfortable.

Blackflame's lair had been found. Far to the north. Nowhere close to where Larek stood near the river Quar.

And yet, high in the sky he could see that shadow.

"Larek!" snapped Sindra.

He looked over to see Dyrra standing now, sword sheathed and leaning heavily on the small ex-Healer, who seemed to be stronger than she looked. Much stronger, if those slaps were any indication.

"At least get the packs."

Sindra helped Dyrra begin to hobble down toward the Quar. Larek stuffed Sebas' workshop pouch into a pocket and began to gather the packs.

***

"Here," said Sindra in her gentle, professional tone. "We'll just ease you down here on your left side."

Dyrra's grip felt tight enough to crack Sindra's shoulder, and her body sweated and shook as Sindra strained to lower the bigger woman slowly onto the soft river grass only two paces from the Quar.

Dyrra's teeth clenched hard enough they might shatter. Pain, yes, but anger and frustration as well.

Sindra leaned down and flared her nostrils in a deep inhalation before pressing one of her yellow Healer's cloths against the wound. Dyrra hissed in protest, but at least her smell was all right. The stink of effort and fighting, yes, and a tangy undercurrent of blood, of course.

But nothing sweet and nothing rotten. Those were the basics any Healer would recognize instantly, even here beside the algae smell of the slow-flowing Quar.

Even more, there were none of the crisp or astringent or pungent smells that would have indicated poison. That had been Sindra's biggest fear. Dyrra's accusation that Keon had used poison in one duel made Sindra expect him to use it in another. Perhaps he didn't have time.

She glanced up as she pulled out a needle tipped with Nilasah's Tears. Perhaps three hours of sun left, and no clouds to mitigate the heat. No sign of the dragon though. That wasn't good. That could only mean the beast dove, and somewhere nearby people were suffering.

At least the sight of it was gone. That alone might keep Larek from freezing again. Sindra had never seen such fear. Not even on the battlefield. The mere thought of it made her check on Larek, still stumbling down the rise toward them, overburdened with all of their packs. The grass rustled beside him, probably Chitter running down instead of riding.

She looked back at Dyrra. Her gray eyes were dull with pain. Her breathing rapid. Her skin shining from the sweat.

"I'm sorry, Dyrra," said Sindra.

"What are you—"

Sindra poked her in the throat with a tipped needle.

Dyrra's eyes rolled back, her lids fluttered shut, and she passed out on the grass.

"That ... was fast," said Larek, puffing for breath.

"Pain and tension make it work faster," said Sindra, now pressing the cloth with both hands. A simple prayer came to mind. One that would staunch the bleeding. Her lips began to form the words...

But no. She couldn't.

She was no longer a Healer of Nilasah. What if she offended the goddess by offering a prayer she had no right to say? What if she made things worse?

No. Not again. Never again.

Sindra had the skills of her training. They would serve her as well as they might serve a chirurgeon. Perhaps better. Perhaps not. But either way, they would have to suffice.

So instead of uttering the words her heart begged her to say, Sindra spoke to Larek as she worked. First, she held the pressure for the same count the prayer would have taken.

"That's why Nilasah's Tears are so effective in a skirmish. Everyone is already tense and charged up. Scratch them anywhere halfway decent and they drop like a bow-shot duck."

Sindra loosened the armor straps around Dyrra's hip with one hand and waved her other hand for Larek's attention.

"I'll need things from my pack. Fetch them as I call for them. First, the yellow powder in the translucent vial."

Chitter said something, which Larek translated.

"Chitter says he can help, if you will cover the wound with dirt or water. Dirt would be better."

"Water will have to do. I'm not rubbing dirt on the wound."

Sindra had the wound exposed now. Not as bad as she feared. Only as long as the width of her hand, and the first half of that was shallow. The second half was another story, deeper and cutting. The sword's point must have gouged through. Or more likely — considering how the armor looked as Sindra had peeled it away — found a seam in the leather.

Still, it wasn't good. The deep part of the gouge slashed muscle. No wonder Dyrra could scarcely pull her right leg forward.

A Healer — a proper Healer in Nilasah's good graces — could close that wound and have it healed enough to walk on by the dawn, enough to fight on by the second day.

But that didn't matter now.

Sindra took the vial from Larek, who also held his enchanted jug out to her. She puffed out a sigh, but took both.

"You can help best by giving me things as I need them."

"Sorry."

"It's fine," she said, pulling the vial's stopper and shaking a tiny amount onto the tip of her right index finger. There was a chant for this too. Dozens of little prayers that all worked together as a Healer worked.

But High Healer Alain had been clear. Sindra was no longer a Healer. She could not say the prayers. Instead as she sprinkled the cleansing powder over the wound, with extra over the deepest part, she said, "What can Chitter do to help?"

"Once it's covered in water or earth, so no air is touching it, he can persuade the flesh to knit."

Chitter said more as Sindra closed the vial, and kissed it before she could stop herself.

"We won't be able to move her tonight, but by morning she should be able to walk on her own."

Sindra leaned back.

"So you don't need me at all?"

"He can't clean it," said Larek. "And anything you can do to help will only speed her healing."

"Of course," said Sindra, handing back the vial and asking for another Healer's cloth.

So this was what her life had come to. All her years of study. Of training. All of her devotion to the Goddess and to those in need.

And now, because her faith had broken when it mattered most, she was nothing more than an assistant to an unbound earth spirit.

Handmaiden to a squirrel.

16

Dyrra lay awake long before she opened her eyes.

Lucala's Jealous Sister had relinquished the sky for the night. She could tell that much by the inside of her eyelids. She could hear a campfire off to her right, feel the kiss of its warmth. She could smell roast trout, and toasted bread and cheese.

The smell alone was enough to make her stomach rumble.

Sindra and Larek conversed in low voices. That was good, at least. Not a prisoner then.

She should have been though, and she knew it. She'd been a damned fool to believe Keon would throw his weight behind a strike begun in the air. That was overcommitting. Never his way. It was the reason he had been a good commander, and the reason he was dangerous in a fight. He always held something back in reserve. Always ready for the enemy to make a mistake.

Dyrra had made that mistake, and it had damn near cost her a leg.

She twitched the leg by reflex. Her body checking to make sure the leg remained where the gods had put it. It responded with a hint of movement and a dull ache.

Only a dull ache?

Dyrra had felt the bite of steel. She knew that. She had felt it many times in her life, and it was not a sensation she mistook.

With the fingers of her right hand she poked at the area. Unarmored, of course, and bandaged, complete with a poultice. All to be expected. But still, the poke should have hurt. The bite from that kind of sword blow didn't dull down to an ache without weeks of recovery...

Or the prayers of a Healer...

Sindra?

Dyrra tried to sit up, but her right hip refused with a complaint of exhaustion. The effort only dragged her onto her left side.

"Stop," said Sindra, and Dyrra could hear the rustling of Sindra coming to her feet.

"Don't bother," growled Dyrra. "I can—"

"Hurt yourself if you don't listen."

Dyrra finally consented to open her eyes. Well past dusk. She could see the filling form of the waxing moon and stared at it until she smiled as though a chastened child. Her eyes sought the vertex of the Great Cross and the star she decided was Ommure's. A brief touchstone of the death she came close to that day.

"Forgive me, Healer," said Dyrra turning to Sindra. "I won't undo your work."

"No," said Sindra quietly. Were her eyes shining with tears? "Not a Healer and hardly my work. You have Chitter to thank."

The spirit squirrel was barking madly, but all Larek said by way of translation was, "He says he only sealed your work, and it only helped because of what you did."

Larek's voice shifted from that translating rhythm he used to the cadence of his own speech.

"And I have to say, I've never seen him do that kind of healing before. Nothing even close."

"Well thank you both," said Dyrra with a solemn nod, determined to change the subject for Sindra. Happily, she had one ready to go. "What happened to Keon?"

"He and his men took off to the north," said Sindra. "No doubt to find some way to capitalize on the dragon sighting."

Larek's turn to look away.

"He'll be back." Dyrra shook her head. "You can count on it. Fortunately I heal quickly."

Sindra brought her food. A whole trout to herself, plus a generous helping of rye bread and that creamy goat cheese.

"Only water to drink," she said as she passed the food to Dyrra. "But you should eat all you can."

Dyrra ate in silence for several minutes, the other two alone with their thoughts as they stared into the fire.

Finally Dyrra cleared her throat to get them to look up.

"I hate to raise this subject, but the dragon. What does it mean that it's down here instead of way off to the north where everyone said it was?"

Sindra looked at Larek. He shrugged.

"Word will spread back. Probably brought by Keon, for a price." Larek tilted his head in thought. "The king will probably take more champions. Maybe four groups total. Send a few scouts with each, then send them out in different directions to hunt down the dragon. One of the groups will find it."

"No. I mean what does it mean for us?" Dyrra searched Larek's eyes. "Do we need to go another direction?"

"South is as good as any other direction. What's it matter, really?"

Dyrra didn't like the resignation in his voice. Not at all. And the tears in Sindra's eyes after Dyrra called her a Healer.

Dyrra had convinced herself that it was only the songs they were running from. That they could not begin to live real lives until their worst failures were no longer flung daily in their faces.

But that wouldn't work, would it?

Not when they were carrying their failures around with them like a talisman of home.

"Well," said Dyrra, "it seems to me that if the dragon wants to come to us, maybe we should kill it ourselves."

"Are you insane?" said Larek.

This was too much. His stomach rebelled at the thought of facing Blackflame again. Of facing any dragon again. He clasped his hands over his mouth to avoid tossing up his half-digested dinner all over Sindra's campfire.

Chitter came closer and placed a paw on Larek's thigh, and the need to regurgitate faded. The acid taste at the back of his throat giving way to the remaining rich aftertaste of the goat cheese. Larek's heartbeat slowed to normal in the process, until he could hear the crackling flames of the fire and the flow of the river over the rushing of his own blood.

Still, Larek sat there, sweating in the pale moonlight. Even though the dragon had not been seen in hours. Even though their camp beside the Quar sat within a warding ring of stones that would keep dragons and mercenaries from so much as smelling them, much less seeing them.

Even though Larek sat as safe as he could be, his insides churned with fear.

That Dyrra and Sindra stared at him with such pity in their eyes did not help. Perhaps they were no better than all the others. Perhaps deep down they hated him for his failure as surely as they hated themselves for their own.

His heart sped its beat again. The world tried to spin around him, but got no more than a quarter revolution before snapping back into place.

"No," he said, shaking his head frantically. Not seeing anything now, just lush green grass made gray by moonlight. "No dragons. Never again. Never."

"Shhh," said Sindra, kneeling in front of him. Her hands gentle on his neck, easing his shaking head slower until she cupped his chin in both hands. Her eyes mere inches from his.

"Shhh," she said again. "There are no dragons here. Only friends. *You are safe.*"

"No." Larek felt some pit-deep desire to shake his head again, but he didn't want to look away from Sindra's green eyes. "Not safe anywhere. Not from dragons."

"Exactly," said Dyrra, from the other side of the fire.

"Dyrra—" began Sindra, a warning tone in her hushed voice.

"But he's right," said Dyrra. "We won't be any more safe from dragons in Velstadt than we are here in Aeralfast. And that would be true if we went as far west as Karwale or as far east as Hrakrash. Dragons go where they want and do what they want."

Dyrra's tone grew sharp. "Until someone stops them."

Larek started shaking again, but Sindra hushed him, stilling him with her eyes, and somehow the shakes and sweats never really took hold of him.

"Dyrra," said Sindra in a slow, careful voice, "I don't think that's helping."

"Of course it's not helping!" Dyrra spat a few words in Karwalish, then said, "Look at us! Running away like muttonheads, as though it'll do us a damned bit of good."

"We all agreed," said Sindra, holding steady to that careful tone. "None of us could find forgiveness for ourselves, or at least a chance to move on, until we left those songs and stories behind."

"But the songs and stories aren't our problem."

That got Larek to turn his head, and Sindra was so surprised that she let him, her hands withdrawing even as she turned herself to look at where Dyrra sat.

And Dyrra *was* sitting up, even though Chitter and Sindra both agreed earlier that she would not be able to sit until morning.

"No," said Larek. "It's the failures they represent. But what difference does that make? The people I didn't save are still dead."

"I cannot raise those I lost," said Sindra. "Not even High Healer Alain can do that. Nor can I mend the limbs maimed by my failures."

"People die every day." Dyrra pointed at Larek. "You took a life today, whether you wanted to or not. And I took more lives the day of the ambush. That's what life means. That we will die."

She turned her focus on Sindra.

"And sometimes we die a piece at a time. An arm here. A leg there. I would have lost a leg today, if not for you and Chitter."

"It was in no—"

"Were I here alone against Keon, and left on my own after the dragon sighting, I would be feverish right now and dying within days. Wouldn't I?"

Sindra flared in a breath, but nodded. "It's not a certainty, but it's likely. Yes."

"And think about this, Larek. Mighty Keon and his men turned and ran at the sight of a dragon's shadow."

"More likely to profit the safe way," said Larek. "By reporting it."

"These are men who risk their lives every day. How much more money would they have made for killing it?"

Larek shook his head.

"They had no wizard. There's no way they could—"

"*But we do!*"

"Do we? I nearly pissed myself at the sight of its shadow."

"Men and women piss themselves in battle all the time. You didn't run."

"He froze," said Sindra. "I'm sorry, Larek, but it's true."

Larek shrugged. He had no interest in denying that.

Dyrra looked deep into Larek's eyes.

"My Ommure is gone. I cannot fix what I did to him. I cannot undo it, and there is no one to whom I can make reparations."

She pulled Ommure's necklace out of her shirt and kissed the golden three-quarter moon symbol of Lucala.

"Now that the *xincalu* has begun, though, I can make up for some small part of it. I can kill Keon. I can avenge the wrongs he did me, and the wrongs I believe he did to Ommure."

Larek nodded, unsure what to say.

"I can't do that in Velstadt."

"Wait—"

"If I go to Velstadt without killing Keon, I will be failing my dear Ommure one final time." Dyrra tucked the pendant back insider her shirt and armor. "I see that now. And that's not all I see."

"No," said Larek. He could barely hear his own words over his pounding heart. The sweating and shaking had hold of him again. Had to bite his cheek to stop his teeth from chattering. "The dead do not need vengeance."

"Their memories do," Dyrra insisted. "And memories are all we have of them."

"That might be true for you and Ommure, but—"

"Tell me, those songs they sing. Do they insult Inga and Taran?"

Larek blinked at that. Stopped shaking for a moment.

"Of course not."

"Of course not." Dyrra raised a clenched fist. "Larek, people do not revile you because you failed to slay Blackflame. They revile you because you still breathe."

His breaths were shaky, but his limbs had slowed to a tremor and his sweat had slowed enough that he could wipe the stinging salt from his eyes with his sleeve. But his mouth felt dry as a hearthstone.

"So I should let the dragon kill me?"

"The dragon has already killed you." She shook her head. "You've lived huddled away in the woods with your fear and shame. Only Chitter for your friend, and so little contact with women you barely notice their touch."

"What?" Larek leaned back so fast he nearly fell.

"An eastern beauty like Sindra holds your face in her cupped hands, stares into your eyes in kissing range? Most men's blood would run hot at such a moment. But you won't let yourself enjoy even that."

Sindra became very interested in the fire, which was just as well because Larek could not look at her just then. But his next words were for Dyrra anyway.

"Are you any better? You've had no men since Ommure."

"No! I'm not. That's my point. I haven't been able to even think about it with all my crimes hanging over me. What about you, Sindra? Have you—"

"No." A simple word, but her voice nearly choked on it.

"We talked about finding new lives down in Velstadt," said Dyrra.

"But I say we won't find anything more than the living deaths we have now. Not unless we find ways to make peace with ourselves.

"And for you, Larek, that starts with the dragon."

"If we all die against the dragon—"

"She's right," said Sindra, still not looking up from the fire. "The dragon has to be first. If I die trying to save people from the dragon, at least I'll die in a cause Nilasah would support."

"And Ommure would call it a glorious death, when I meet him again in the Underworld. Enough, perhaps, to earn his forgiveness."

"I don't know..." said Larek.

"The dragon dove today," said Chitter. "I saw it."

"The dragon dove?" said Larek aloud.

"One moment it was high in the sky," said Sindra with a nod, "the next the sky was clear. You know what that means."

Larek stared into the fire, heard the memories of people screaming and running before the dragon's black fire caught them.

"People are dead."

"And more will follow. Blackflame has never hit an area only once before moving on."

"Well, wizard," said Dyrra, "do you have the courage to face your fear and give the skalds something new to sing about?"

"No," said Larek, giving voice to the thousand tremors plaguing his guts and shivering up his spine.

"But maybe I can find it."

17

———

Larek's dreams that night were fitful, and all variations on the same theme. He watched Inga and Taran die over and over, consumed in black dragonfire. Each and every time they screamed for his help, their screams echoed by hundreds of farmers and innkeepers and grooms and more. All imploring Larek to save them with his spells.

Always he tried to save them. And always he failed. His voice cracked and broke as he chanted against dragonfire. The wave of power that should have flowed out of him reduced to nothing more than a vague ebb. Enough to keep the worst of the flames from him, but no more than that.

Enough to let him live and function. And the dead all hated him for it. Their hate like ashes in his dry mouth.

For the first time in memory, Larek felt grateful for the red rays of dawn, pulling him from his sleep with their light and simple warmth. For all they resembled distant fire, they had at least the secondary color. The natural color. The color of fire sparked by lightning or flint or spell.

Not the black flames. Not the fire that had named the dragon.

Larek sighed with something close to relief. He tried to savor the sensation through another breath, but he could smell Sindra seasoning hard-boiled eggs and bread as she warmed them over last night's coals.

Dyrra was already up and packed, which was odd. Her hip stiff as she moved, and her gait slow, but she limped about with determination. And she stayed within the wards he'd set before sleeping last night.

Even odder, though, was Chitter. Asleep. Actually asleep, curled up on the thick grass beside Larek's bedroll like a natural flying squirrel. A pet, instead of an earth spirit. Healing Dyrra must have taken more out of him than he admitted.

"Good, you're awake," said Sindra, with her usual morning cheer. "We can finalize our plans over breakfast, but first, I meant to ask you something last night."

"Why," said Larek with a yawn, "is last night the first time I cast wards on this trip?"

"They do seem useful."

"They are. Mind if I wake up before I answer?"

"Don't take too long," said Dyrra, "or there won't be any breakfast left for you."

Larek grabbed his everfull jug from beside the fire, held it high, leaned back, and opened it. Icy mountain water streamed over his face and bright red hair, shocking the rest of the sleep out of him with a sharp cry.

He straightened up and held the jug upright so it stopped flowing. He shook the water off his head, dried his forehead with the sleeve of his light brown travel tunic.

He brought the jug to his lips and drank away the taste of his dreams. He capped the jug.

"Awake?" said Dyrra.

"Good enough," he said. "Those wards are tricky. They keep people or animals — or anything as far as I know — from noticing whatever or whoever is inside them. Predators or prey, doesn't matter. As far as they're concerned, what is within the wards is not worth noticing. Like any other empty patch of grass here beside the river.

"But like I said, they're tricky. There are only two ways to make them work. The first involves casting certain spells on the rocks ahead of time to prepare them. That takes days, and they only work once. The second needs the rocks to all be about the same size, shape, and color, and they have to be local to the area where the spell is cast."

Sindra glanced from her cooking to the half-dozen rocks encircling them. Each perhaps the size of her fist, ghostly white, and oblong. "How did you manage to find them?"

"I didn't." Larek pointed to the sleeping earth spirit. "Chitter did. If there are qualifying rocks around us, he can let me know. In this case, we were next to a river, and rivers are great sources for this type of spell."

"Should we be worried that Chitter sleeps?" said Dyrra.

"I don't think so. He goes to sleep every so often, but I've never spotted a pattern to it. In this case, it's probably because he did a lot yesterday. Even more than I did, in some ways."

Dyrra's mouth puckered as though Larek's words tasted sour. She put her hand on her hip, where even the green leather armor had been sealed again by Chitter. She stopped limping about and eased herself down to a sitting position.

Sindra caught that and smiled, but hid her smile from Dyrra. She set an egg aside for Chitter, then began handing around spiced rye bread and eggs. And the three of them passed the everfull jug among themselves as they ate, drinking straight from the jug.

"So," said Sindra, "how do we catch a dragon?"

"We'll need horses," said Larek. "Dyrra's not at full speed, and even if she were we won't catch a dragon on foot."

"You said they smell magic," said Dyrra. "Maybe we lure the dragon to us?"

"I don't know how far away they can smell it. It might not have been able to smell the pavilion yesterday, but we couldn't take the chance. I know that if we can't even see it in the air, it won't find us by the smell of anything we carry."

"What if you cast spells?" Sindra pushed her words out around a mouthful of egg. "Would the magic entice it?"

"Perhaps, but I wouldn't count on it." Larek looked away from them and into the sky above, bluing as the sun rose. "After all, there's never been a dragon slain without a wizard playing a major role in the death. There's no reason to assume Blackflame doesn't know this. Why would it take an unnecessary risk?"

"Why wouldn't it want to kill you when it thinks it has the advantage?" said Dyrra. "If it thinks you look weak—"

"If it even knows I'm here." Larek shook his head, driving away the old words before they could overtake him. "Look. Where did it dive?"

"West of here," said Sindra. "Hard to gauge how far. If I had to guess, I'd bet it hit near Neton. It's a river town, but they have some outlying farms."

Sindra furrowed her brow, but her eyes rolled up to the right, her head moving slightly as though searching her memory or perhaps doing tricky math.

"It's about three days from us on foot as we are now. One on horseback, if the ground stays steady."

"Then that's where we should start," said Larek. "But we still have to get some horses."

"And pay for them how?" said Sindra. "I told you we should have gotten them while we could get them cheap. What are we supposed to do? Trade the pavilion for them?"

"That workshop could be worth a thousand horses," said Larek. "Probably more."

"But what good is it if we can't catch the dragon?"

"Well," said Dyrra, drawing out the word until she had their attention. "I was going to save this for a surprise down in Velstadt, but…"

Dyrra threw a heavy leather pouch onto the ground. The tie came loose when it hit, and two cubic golden marks rolled out of it. Each no broader across than the nail of Larek's smallfinger, yet with five of its sides engraved with the images of past monarchs. The sixth looked like King Harlan III, from a sketch taken in his youth.

Even one of those gold marks could have paid for a week's good lodging for the three of them. And if the pouch was full…

"Where did you get that?" said Larek.

"Found it in a cabinet inside Sebas' pavilion when we were searching for the key." Dyrra smiled broader than Larek would have believed she could. "I wouldn't be surprised if it's not the only one tucked away in there, either."

"That's enough for—"

"Not just horses. *Good* horses. And more besides. If we're going to do this, let's do this right."

"And the bandits who will see our horses as targets?" said Sindra with a mock innocent expression. "What about them?"

"If we can handle a dragon," said Dyrra, "I think we can handle a few bandits."

"And if we can't," said Larek, "then the bandits won't matter anyway."

***

THE MORNING WARMED EARLY ON THE WALK BACK NORTH TO LILLIKAN.

Normally, that would have made Sindra happy. Bright blue skies, no clouds in sight, fresh green land and smells all around her. Birds singing in the background. The sort of morning that would have put a spring in her step on most days, especially with a decent road underfoot.

Of course, as far as Sindra was concerned, they hadn't seen any bad roads yet. Not really. Yes, the road north of Lillikan had not been good. Too many wagon ruts, too many broken places where she had to be careful of her footing. But as far as Sindra was concerned, any road at all was easier than traipsing across the countryside at a high pace.

She had done that a few times in her days as a Healer.

But even under blue skies on a decent road, with spiced eggs and bread in her belly and people she could call friends by her side, Sindra had trouble keeping sincerity in her smile that morning.

Maintaining the smile in the first place was important. It was an early lesson taught to the apprentice Healers. "Cheer can spread as fast as a fever." Already on this trip she had seen her smile worm its way past the worries and tempers of Larek and Dyrra until they reflected it back at her.

No small accomplishment, particularly in Dyrra's case.

But this morning Sindra's smile would not be enough, especially when her own worries tried to wipe it from her face. Larek may have worried about the dragon, and Dyrra may have worried about Keon, but Sindra worried about Neton.

Blackflame had hit near Neton. She was sure of that. As nearly as she could remember the layout of this portion of Aeralfast, Neton had to be the closest town along the Quar. Hundreds of people. Maybe a thousand. At least a score of nearby farms, any one of which would have enough sheep or goats or cows to attract a hungry dragon.

But what did it do? Hit them all at once and eat everything? Gorge itself before it returned to the skies and its rest in some secluded spot?

No. Not likely. The last time Blackflame came, it hit the same area two or three times before moving on.

It would come back to Neton, probably today. Possibly tomorrow. But either way, the people of Neton would know it was coming and could do nothing about it. Any local warriors or wizards powerful enough to hope to stand against it would be off at the tournament.

And even if Keon rode north at speed to carry word of the dragon, the response from the capitol would be too slow. No less than three days, and that assumed swift, decisive plans and action. Four or five days were far more likely.

Too long a delay. The people of Neton could do nothing but huddle in their homes. If they tried to flee, they might become appetizers for the dragon on its way to their herds. If they tried to fight, they would die.

Even hiding they might die. The dragon might burn their homes for its own reasons. It had done so before.

Sindra had heard the accounts of the time Larek fought it. Not just the songs, but reports from the Healers dispatched to aid the survivors. Some of the farms burned had no livestock, or at least none that would draw a dragon's interest. And yet the dragon had burned them to the ground, left none alive.

No pattern. No certainty. Only that one strike would not slake it.

No. Neton would suffer again, and perhaps again after that before the three of them could even reach the area.

And when they did, there would be survivors. There would be wounded. There would be people in desperate need of aid.

In desperate need of a Healer.

And all they would have was Sindra.

Dyrra's words about confronting their failures sounded wonderful. An oration worthy of a noble. But Dyrra and Larek could not understand the basic difference between their failures and hers.

Dyrra could still swing her sword. And her stiff hip seemed to improve with every mile they walked.

Larek could still cast his spells. He even had Chitter to help him and consult with him.

But Sindra's "power" was no longer hers to call.

Cast out of her order. Warned by no less than High Healer Alain himself to never again utter the supplications of the Healers of Nilasah.

Easy words to accept when crying in the streets of the capitol, staring at the devastating compassion in the High Healer's eyes. But what would Sindra do if surrounded by those who suffered under the predations of Blackflame? Would she confine herself to the physical skills she had been taught, knowing they would only do so much? That those skills might not — would not — be enough?

She had heard the stories. The tales of those who had been cast out, yet tried to speak the prayers and heal anyway. They failed, but that was not the worst of it.

They all, and every one of them, were said to have sickened and died before the next sunrise. It was said that Nilasah knew her own, and only trusted her gifts to those who had proven their worth.

That was a lot for Sindra to risk, knowing that the prayers would not help anyway.

But those tales told of failures through greed or self-importance. Those men and women who put themselves before the goddess in their hearts and in their minds. That was not Sindra's failing.

At least, she didn't think that was her failing. But her own memories of that night. The chaos. The confusion. Could she really be sure?

And even if her failing *was* different, did it matter?

And even if it did, what then?

Even if Nilasah consented to hear the healing prayers of a failure like Sindra whose only desire was to grant succor to the suffering, would She answer? Could She? Could Her beneficence flow through so flawed and unworthy a vessel as Sindra?

Or would Sindra sicken and die anyway, unable to channel Her Divine Grace? Or simply for the arrogance of the attempt?

These were the questions that plagued her into silence as the trio walked back north to Lillikan, on what should have been a beautiful, hopeful morning.

———

THE GATES OF LILLIKAN STOOD CLOSED, COMPLETING THE TOWN WALL composed of shaved tree trunks, cut to interlock tight and shaped to sharp — though worn — points at the top. Easily five times Larek's height.

He found the sight just as intimidating here under a too-bright-and-hot mid-day sun as he first had near dusk only a couple of days ago.

But this time it felt worse. Larek's growling stomach fell at the sight of the closed, iron-banded gates. He was tired and sweaty from the hike, and had been looking forward to a good meal before they took to horseback. He imagined he could smell baking bread from where he stood, a good two dozen paces from those gates.

Those closed gates. And that was the problem. There was only one reason a town built for trade would have those gates closed on so inviting a day.

They were hunkering down against the dragon.

But that did not make sense to Larek. If they saw the dragon dive, they had to know it did so some distance away. And if they did not, then they must have seen it fly out of sight.

True, a dragon in the area at all was cause for alert. But they were behaving as though they expected it to come after them here.

Sure enough, when Larek ran his eyes along the tops of the walls, he noticed crouching crossbowmen watching the skies. A glance at the fields on either side showed mostly level stretches of green wild grass, with the occasional copse of ash and cherry trees.

But no people out among them.

"Young," said Chitter in his ear. The earth spirit had finally roused an hour ago, though he still did not seem quite as spry and active as usual, despite assurances that he was fine. "The guards. Both of them."

Larek looked back at the two pikemen, and sure enough, they were both young, rather than one young and one ... experienced. That had to mean something. Was Barth in trouble for his kindness to them?

Or was Larek reading too much into this? Barth had been guarding the northern gate last time, and here Larek stood at the southern gate.

Still, those young guards looked wary, not welcoming, which was not a good sign. Nor was the tipping of their pikes as the trio approached.

As the guards took their positions, Larek decided that the one on the right was the clear leader between them. He held his pose one step forward of his fellow, his heavy jaw in a confident thrust.

"Problem?" said Dyrra to the pikemen, loud enough that Larek saw two of the crossbowmen glance down from their high perches. Her hand was on the hilt of her sword.

"Lillikan is closed." The speaker, as Larek expected, was the one on the right. "Go around or go away."

"Point those pikes away from my friend Larek," said Dyrra, who started to take a step forward when Sindra stayed her with a hand on the shoulder.

Why *were* both those pikes pointed at Larek? Was this about the duel?

Larek's stomach quit growling then. It was too busy trying to sink down his dark pants and into his walking boots.

Sindra took a step forward and raised empty hands to show she meant no threat. Her words came out soft, but carried, which Larek found an impressive trick.

"Please. This isn't for us. We saw the dragon dive yesterday. I believe it attacked Neton."

"So you're running north," said the guard leader, tone matter of fact. "Smart. But you three have to go around Lillikan all the same."

"No," she said. "You know the reputation of Blackflame. He will strike there again today or tomorrow. He might even strike a third time before he vanishes into the skies."

She had their interest now, both guards' attention more on her than on their weapons, whose tips began to waver enough to give Larek a small sigh of relief.

Sindra continued, "We want to go help the good people of Neton. To do that we need horses—"

The guard leader snorted, breaking the pattern of her words. Both pikes steadied their aim at Larek.

"You want horses so you can flee faster? Don't blame you. But don't try that—"

"Do you give my friend the lie?" said Dyrra, tone even darker than her expression.

"I'm saying you have the murderer Larek Dragonbait with you, and he is not welcome in Lillikan."

"Dragonbait?" said Dyrra.

"Murderer?" said Sindra.

Larek could say nothing. However low his jaw hung, it seemed that no words had any interest in escaping past it.

"He murdered Sebas in front of—"

Apparently that was enough to stir some words in Larek's brain.

"Sebas challenged me to a duel in front of an inn full of witnesses. He repeated his challenge in front of what looked like half your town. And he was the one throwing lethal spells. All I did was turn one of his own spells against him. If anything, he murdered himself."

"That isn't the story the townsfolk tell," said the guard leader. "And while Sebas might not have been well-loved here, he was one of us. If you were anyone else we'd have you before a judge. But you're the Dragonbait, so stay out of our town or we'll kill you where you stand."

Chitter tapped Larek on the shoulder, and pointed for him to look up.

Two dozen crossbows. All trained on Larek.

———

DYRRA FLICKED HER EYES ACROSS THE TWO DOZEN TRAINED CROSSBOWS atop the high, spiked wall, and tried to remember the last time she had gotten to fight from a superior tactical position.

Nothing. She wasn't sure she ever had.

The two pikemen in front of the gate were nothing more than an irritation. She was sure of that. They held their grips too tight. Their stances stiff, unready to adjust to an enemy who acted against their expectations. She could even smell their sour fear sweat from a dozen paces. They were spitting accusations to hide their inexperience.

And likely the terror that Dyrra would draw her sword of war.

She could kill them both before either could offer a serious threat. Even here under scalding glare of Lucala's Jealous Sister, which narrowed Dyrra's vision and slowed her hand more than she liked to admit.

But what good would killing the pikemen do? The gates would still stand closed, their iron bands no doubt reinforced on the inside, as the northern gate had been. And then there were the crossbowmen...

No good.

Larek probably had a spell that could spoil their first shot. But would he think to cast it? Or would he rather let them kill him out of some twisted sense of honor? Even if he did cast, would he act to stop their second shots? Their third?

She spared a glance to assess him. Pain in his eyes. The shock over his new kenning. Dragonbait. What idiot had...

Keon. Of course.

Didn't matter. Bad enough that Larek had to suffer insults he felt he warranted. But an unjust kenning was a step too far, especially from the lips of a muttonhead.

Dyrra drew her sword, causing at least a third of the crossbowmen to reconsider their choice of targets.

"Deny us entrance if you like, but I won't stand here and listen to—"

"Wait," said Sindra.

Dyrra bit back the rest of her words, but doing so left a bitter taste in her mouth. She glared a warning at Sindra to let her know that her temper would bide only so long.

"You wrong Larek when you call him murderer and dragonbait," said Sindra, seemingly infinite patience in her voice. "Sebas forced him to fight, and Larek won fairly. And if Larek were dragonbait, why did he live so near the capitol for so many years with nary a sign of dragons?"

"The dragon found him the last time it rampaged," said the guard leader, "and it found him again this time. Every hour he stands in our shadow is an hour he threatens us."

Dyrra could hear some commotion on the other side of the wall. Raised voices arguing, though muted by distance and wood.

"We are not here to bring you trouble," said Sindra. "I am no warrior and I am no wizard. You are not proscribed from allowing me entrance. Let me friends wait out here and I will come purchase—"

"He leaves or he dies."

From the corner of her eye, Dyrra saw Chitter dive into the ground behind Larek's boots.

"If he dies, the two of you are next," said Dyrra. "And if you think the rest of you are safe up on that wall—"

"HOLD!" cried a voice from atop the wall.

Dyrra gave her sword an impatient twirl, and was gratified to see four more crossbows turn her direction. She already knew which way she'd dive, if necessary.

But then Barth leaned over the wall.

"If you could all stop threatening each other for a moment," he said, voice craggy with an irritation familiar to Dyrra. The sound of a soldier sick of politics. She'd heard that tone in her own voice many times.

Sindra looked at Larek. He shrugged, which made the pikemen renew their grips. Dyrra would have bet that they would piss themselves if he so much as raised a hand.

While she amused herself with that mental image, she could hear arguing atop the wall in voices that tried to hush and failed. She could not quite pick out any of the words though.

Finally, Barth leaned over again and said, "Sindra, will you swear not to cause any trouble if you are admitted into Lillikan?"

"I swear by Nilasah, may She restore me to Her favor, that I only seek entrance to purchase horses that we will ride in service of others. I further swear that I will cause no trouble nor begin any arguments within the walls of Lillikan, though I will defend myself if I must."

"Good enough for me," said Barth. He turned to face someone on the wall that Dyrra couldn't see and said, "As a citizen of Lillikan, I take responsibility for her actions and behavior within the township of Lillikan today. Her deeds will be as my own, and I shall share equally in the punishment for any crimes she might commit."

Shocked murmuring from up atop the wall, but Dyrra didn't care. In fact, she smiled and sheathed her sword as she heard the thumps of support braces coming down. Moments later, the squeak of pulleys began, and the gates began to open.

The pikemen had yet to lower their weapons, but they shifted on their feet uncertainly.

Dyrra spat. She wouldn't even need her sword to kill these two. They had no business on guard duty. No one should stand guard who has never swung her weapon to kill.

As the gates swung wide, Barth was waiting for them. No armor this time. Simple tunic and pants, but the boots gave him away. Those were boots that had seen campaigns full of marches and skirmishes. Worn to the perfect fit. Mended and repaired as needed.

Dyrra understood the boots, and in that moment she understood Barth.

Half again her age, a good sign in a warrior — still alive, and in good shape by the look of him. Fit, strong, and not permanently disfigured. Old scars on his hands, and one more creasing his short, graying black hair. That one had the look of a sword blow that had split armor on its way in.

She gave him a Karwalish salute, a smack of the back of her sword hand on the palm of her other that echoed in its respect.

Barth had been stepping forward, but stopped short. A smile lit his eyes — hazel, if Dyrra could judge at this distance under the cursed light of Lucala's Jealous Sister — and barely touched his lips. But he returned the salute, and his rang out just as loud.

Sindra looked back and forth between them, confused, and Larek had his head bent toward his shoulder, where Chitter — whose return Dyrra had missed — spoke fast and soft.

"Thank you for this," said Sindra.

Barth rushed a nod and said, "Is it true you're going to Neton, after Blackflame?"

"And to help the survivors," she said and Dyrra nodded confirmation.

"Then we should hurry. And we'll need a fourth horse. I'm coming with you."

18

LAREK AND DYRRA WERE TOLD AT CROSSBOW POINT THAT THEY HAD TO wait a thousand strides down the road while Sindra and Barth bought the horses. Dyrra looked inclined to argue, but Larek began walking and gave her no choice but to follow along.

He had been hoping to at least find a comfortable place to wait. From the way Dyrra blinked and squinted and sweated, he suspected that the bright, hot sun was as hard on her as it was on his scars. And she didn't have a floppy hat like he did. He also noted that Dyrra no longer limped or showed any sign of stiffness in her movements, but though that pleased him it did not affect on his line of thinking.

He wanted a place to rest out of the hot sun. But as they walked he noted that there were no shade trees near the road for quite some way.

Well, Larek had an answer for that. He had a theory to test about his latest acquisition and this would be as good a time as any to test it.

But first, he needed some answers.

Once they had counted off exactly the thousand mandated steps — and Dyrra counted them aloud — he turned to face her and was surprised to see a patient look on her face.

"Let me guess," she said. "'Dyrra, Barth announces he's coming with us and you just accept it? You? Who didn't even want Sindra along with us?' Something like that?"

Larek smiled. "I was also going to throw in a, 'but we don't even know anything about this man. He could be working for Keon.'"

"He isn't," said Dyrra with a confident shake of her head, enough to make her pony tail with its blade at the end whip back and forth. "And I do know him." She frowned. "Well, I know his type anyway."

"The same way I could pick out what kind of wizard Sebas was from the way he moved and spoke in the inn? You can figure something similar out about other warriors?" He frowned. "Then why didn't you—"

"I read him wrong at the gate that first night, I admit." She shrugged. "The uniform distracted me. I figured him for a career guard, the type who grows old in the job because he never sees any action. That's why his behavior threw me. Didn't match.

"But today I saw those boots, and it all came together."

"His boots?"

Dyrra nodded. "Take a look at them when he meets up with us. Those are boots that have been through a war or two or three. But he's seen more than four decades or I'm pale as an easterner."

"And he's still in one piece..." said Larek as he began to understand.

"Fit too." Was that a hint of a smile in her eyes? "Moves well. Once I saw those boots, his behavior made sense to me." She nodded. "He'll be a help when the fighting starts, or I don't know which end of the sword to hold."

Larek could think of no reason to dispute her, at least not at this time. So instead he pulled the pavilion's cool, silver piton from a belt pouch and stabbed it into the earth among the fresh wild grass on the east side of the road.

It only went halfway in.

"What do you think?" he asked Chitter. "Deep enough, or should I try it again?"

"It wasn't any deeper than that when I pulled it out after the duel," said Chitter.

"I could do it," said Dyrra, pacing. "I could shove it in deep enough to hold a tent rope, even without a mallet."

"No," said Larek. "Unless I read the spells wrong when I examined it last night, I need to be the one to do it."

Larek pulled the tightly stuffed cheap burlap pouch from his belt. He took a deep breath and gestured for Dyrra to step back. She did, but didn't stop pacing.

Larek brought his fingers to the laces, grateful to his old master for the emphasis on languages in his studies. He had met wizards who spoke only the local tongue of Aeralfast and ancient Aarkadian. But Larek also spoke Thelmastii, Florese, Chaldish, Chelas, and a half-dozen others.

If Larek were to guess, he would have guessed that Sebas' master had only emphasized Aarkadian. It was the language Sebas had relied on for his spells during the duel, and it would explain the safety design of his workshop.

Which was a clever enough. Larek had to give Sebas that much. Many wizards trying to puzzle out the spells would have looked for a triggering incantation. And, in truth, Larek had spent a good deal of time and effort doing just that, perhaps the whole time Dyrra had spent in prayer to Lucala by the firelight last night.

Oh, he had found what looked like a trigger quickly and easily. But that bothered him. It was too quick and too easy. Sebas had warded part of his workshop off from the rest of it. This was not a wizard who left his triggers in the open for anyone to find.

And so Larek had gone over the spells time and again, until he realized that more than a portion of the "trigger" was a ruse. That whole part of the spell was a trap. Casting its incantation while opening the pouch would channel all of the power in the workshop — more than a year's worth of spellcasting — into an explosion that would likely leave a crater deep enough to sink all of Lillikan.

However, engraved on the piton were two words that would look like a name to anyone not well versed in Chaldish. *Ila Onosa.* In fact, Larek had met more than one woman named Ila in his life, though their names were accented on the first syllable instead of the second.

But when said with the proper inflection, the two words meant "welcome home."

Once he realized that, Larek had shifted his attention from the trigger to the release, and found in it two false words of Aarkadian. *Piraila Otonosa.* Aarkadian was a rich and ancient language. Few who spoke it in the modern era knew the whole of the lexicon, and from context, most wizards would have assumed that the words involved organizing the placement of stone.

Wizards who weren't looking for two words of Chaldish, disguised among the Aarkadian. Two words that would tie the released spell to the piton, if the piton were also placed by the wizard opening the pouch. And opening the pouch was the actual trigger. It simply wouldn't work without the Chaldish.

At least, those were Larek's conclusions, and he felt his face try to redden further as he continued holding his breath in anticipation while going through all the steps yet once more in his head.

But then he could wait no longer. Larek closed his eyes. He expelled all his air saying the words *"ila onosa"* as, he unknotted the pouch and pulled it inside out in a single quick movement.

No explosion.

Larek opened his eyes a crack.

There stood the pavilion, tall as that of any countess, and bright red with gold trim and filigree.

Dyrra thumped him on the shoulder hard enough to jerk him forward.

"Good work!"

"Thank you." He gave her a sidelong glance as he rubbed at the shoulder.

"If you were wrong, that would have killed us, wouldn't it?"

For all the inflection in her voice, she might have been saying that a cloudless sky at night meant we were all blessed by Lucala.

"We were in no danger." He shrugged, while Chitter twitched his tail doubtfully. "I think."

"Well, try not to get us killed before we face your dragon."

And with that, she threw back the tent flap and entered the pavilion. Already Larek could smell the fragrant fruits within, and the lingering smell of ... was that the eggs, bacon and toast that Sindra had cooked yesterday?

Was this workshop in stasis while put away?

Stasis — true stasis — was only a theory as far as Larek knew. He had read some speculations about methods for extending preservation spells, and a few wild conclusions about hypothetical open-ended paralytic spells, but never anything that extended to practical application.

But the possibility of a closed workshop being in stasis? Larek had never thought about that before. Had never read anything along those lines either. Workshops were so basic a wizard's tool that he had never heard of tracing the development of their spells the way a scholar might trace the development of a word.

Larek, like most wizards he knew of, had always left his workshop open. And in closing it for travel he had removed anything perishable.

Could Sebas have stumbled onto the secrets of stasis?

Now Larek really wanted to get past that warded purple wood door.

But that was a task for later. Assuming there was a later, once he had faced the dragon.

Still, the possibilities gave him something pleasant to think about as he followed Dyrra into the pavilion, where no doubt she was foraging for lunch.

SINDRA KEPT HER CHESTNUT GELDING TO A SMOOTH, EASY GAIT AS SHE and Barth passed through the gates and out of Lillikan. The mid-day sun felt more cheerful to her now. She had all but forgotten the feel of riding. The warm strength of the horse beneath her, the slight rocking of a walking pace. The smell of hay and musk.

Just like her first day as an apprentice Healer, half a lifetime ago. She and five other new apprentices, none past their eleventh year, four girls and a boy. All of them skinny and scared and excited in their fresh white kirtles. Proud of the soothing hand of Nilasah embroidered over their hearts. Fidgeting and feeding off of each other's nerves. Away from their parents for the first time. Though their parents all still lingered just inside the inn behind them, watching through the windows, as nervous as their children.

A fall day, and the rains had come early, pouring down past the stoop so heavily the drops broke into low mist as they eroded the road to mud. Even now, so many years later, when Sindra thought of the smell of rain, that was the morning she remembered.

Then their escort arrived — six guards, six spare horses, and Instructing Healer Deramu leading them, with all his grace and poise. The way Sindra remembered it, Deramu threw back his hood and the sun broke through the clouds, shining on his golden hair and driving off the storm.

At least half the girls fell in love right then, Sindra included. Not that he would have noticed. He was three times their age and they had the quicksilver emotions of youth.

But Sindra still smiled when she remembered his strong hands lifting her onto the bay mare. And even though her horse was led by a guard, she still felt like a lady and a knight and a king's messenger all at once. That anything was possible with a strong, beautiful steed supporting her.

That feeling was distant now, tucked away toward the back of her mind. But it still lingered to this day, and it kept the smile on her face as she followed Barth past the gates.

It turned out that they had not needed to buy Barth a horse. He had one. A gray stallion he called Baron, several years older than the steeds she had bought today.

Sindra had asked about the name. He had said, "A baron was always sending me into danger. I figured a baron should be getting me out of it again."

Barth had only nodded when Sindra chose her gelding, and again when she found a black stallion that she thought would suit Larek. But he insisted on picking out Dyrra's mount. A roan stallion easily the size of his own. Said it was a horse she would be able to rely on "in the thick of things."

Sindra wondered about that, much as she wondered about the understanding she had seen pass between Barth and Dyrra around the time that he announced he was coming along to fight the dragon.

Sindra wasn't sure it was a good idea. She was pretty sure Larek doubted the wisdom of it as well. But Dyrra had not hesitated to agree.

Some kind of recognition between old soldiers? That was the closest she could come. At least, until she had a chance to ask Dyrra.

Still, he had impressed her in town. She would have sworn that he had gotten them to the stables faster than the guards had been able to re-close the gates, and before she could draw breath to ask about horses he had told the stablemaster the sort of horses they needed and hinted at what they would need to do.

Eliminated more than half of the stock before Sindra could even consider her choices, but she trusted to Dyrra's confidence in him. It helped that he negotiated an excellent price without much haggling. That pouch of gold marks Dyrra had found remained more than half full.

Sindra was beginning to get the idea that Barth was respected in Lillikan.

Once they had the three new horses — and Barth had reclaimed his own from the same stable — they paused near a small house toward the eastern edge where Barth had left her outside with the horses.

He returned quickly, but now clad in chain mail armor, carrying a round shield and a spear in addition to the sword on his belt and the pack slung over his shoulder.

He even brought food. A loaf of good bread, and enough beef to share with Dyrra and Larek when they met up, plus a few apples and a good half-dozen carrots. He had wanted to stop for more, but Sindra told him they had plenty.

She had not mentioned the pavilion. Even now, riding south alongside him, she wondered if their using Sebas' pavilion would bother him. Assuming Larek had managed to figure out the spells. He had sounded confident enough last night, but she knew...

They barely passed through the gate when she saw the pavilion, off to the side of the road as though expecting a tournament to spring up around it.

"Is that ... Sebas' pavilion?"

Sindra had trouble reading the tone in his question. She heard surprise, but not opinion. She decided that honesty was the best option.

"It remained after the duel. Seemed a shame to let it go to waste."

"Your Larek understands it to the point of safety?"

"It wouldn't be open if he weren't certain." She craned her neck. "And I don't see him or Dyrra, so they must be inside."

Sindra glanced at Barth. His brow furrowed, but his eyes, lips and cheeks gave away nothing.

"Does our using it present a problem for you?"

"For me?" Barth laughed, a rich sound of honest amusement. "The bastard had me fired over Dyrra's armor. It'll be a pleasure to sleep under his fancy roof."

———

THE FOUR RIDERS TROTTED SOUTHWEST ACROSS BROAD GREEN FIELDS and up and down hills and rises and past groves of oak and ash all through the afternoon sun. Dyrra had assumed at first that they would follow the road down to the river before turning west toward Neton, but Sindra insisted that the route was too slow. That they would arrive sooner if they cut directly across the land.

Sindra did not sound happy as she said it, but certain that she knew the way.

Larek had hesitated, but Dyrra simply shrugged and started riding the direction Sindra was pointing. Dyrra had ridden many horses on many campaigns, and few were the number of times she had actually gotten to travel by roadway. She had yet to meet a horse so fragile it couldn't pick its way across decent land.

And the roan stallion Barth had chosen for her was a worthy horse. But of course he chose her a worthy horse. Just another way he could prove that he knew his business. As though Dyrra had any doubts. The uniform might have thrown her in their first meeting, but she understood him well enough now.

And the roan stallion was excellent. Big and strong and beautiful, in another place it would have been reared as a proper warhorse. She named it Glint, after the glint in the eye of Lucala. Glint had smelled freshly bathed when she mounted him, but as the afternoon wore on, she began to smell hints of his sweat.

Less from him, though, than from Larek's black stallion, Fal, or Sindra's chestnut gelding, Nut. Barth's gray stallion, Baron, seemed to have similar endurance to her own, however. If Baron had begun to sweat, Dyrra couldn't smell it yet.

At least they all seemed to know how to ride horses. Dyrra had half-expected Larek to start off at a gallop and wear his mount out too soon. But he clearly understood the traveling value of the trot. And from the comfortable way Chitter sat on Fal's head, Larek had taken the squirrel-spirit riding many times.

To Dyrra, the most surprising part of all this was that she was riding to war while following a Healer.

Technically, she was not. She knew this in her head, but warriors did not live in their heads. They lived in their guts. And her gut told her that riding to face a dragon was riding to war. And while Sindra might not have held the title of Healer, Dyrra had never met anyone else so focused behind following the beliefs of Nilasah.

So many of these easterners paid lip service to their gods. Oh, they prayed for their rains and they prayed for help when the needed it, but they did not seem to truly understand devotion. Not the way the Karwalish understood it.

Here in the east, they thought Lucala was just the moon. But Dyrra knew the truth. Knew it the way her heart knew how to beat. The way her lungs knew how to breathe. Lucala was the moon, yes, but Lucala was everywhere, and most of all, Lucala was in the hearts of her followers.

Dyrra did not pray every night out of some sense of purpose. Nor out of habit. Nor a desire for aid, or anything like that. She prayed because it was time to pray. She prayed because her devotion to Lucala sustained her every bit as much as food and sleep.

She could not go without food. She could not go without sleep. And she could not go without prayer.

And out of all the easterners Dyrra had ever met, only Sindra seemed to understand that. Sindra lived with the same complete devotion to Nilasah that Dyrra felt for Lucala. There was no craft to it. No artifice.

How the Healers of Sindra's order could not see that, Dyrra did not know. It made her think less of them because it seemed so obvious to her. Nilasah was part of Sindra as Lucala was part of Dyrra.

As magic was part of Larek. She understood that now too.

And that understanding, as much as anything else, was why those two were the first people she had known in years that she could comfortably call friends.

So yes, technically, it was not a Healer Dyrra was following to war, but an ex-Healer.

But even that phrasing made Dyrra snort. Sindra may have led their ride across the plains of Aeralfast on the most direct route to Neton possible, but Dyrra was not actually *following* her. Once they found this dragon, Sindra would not be issuing any orders.

In fact, none of them would be issuing orders.

Dyrra wondered if that would pose a problem. It might.

Perhaps they could plan their way past it? That would never have worked with a volley of soldiers, but they were no volley, and only she and Barth were soldiers. Larek would hang back to cast his spells anyway. He would not trip them up.

But Sindra... If there were wounded near the dragon when the time for battle came, would Sindra rush to help them despite the risk? Despite the way her presence might complicate the battle?

It seemed likely. The sort of thing Sindra might think she had to do to atone to her goddess.

Well, if she did, Dyrra sincerely hoped Nilasah didn't ask her to die for the cause.

THEY PRESSED ON AS FAR INTO THE SUNSET AS THEY DARED, FOLLOWING Dyrra's sharp-eyed lead toward the end, but Larek was glad when they called the halt for the day. They found a wide clearing between two groves of elms, where the ground was smooth and level. Sparse, stiff, yellowing grass, but a pleasant, nutty scent to the air.

Stopping at all was not ideal, but necessary. He knew that. Yes he wanted to get to Neton at speed. But he wanted to get there intact. The horses needed rest, and the brushing and rubbing down they had gotten immediately after the halt had been called.

Besides, Larek could tell he was not the only one saddle-stiff. Sindra may have known more about riding than he did, as comfortable as she had looked on her horse, but after an afternoon's ride with only a single break, her legs looked as unhappy as his. She began extending them and contorting herself in ways that strained her kirtle, but from the pleasure in her expression must have had some healing value.

Still, stiffness and soreness and lack of light aside, stopping for the day only gave Larek time to think about what he was doing.

He was riding to face the dragon. To face Blackflame. Again. Yes, he had grown in his magic over the past ten years, but no doubt Blackflame had grown in power as well.

It was said that dragons did not age as men or animals, to reach a peak of vitality before they began to ebb and decay. Dragons were said to have no upper limit on their power, if they survived long enough without brave heroes killing them.

Ten years was not much time on the scale of a dragon's life, but could Larek possibly be lucky enough that his power had grown faster than the dragon's?

He doubted that sincerely.

This was a fool's errand.

So while Chitter pulsed soothing earth power through him to relieve the aches and stresses of the half-day's ride, Larek said to the newest fool, "So Barth, what has gone so wrong in your life that you're willing to die fighting a dragon?"

"I don't plan to die against the dragon." Barth didn't look up from setting up his bedroll. "I plan to see us kill it."

"Just so," said Dyrra, who hesitated with her bedroll in her hands. "Are we setting up the pavilion?"

"I'd rather not," said Larek. "Hard to be certain how the horses would react. Putting the pavilion away in front of them was one thing. Making it appear out of nothing has a better chance of spooking them. And they're going to be dealing with shocks enough soon."

"I'll get a fire going then," said Sindra, who now moved as though the ride had not bothered her after all. The result of her contortions? Or some small blessing from her goddess? No way for Larek to know for certain.

Chitter scampered off to gather the driest firewood, but Larek refused to get distracted. After setting up his own bedroll he returned to his question.

"None of us plan to die," he said to Barth. "But only an idiot would deny the risk of what we're planning. And I don't think you're an idiot.

"I owe it to the dead to try for that dragon again. You know that because I know you're heard the songs and stories, and you can see my scars even under the fading light of day. In fact, I'd wager you've heard all our stories and songs a thousand times. And yet you ride with us to match yourself against Blackflame. That can't be some childhood dream or life's goal or you'd be off at the tournament.

"So while I welcome you among us, and I'm grateful for your help, I can't help but wonder. Why?"

Barth chuckled, a dry sound.

"Guess it's the nature of you wizards to ask that question. Warriors, we're taught not to worry about why. Only about who, what and how."

"Not about when?" said Sindra.

"When is always now," said Dyrra, sharing a nod with Barth. But then she raised an eyebrow. "But some of us worry about why all the same."

"You must have been an officer," said Barth with a snort. "I never was. The farm I grew up on changed liege lords at least a half-dozen times before I quit going home. I fought in the service of three different barons, and not one of them allowed officers from the common folk.

"But it wasn't the farms that were valuable. They came with the mines dug into the Miser, most northern of the Seven Peaks and the most contested."

"I had to heal for some of those battles," said Sindra. "Vicious, they were. I'd never seen such hatred."

"Vicious," said Barth. "Pretty word for it. I always just called them ugly. Have you ever heard about the rules of war?"

Sindra nodded. Dyrra snorted. And Larek's, "Yes," was suspicious, hearing the hints of a story behind the question.

"Bet you've heard how they make war 'fair,' and keep things 'from getting out of hand.'"

"Something like that."

Barth chuckled. "They're fancy things agreed to by fancy people who never have to do the fighting. Something to make them feel good about themselves over their evening brandy while sending their lessers out to die."

"I have seen them adhered to," said Dyrra, holding up one finger. "Once. And that whole conflict lasted only three days."

"Three days is longer than I've ever seen. Usually they start fraying at the edges within the first few hours of the first battle."

Barth shook away a memory. Sindra sparked a fire within a ring of stones set up by Chitter. Enough to cook by without making Larek uncomfortable, which was no small feat. The nutty smell in the air grew stronger with the fire, and Larek wondered how it would flavor their dinner.

But he only wondered for a moment, keeping most of his attention on Barth who, like Dyrra, now sat on his bedroll. His face took on a haunted look in the yellow light of the campfire.

"You don't need to hear the stories. You don't want to. Trust me. No battle is ever pretty, but out by the Miser you have people who've been killing each other for generations. If you went out there to visit you'd think they were different countries, that somehow they weren't even part of Aeralfast.

"But they are. It just doesn't mean anything to them. Not even the barons mean anything to them, and the barons are the ones demanding that they fight.

"At this point, they'd fight without the nobles. They'd fight without gold. They'd fight just because they've grown to loathe one another.

"I was the same way." His eyes flicked to Dyrra, then back to the fire. "I'd like to say I wasn't, but I was. I grew up in it. The hatred was all I knew. I swear we must have sewn it into the ground of our farms."

"But something changed," said Sindra.

Larek would have sworn she wasn't paying attention. That she was digging out food and pans to prepare dinner, and yet her soft words came just as Barth had lapsed into the sort of silence Larek was very familiar with.

"We had a new officer. Some fostered noble from some important family. Never knew his name. Never cared. We called him Lord Vest, because he wore this bright yellow vest over his armor. Like he had no idea what a target it made him, or what blood and dirt would do to his fancy fabrics. Sebas reminded me of him that way.

"That doesn't matter though. What mattered was that Lord Vest was in charge of my company" — he glanced at Dyrra — "It's like a volley. Anyway, he was in charge, and the baron's knights made it clear that Lord Vest had to come home intact or our families would suffer. To make that more palatable, we were given an 'easy mission.' We were supposed to guard a pass that the scouts said was clear.

"It wasn't. Not a big company or anything. Just a handful of soldiers on their way to sabotage a key well. We took them down easily enough, and Lord Vest was all puffed up with pride at his 'victory' and the 'prisoners' he'd taken.

"Except we didn't need prisoners. Not from the common soldiery anyway. Our real leader — the one we actually took orders from — was this grizzled old veteran we called Kank. He told Lord Vest what we needed. Information."

Barth lapsed into silence for a moment. Larek thought that might have been the end of the story, but then he realized the only sound he heard came from the popping of the fire. Even Sindra had stopped preparing dinner, though she didn't look over.

Dyrra merely looked at Barth. No judgment. Just patience.

Eventually, Barth continued.

"We got the information we needed. Troop movements, how they knew about the well, and more. But that wasn't because of the pain. That was because of the only real rule of war acknowledged in the shadow of the Miser. Tell us what you know, and make us believe it, and we'll kill you quickly.

"Lord Vest couldn't take it." Barth's eyes darted to Dyrra, then back to the fire. "Never seen a man vomit up that much. Kept vomiting past the point of bile. We had to get him to a Healer once we saw blood in it, but he wasn't ill. It was pure disgust.

"I still remember the sight of him, pale and weak and tottering as he stood before the lot of us. 'Monsters' he called us. And the way he said it. Like it wasn't an insult. Like he had found the most horrifying thing he could imagine, and it was the troops serving under him.

"Most of the guys laughed. Wanted to call themselves the Monster Company.

"Me, I deserted that night. Just ran and kept running."

"I imagine," said Keon, stepping into the firelight, "that there must be a price on your head as well then."

Just inside the limit of the growing darkness at the edge of the firelight, Larek could see the rest of Keon's men, weapons out and ready.

19

If Keon had to catch her by surprise, at least he had found Dyrra where she had a reasonable place to fight. Smooth level ground under stiff grass, without too many rocks to trip over.

Lucala rose overhead, though in that form She was still not much more than a sliver. Very little extra light for the others, but for Dyrra the blessing of fighting under her goddess. Decent light from the fire, too. Should be enough for the others to see by, to watch for treachery.

Dyrra didn't need the firelight, of course. The stars were more than enough for any woman of Karwale to see by, and no number of years in the east could diminish that.

Keon wouldn't need the firelight either, though he would be helped by it. Dyrra remembered from her days fighting under him. Keon the half-blood did not see as well at night.

Suited a *daywalker* like him.

If this was to be where she had her final fight with Keon, she could have done a lot worse.

Still, Dyrra cursed herself for letting her guard down. Larek's wards of the previous night must have made her sloppy.

Or was it just Barth? Another warrior riding beside her. One who knew...

No. She had no time for such distractions right now.

Barth already had his hand on his sword, looking at Dyrra to follow her lead. She gave him the barest shake of her head. She could only just hear Sindra set down her pans near the crackling fire.

"I seem to recall," said Larek, looking around at Keon's soldiers but not standing up, "that we had an agreement."

"We do," said Keon. Green vest and pants this time, a brighter shade than Dyrra's leather armor, and she could still see the chain mail underneath his collar. "But we don't have any agreement about your new friend, and he just confessed to desertion. I hear that's as big a crime here in Aeralfast as it is in Karwale."

"Maybe from the king's army," said Barth, edging one hand toward his shield. "But out in the shadow of the Miser, no one cares. We breed too fast. There are always more soldiers."

"That's what any deserter would say," said Keon as he made a show of looking over the campsite. "Do you know I can tell which horse is whose by the way you hobble them?"

"Are you here to fight or are you here for tavern games?" said Dyrra, standing up. "Either way, Barth is with us and he is not going with you."

"I like the idea of a fight," said Barth, also coming to his feet, round shield now in one hand. "Be good to stretch those muscles before I face a dragon."

Keon laughed. "Oh, this is too *much*. Dyrra, a dragon? Really? Alongside the Burned Wizard?"

"No, Barth," said Dyrra. "This is between me and Keon. I called for *xincalu*."

Barth frowned and lowered his shield, which impressed Dyrra. She wasn't sure he would have heard of the Karwalish practice.

"Well, Keon?" she said.

Keon sighed.

"I knew you'd go back to Lillikan. I even figured you'd want horses, once you knew I was after you. But I can't believe you rode *toward* the dragon. Do you know how much you just cost me? I had to send a *rider* to the capitol to carry the news instead of bringing it myself. That's profit cast into the wind."

"And here I thought you were all about safe profits," said Larek, his voice droll enough to make Dyrra smile.

"Normally yes," said Keon, as though he had finally found someone rational to speak to. "But it's this *xincalu* business. If I let some dragon kill Dyrra instead of doing it myself—"

"I can't imagine a bounty hunter gets much respect anyway," said Barth. "Even from his own men."

"Tie back your dog," Keon said to Dyrra, "before someone beats it."

"Listen to me," said Larek, loud and directed at Keon's men rather than Keon. "Your countrymen are suffering under the predations of the dragon Blackflame. Yes, the dragon that gave me these scars."

He gave them a moment to look over his scars.

"We ride to Neton because someone must kill that dragon. Ride with us if you will, but if you won't at least don't hinder us."

"Pretty words," said Keon, projecting his voice over the murmurs of some of his men. "But you don't need to worry. My men won't do anything to you or your pretty needle thrower there. And as far as I'm concerned, if Dyrra's dog wants to slap his shield to join your agreement, I'm willing to let it include him. Do you know what that means, old man?"

Barth glared hard enough to split stone, but he said, "I know, boy."

Barth thumped his shield.

Dyrra noted that most of Keon's men lowered their weapons.

"Well, then, Dyrra," said Keon. "Shall we finish this before the dragon comes along and eats us all?"

DYRRA MET KEON'S EYES ACROSS THE FIRELIGHT AND LET A SLOW SMILE spread across her face. She drew her sword of war slowly, first with a single hand, only bringing her second hand into play when she gave the blade a spin. But she held back from her battle cry this time. Saving it for the right moment.

Barth scooped up his bedroll and pack with his shield and cleared the dry yellow grass between them. He dropped the bedroll near Larek, but kept his hand on his sword and his shield ready.

Six paces of space now between the fire and the arc formed by Keon's men. Plenty for a sand dancer.

Larek made a noise that sounded like choking, but Chitter must have understood because he leapt down and ran for the fire. It gave a loud pop, and a flicker of curiosity passed through her as to whether that was one of the logs or something the earth spirit had done. Either way the fire appeared unchanged.

Sindra crouched, and from the corner of her eye Dyrra could see the gleam of a drugged needle in her hand.

Clearly the others trusted Keon as far as she did. And he knew it. She could tell by the way he stood there, giving them time to make their preparations.

He waited until all the movement had settled before saying, "Such stories she must have told you all about me to engender so much mistrust. Well, don't worry. I don't need tricks to kill a slow sword like Dyrra."

He whipped out his own sword of war with a spinning twirl, as though to remind Dyrra that he knew a thing or two about sand dancing himself.

As though she could have forgotten the fighting skills of her old commander.

He would expect her to attack. To leap and scream her battle cry. So she waited, spinning her sword through a lazy, nominally defensive circle before her.

Whispers hissed through Keon's men. Speculating, perhaps. Or gambling. The same was true the world over. Soldiers would bet on anything.

"I almost forgot," he said, switching his sword to his usual one hand grip. He pulled a dagger from his boot, holding it by the tip in a throwing grip.

Dyrra crouched low and spun her sword faster, forming a near-solid shield between her and that dagger, in case he threw it.

Keon cast the dagger aside, point first into the ground near the feet of one of his soldiers.

"Can't have anyone saying I cheated and poisoned you." He smiled. "Any last words I should bring back to your daughter?"

Dyrra blinked. The smooth circle of her spinning sword faltered.

"I found the temple you and Ommure gave her to. She has your eyes, but his jaw, the poor thing. I've even seen her train. Quick for one so young." Keon snorted. "Must have gotten it from Ommure."

He was bluffing.

He had to have been.

Surely no one would have told him where to find her, if only to keep the information from Dyrra. Warriors were never allowed to know their children, not until they were of age. Not until they had survived their first battle. Then, and only then, were they told their parents' names and deeds. Then, and only then, could they seek out their parents if they chose to.

As Dyrra had.

As Dyrra never expected her daughter to. Not with the deeds she had left behind her.

That was half the reason Dyrra had left. To spare her daughter her mother's shame. She would hear the stories, yes, but never confront them. Never meet any of the participants.

And now Keon had found her.

Was it possible?

Keon's smile spread until a hint of parted teeth showed, and Dyrra's heart sank.

She knew that smile. She had seen it too many times. It was the smile of a truth uncomfortable for the listener. She had seen Keon use it many times. To enforce behavior in his troops. To force compliance from suppliers. And only when Keon was certain of his information.

"No last words for her? I'll just make something up then."

Dyrra had a plan for this fight, when it came. Draw Keon in. Force him to commit himself to an attack, then kill him through the opening he left.

But as she stared at that haughty grin, those mocking eyes... As she imagined Keon telling her daughter lies that were even worse than the awful truths of Dyrra's life... As she pictured him offering the young girl a place in his company when she was ready to take it...

Everything came together hard in Dyrra's throat. A great lump of fire that gathered there even as tendrils of this flame burned through her limbs. Her guts. Flared and consumed her thoughts.

Then hotter.

Wilder.

Demanding release.

The only release she could give it.

"KEENARACH!" SCREAMED DYRRA.

She leapt high in the rising night. Blade spinning. Limbs shaking with the need to kill. Crush. Destroy.

No Keon where she landed in the dry yellow grass. Gone.

She swept a leg behind her like a scythe. Turned with it. Blade cutting across at head height.

Forced Keon to abandon his strike. He dove right, between Dyrra's sweeping leg and blade. Rolled to his feet two steps away.

Keon speaking now. Words just noise. Like the chatter of his men. Like the roaring of the campfire.

Dyrra heard none of it. Nothing. Silent world. Empty world. Everyone, everything around her just ghosts. Only three things were real.

Keon, soon to die.

Dyrra, soon to kill him.

Lucala, watching all from on high.

She knew this like reflex. No thought. No plan. Only action.

And prayer. Somewhere deep inside her, Dyrra was praying

words she could not say. Could not think. Words for Lucala. Words for Ommure. Words for the daughter she had never met.

But even that was too deep to touch her then.

Keon lost his moment trying to gloat. Trying to hurt her with words she could not hear.

Her lunge came in fast and true. His parry ugly. Awkward. His feet out of place.

Dyrra spun fast, hilt high and sword pointed straight down to catch any strike.

Keon's swing was weak. Low. Rushed. Driven off without notice.

But her blade struck true. Not her sword. The blade hanging from the thong she used to tie her hair back. It cut Keon's right cheek open, exposing teeth. Dripping blood.

Blood.

Blood was real too.

She could almost taste it.

Dyrra finished her spin with a thrust for his heart. But Keon had his feet back. Hard parry jarred her arms.

No pain. Too much rage.

Blood in her eyes. Keon spat. Dyrra fell backward in a roll. Blade tucked sideways. Came up wiping her eyes on her armor.

Keon leapt. Coming down on top of her. Spitting more blood. Thrusting for her throat.

She rolled left. Kicked at his knee. Hit his shin. Brought her blade back in time for another parry. And another. Fast attacks. No time to set her feet.

Dyrra fell right. Turned it into a roll. Came up thrusting.

Nothing.

No Keon.

Dyrra dropped flat. His blade swept past where her neck had been.

Deep within her, prayers built toward their crescendo. Live or die, she needed forgiveness. Live or die, she needed to set things right. Live or die, she needed to kill Keon. Had to kill Keon. For herself, yes, but for Ommure. For her daughter.

And for Lucala, Whom Keon spat on by worshipping her Jealous Sister.

She kicked at Keon's groin. Forced him to jump back. Used the momentum to roll backward to her feet.

Keon attacking again. Wide sweeps like a sand dancer.

A trap.

Dyrra spun counter. Swinging for his sword of war. Buying space for her hair blade.

Keon shifted high. Missed her sword. Cut loose her thong.

Dyrra's wiry hair now wild about her face.

Keon laughing and drooling blood. Slipped a stab past her half-blind guard.

Gashed her armor. Blood from her right arm. Shaky now. The limb's fire leaking out with blood.

Dyrra spun a defensive circle. Too slow. Erratic. The cut too deep.

Keon pummeled her. Hard strikes. All easy parries, but taking a toll. Strength ebbed from her arm.

Keon boasting again. Still no sound reached her. Fear mixed with her fire now. Her vengeance — perhaps her justice — fleeing with the strength of her right arm.

More sweeping strikes. More shaky parries. Each weaker than the one before. Little by little he wore her down. Their swords repeating the same motions as though linked. Each driving her back and back.

Then Keon broke the pattern.

Keon thrust for her belly.

The campfire vanished. Lucala's shine only now.

Dyrra felt Keon's blade push through her leather armor. Colder than Larek's jug water. Twisting. Spilling her. Her right arm gave out entirely.

But the fire still burned in her left arm. Even as the cold spread through her guts. Even as his thrust seemed to last forever.

No thought left. No skill left. No prayer left. Nothing but the sliver of Lucala up above, the enemy before her, and the sword still held in her left hand.

A left hand she could no longer feel.

And the fire of her fury.

With everything she had left in her, Dyrra thrust that fire at Keon. Stabbing for the throat.

The fire rushed out of her.

Around her the world grew dim.

The cold in her belly faded. The fire of her rage long gone. Even Keon, invisible as the night swallowed her up.

Only the sight of Lucala overhead. Beautiful Lucala. There was a prayer for this too. Dyrra was sure of it. She tried to give it voice.

But the only word that slipped past her lips was, "Ommure."

20

LAREK WAS READY THE MOMENT CHITTER EXTINGUISHED THE CAMPFIRE. Dyrra and Keon could talk about honor and duels all they wanted, but Barth's story had proven a point.

Battlefield honor rarely lived beyond need.

Larek knew Dyrra could see well enough to fight even with nothing more than moonlight to aid her. In fact, he wouldn't have been surprised if she could have read a book in a sealed mineshaft.

Whether or not Keon could see without the firelight didn't matter. He probably could though. He looked at least half-Karwalish, so his eyes probably adjusted.

Either way, it didn't matter. Larek's plan was clear. When the duel was about to end, Chitter was to extinguish the fire, eliminating the risk of last-second "help" from Keon's men. It also made what Larek was about to do more dramatic.

Chitter extinguished the fire.

The campsite plunged into darkness.

Mercenaries cried out in shock and surprise. Swords hissed out of scabbards.

Larek stood, raised his hands high, and cast a spell he had not cast since his days as an apprentice.

He snarled out harsh, Thelmastii syllables that accompanied gestures no one else could see.

And a great globe of red fire appeared ten feet above him.

As wide across as his outstretched arms it was, and its light cast a red hue across the teeth displayed by two dozen dropped mercenary jaws. Larek knew that every one of them could feel its heat. Hot as a forge melting iron and smelling of burnt peppercorns.

Too hot. Too close. Did they see Larek's knees shaking? See the way he sweat gushed down his face? Surely they heard his pounding heart.

Fire was bad. No more fire. Why was he doing this again?

No.

They all stared at the ball of fire. They couldn't hear his heart over its roaring flame. They all had to know what would happen if he merely dropped it on the dry, yellow grass at their feet.

To say nothing of what would happen if he dropped it on them. Or swept it through their ranks.

"Now," Larek said in the most impressive voice he could manage, "the duel is over. If Keon can walk, take him with you. If not, take his body. But if I see a single threatening movement..."

Every weapon held by a mercenary dropped to the grass. Swords, maces, spears, even crossbows. As one they raised their arms in surrender.

But their Healer rushed to check on Keon.

And Sindra rushed to check on Dyrra.

DARKNESS. THEN LAREK WITH A GREAT BALL OF FLAME. ITS HEAT HIT Sindra in a wave that smelled like peppercorn.

Larek with fire. The last thing Sindra expected to see.

He was saying something to the mercenaries, but Sindra had no time to listen. The moment her eyes adjusted to the red flame of Larek's fireball, she saw Dyrra.

On her back. With a sword sticking out of her guts.

Reflex faster than thought. Sindra grabbed her Healer's kit from her pack. A kit she was not supposed to have. A kit that could kill her if she used it. Not immediately, but by the wasting curse that befell all failed Healers who tried to take up the mantel without Nilasah's blessing.

But like that night, not so very many months ago, Sindra did not have time to think.

She rushed to Dyrra, passing Keon, who looked dead. Dark skin blanched. A sword jutting up through his jaw and out the top of his head.

But Dyrra. Dyrra yet lived. She was unconscious. Shaking. Mumbling something about Ommure and Lucala. Sweaty. Feverish.

Sindra cut the buckles on Dyrra's leather armor. She pulled clear from Dyrra's torso as much of the armor as she could, swept the rest aside as she tugged the sword free.

More blood. Too much blood. On Dyrra's right arm, too, but the arm was not the problem. Even with minimal attention the arm would heal with time. But that gut wound would kill her.

It stank, for one. Not just with blood or sweat, though there was plenty of that in the air. No, the sword had slashed her bowels.

This was bad.

Normally a slashed gut took time to kill. Sindra had hoped to clean the wound, and bind it, and get Dyrra to a real Healer. But the smell told her traveling was not an option.

Fortunately, there was a real Healer somewhere nearby…

The thought made her glance. Keon's Healer stood beside his fallen employer, shaking his head. Not a drop of blood on his pristine yellow kirtle, to say nothing of his pale skin and hair.

"Help her," said Sindra, trying to staunch the bleeding. "We can pay, if that's your worry."

"Keon paid me not to heal Dyrra."

"Keon is dead." Sindra spat the words at him, unable to believe that a Healer would take money to not do Nilasah's work.

"His men are very much alive, and all of them know about the arrangement. They may be afraid of your wizard, but I can assure you they aren't afraid of me."

He started to walk away, but turned back to say one more thing.

"For whatever it's worth, I'm sorry. She fought bravely."

The Healer tossed an envelope at Sindra's feet, then walked back toward where the other mercenaries waited.

Sindra looked back at Dyrra. The bleeding would not stop. And the smell was getting worse. Dyrra's life was draining away right before Sindra's eyes, and that bastard would do nothing but give her a letter?

No. Dyrra could not die like this. Not if there was any justice in this world at all. Not if Nilasah truly embodied the compassion that Sindra believed She did.

There had to be something. Someone.

Perhaps Chitter could...

No. If Chitter could do anything about this, he would already be over here helping.

No aid was coming. That thumping sound was not hoof beats. It was her heart. That was not sweat in her eyes. It was tears. That was not fever flushing Sindra's cheeks and forehead. It was fear.

Because Dyrra's only hope lay on Sindra.

No. Not on Sindra. It couldn't be on Sindra. Sindra wasn't a Healer anymore. Sindra was a failure. If Dyrra's life depended on Sindra, Dyrra would die.

No. Dyrra's hope had to lay on Nilasah.

"Please," whispered Sindra to the goddess she had failed. "Please do not let her die. Not like this. Nilasah, I have devoted my life to you. I have given over everything I am in your service. And I failed you. When need pressed me most, I thought only of those things I could *do*. The tinctures and poultices and herbs and stiches. All the skills I had learned.

"But I forgot what mattered most. Your light. Your love. Your beneficence. It is You who fills our bodies with air. You who flows the blood though our veins. We live. We love. All because You make it possible."

Sindra held her hands over Dyrra's twitching form. "And now I beg you from the depths of my heart, from the very essence of my soul. I plead with you. Fill this one with air once more. Give her life to live and love to enjoy. Not for me, but for her. For the daughter she has not yet met. For Larek who will need her to save lives. For Barth, for in his eyes I see the seeds of love for her.

"I have been called faithless. I have been cast from Your holy order. But never once have I felt my calling waver. Never once have I strayed from my need to help others. I beg you to see past my unworthiness and through to the ember of Your love that shines from deep within me.

"Hear my prayers once more, not for me but for another. Hear my prayers once more, that this one may rise and save yet more lives. Hear my prayers once more, that she may spare people from pain and suffering under the yoke of a monster."

Sindra drew a deep breath.

"Hear my prayers once more, even though it means you take my life. I will pay that price for Dyrra. I will pay that price for her daughter. I will pay that price for Larek. I will pay that price for Barth. I will pay that price for those she will aid.

"And most of all, I will pay that price for You. For if I am not to heal in Your name, I have no purpose in this world at all."

And with that, Sindra opened her Healer's kit and began to work.

LAREK STOOD IN THE CENTER OF THEIR CAMP, HIS FOCUS SPLIT BETWEEN keeping his ball of fire burning high in the air and ready to strike, and watching the mercenaries who showed no interest in doing anything that might make Larek bring that fire down.

Which was good. The last thing Larek wanted to do was start burning anything, least of all people. He still awoke sometimes in the middle of the night with the smell of burning flesh in his nose. Part of the reason he had chosen this spell was the peppery scent.

Every little separation from those memories helped.

Still, merely having that much fire around terrified him. But he held his nerve in check, however badly it made him sweat and tremble, because he knew that fire scared everyone present.

The chances were very good that at some point, every one of those mercenaries had seen someone burn to death. He could even see his own horror reflected in the eyes of more than a few.

But Sindra was over with Dyrra now. And that Keon's Healer had already returned to stand among the mercenaries — without Keon next to him — meant that Keon was likely dead.

So something good had come out of this, at least.

Larek hoped Dyrra suffered only a minor injury. Something Sindra could bind and Chitter could help with. Have her back on her feet by morning.

Except that Chitter stood beside Larek, watching the mercenaries. That meant that Chitter could do nothing to help.

That meant that whatever Dyrra had suffered, it was bad.

And it certainly didn't need spectators.

"Why are you still here?" said Larek, addressing all of the mercenaries at once.

"We can't leave without Keon's body," said the bravest of them. Probably the second in charge, after Keon.

But none of them looked in a hurry to go claim their fallen leader, for which Larek could not blame them. Some of them could probably see the fear in Larek's eyes, and whether they could guess the reason for it or not...

Then Larek remembered what he had said when he drove them off the first time. "Leave now with your lives. Or stay, and find out just how much the Burned One has learned about fire." They probably believed Larek was not afraid of the fire, or of them, but of what he, himself, might do.

Larek could work with that.

"Barth," he said, holding his voice as steady as he could in a pretense of casualness, "would you toss them their leader's corpse?"

"Happily."

Barth dropped his shield and closed the distance to Keon in three quick strides. He pulled Dyrra's sword free — which took some effort — then heaved the body of Keon toward the mercenaries. Two of them proved bold enough to step forward and claim it.

"Now leave," said Larek.

Some of them bent for their weapons.

"*I said leave!*"

They abandoned their weapons and hustled toward the large grove of elms behind them, where no doubt their horses were waiting.

"The fire, if you would," said Larek to Chitter. Chitter spat back onto the wood the flames he had sucked out earlier.

Once the campfire was going, Larek released the spell he held in check, and the ball of fire dissipated harmlessly. He worked his fingers and elbows to rid them of a prickling sensation he realized he was feeling as he lowered his arms.

Barth was already kneeling beside Sindra and Dyrra, whose torso lay bare to show her bloody stab wound. Barth looked solemn.

Larek ran over.

"It's bad," said Barth in a hushed voice, only just loud enough for Larek to hear over Sindra's quiet praying. "That smell. It's like poison for her blood. If Sindra can't help her she won't last long."

As far as Larek could tell, Sindra took no notice of him or Barth. Her lips flowed in a constant stream of prayers, loud enough that Larek could hear them, but not loud enough for him to pick out any of the words.

The unburnt sections of Larek's face blanched. Sindra was trying to Heal.

Sindra's eyes were closed as she worked. Her hands moved about Dyrra's body freely. Sometimes they rested, one on her patient's forehead and one near the wound. Sometimes they stroked along the skin of Dyrra's ribs and stomach as though brushing away dirt.

Sometimes Sindra reached into her bag, her hands seeming to know where to find what she needed. She would pull out a vial and empty its contents into the wound, or on Dyrra's forehead. Or she would take a pure yellow Healer's cloth and hold it over the wound for a moment, before crumpling it and flinging it over her shoulder to land in the fire.

And more yet. At least once Larek saw Sindra spread a paste over her hands. It seemed to have no immediate purpose. It made no change in the cadence of the prayers. It led to no specific movements with her hands. And yet she did it anyway, so it must have had a purpose. Perhaps...

And then Larek realized what he was doing. He was trying to puzzle through Sindra's actions as though they comprised a spell with secrets he could unlock. That was not how true Healing worked.

A wizard could transform wounded flesh, but not mend it. Or at least, no wizard Larek had ever met had claimed this power. The closest any had come was a pure transmutation of the person into another form. The example Larek had seen had been a frog, but in theory it could have been a cow or a horse or anything else.

The frog had been whole, but when the man was restored to his humanity, he still bled from the wound on his arm.

Elementals had some small talent for healing. Earth spirits like Chitter could mend some cuts and breaks. Water spirits could cleanse, as could fire spirits, though their method was said to be more painful. And Larek believed it.

But true Healing, only those blessed by Nilasah could accomplish that.

For all his spells, Larek could offer no more help than Barth, who knelt in prayer beside Sindra.

Larek was unused to prayer. When a man creates his own miracles, he feels little need to ask others for them.

But this was not for Larek. It was for Dyrra. And as for the blessing of Nilasah, Larek suspected that Sindra could use all the help she could get.

Larek knelt beside Barth, and sought within himself for the right words.

21

———

THERE AT THE EDGE OF THE CAMPFIRE LIGHT, SINDRA KNELT ON THE
dry, stiff yellow grass. The pale color a reminder that her own yellow
kirtle was not the true garment of a Healer, but of a cast-off. The
embroidered soothing hand of Nilasah long since ripped away.

Larek, Barth and Chitter were around her somewhere, but
whether they were next to Sindra or keeping back a solemn distance,
she would never have known. For her, there was only Dyrra. Dyrra,
shaking and sweating and muttering too soft to hear. Dyrra, who had
lost so much blood. Dyrra, whose insides had been twisted even as
Keon thrust deep his blade.

But that was only the physical side of the matter. And on the
physical side, everything that could have been done, had been done.
The poultices were in place. The tinctures applied. The ointments
rubbed in, and the right potion tipped past Dyrra's lips.

The mixtures left an astringent smell in Sindra's nose, so much
better than the smell of blood and spilled bowels.

And as Sindra had worked, she had petitioned all the proper
prayers at every step, pouring as much of her heart into every word as
she had to give.

It might have taken an hour. It might have taken a full day. She had no way of knowing. No attention to spare to gauge the passage of time.

Were Sindra still a Healer, she would know how long she worked. In fact, she would be done. She would have already completed all that a mortal could do. She would have moved on to the next patient. Or at least seen to Dyrra's arm. Or perhaps taken a small meal, as so many Healers did between patients to maintain their strength.

But not this time. Not this patient. Not this ex-Healer.

Any moment now, the wasting curse might set in. Any moment now, Sindra's life might ebb away. And if it did, Sindra intended to pass every second that remained to her begging Nilasah to save Dyrra's life.

And so she prayed. She prayed to Nilasah with every word and thought her soul could conjure. From the long formal prayers of the Order, to the private prayers every apprentice Healer came up with on their own, and finally down to short, simple supplications every peasant learned from her parents.

When those were gone she relied on whatever words could come to her beleaguered brain that might move the Goddess to intervene.

And when she ran out of words, she prayed by feeling alone, desperately expressing her need for Dyrra.

And when even her feelings were spent, she gave her focus. She gave everything to the dream of Dyrra standing beside Larek and Barth, triumphant over the body of Blackflame, surrounded by the people they saved, including a small girl with Dyrra's eyes, looking on her mother for the first time.

And when even that pressed Sindra's mind too far, she gave her breath. Her heartbeats. Each and every pulse of her own life became a plea for Dyrra's.

Until at last, even the sight of Dyrra began to fade. Dyrra, the ground beneath her, even Sindra herself seemed to be fading into blackness.

Sindra knew what this had to be.

The wasting curse, come upon her at last.

Prayer was every bit as uncomfortable for Larek as he thought it would be.

Kneeling in the dimness at the edge of the campfire light, with dry yellow grass trying to poke its way through his dark brown travel pants and his knees stiffening from the supplicating position.

Worst of all, he did not really know what to say.

Yes, he knew the same basic prayers that every peasant boy learned, but he could not bring himself to say them now. In such a serious situation, he could not bring himself to say something like, "Sweet Nilasah, gentle Love, send Your healing from above."

And that was the only one he knew that didn't have to do with fever or sickness.

Spells made so much more sense. They were organized. Clear. Balance the formulae, manipulate the proper reagents (as needed) and project the power. Spells took work and skill and research, but they followed a structure that made sense to Larek.

But prayer. Prayer was like a child saying rhymes to change the world. Those rhymes did nothing of themselves, but if the child was lucky, something might happen.

Keon's Healer would not help Dyrra. Sindra was trying, but Larek could not shake the image of her as the child saying rhymes and trusting to luck. Or hope.

And if Sindra were just a child saying rhymes, how much less was anything Larek could do?

Worse, none of these questions seemed to plague Barth. He merely knelt there beside Larek, his mouth moving with words he gave no voice to. Prayer. Another child saying rhymes.

But perhaps if enough children said rhymes to bring the rain, some weather god might listen where a wizard would only smile.

And so Larek did his best, saying words that amounted to, "Please, Nilasah, save my friend's life," and repeated them as often as he could. Inside, he felt himself shift from earnest desperation to embarrassed and silly and back again.

Back and forth his emotions went as he kept up his "prayer" filled vigil. For hours.

Until Sindra collapsed.

Larek fell as he reached for her, his stiff knees not unfolding fast enough. But he had his hands on her shoulders, and lying there next to her, he shook her.

"Sindra! No! Not you too!"

Her breaths were shallow, almost gone. Her eyes were closed. Not moving.

Larek managed to get his knees under himself about the time that Barth realized what was happening. Larek pulled her into his lap. Patted at her face, saying her name over and over.

"Try a hard slap," said Barth. "Jolt her."

Larek gritted his teeth against striking her, but gave her a hard slap.

She did not so much as flinch.

"No," said Larek, but it was more of a lament than a denial. How could Sindra be dying? Sindra with her honest cheer. Sindra who found delight in the simple details of nature. A flower here. A bird-song there. Sindra, who managed to make even grumpy Dyrra smile.

Beautiful Sindra, staring into Larek's eyes and understanding when he suffered from spell exhaustion after the duel with Sebas. Just before she opened the everfull jug onto Larek's face.

Spell exhaustion.

Did Healers suffer from something similar?

Larek had never seen it. Never heard of it. But then, Larek had never haunted battlefields nor socialized with Healers. Sindra never spoke of it.

But what other hope did Larek have?

"Chitter," he said. "I need the jug! Now!"

SINDRA STOOD ON A CHILLY BATTLEFIELD, LESS THAN A HALF-DAY'S HIKE from the Seven Peaks. What grass might once have grown there now trodden down to mud and blood. She smelled the fire and death of war. Heard the clashing steel behind her — clashing that should have ended before the sun set, yet continued now into the full moonlight — heard it as plainly as the pleading cries of the wounded around her.

And so many wounded. Acres of injured and dying men and women filling the ground as far as she could see.

And before her, the yellow tent of a Healer. Two peaks. Large enough to sleep a dozen, were it used for anything other than its purpose.

The one in front of her was not the only Healer tent at this battle. There were six others. She remembered them. She could name each of the Healers working here. Knew how long every one of them had held the rank of full Healer. Most for three or five years. One for a dozen.

And one, who had held the rank for just over half a year before this night. The Healer whose tent sat before her now, aglow from within with candlelight.

Sindra's own tent. For this battlefield, this night, was the site of her failure.

Sindra forced a deep breath through unwilling lungs, and pushed through the flap into her tent. Time to go to work.

No. She was already at work.

Within the tent she saw herself, as she was that night. Embroidered hand of Nilasah still in place on that version of the kirtle she wore. Golden hair tied back. A dying man on the white-sheeted table before her. Gut wound. Bad. The blade had been twisted, and the bowels and stomach both slashed.

Around the tent waited others, with surface cuts and simple breaks and other minor injuries. The apprentice Healers tended to them, staunching and setting and evaluating which patients they could help and which had to wait for their Healer's attention.

Sindra looked at herself, the younger her, whose hands flew as she worked with confidence. Whose prayers flowed out with smooth efficiency.

A cold feeling descended through Sindra as she watched her younger self work. This was it. This was the moment it all began to go wrong. It had to have been. The man on the table before her was Ser Jehnus. Big and strong, with his chestnut curls and beard, both matted with sweat and blood as he lay on the table.

The first of her patients to die that night.

Ser Jehnus was the third son of a count, fighting the squabbles of barons to make a name for himself. He had done well before that night. Rumors said that he was to be invited to the capitol, for a position in the King's Army.

His wound was bad. Certainly fatal, except that he had been near a Healer's tent when he suffered it. Sindra had gotten to him quickly. The corruption had not yet set in. The Healing should have been a simple matter.

But Sindra could see the truth in her own eyes as her younger self worked. So aware of how many needed her help. Already, she had started thinking ahead to the next patient. Already she had prayed to Nilasah with only half her attention on her prayers.

Already her failure had begun.

Sindra tried to interrupt. Tried to get her own attention, but it seemed she was a ghost in her own past. None could see her, nor hear her, nor feel her.

So Sindra tried to address the only one who might be able to help. Nilasah. Sindra stood there as her younger self failed and began to offer the right prayers to Nilasah, with the sincerity and focus she had lacked when last she stood in this tent.

She completed no more than the first line before Ser Jehnus turned and looked her in the eye.

"No good praying now," he said, his baritone too strong for his injury. "You've already killed me."

Shock washed over Sindra in another wave of cold. This one seemed to steal all the blood from her face.

"Then may I pray for your soul?"

"My soul has long since gone wherever it will go."

"Then what can I do? There must be something."

"You can die, as I have."

Ser Jehnus turned away from her, back to his suffering.

"No! Wait!" She rushed to his side. Took his hand, half-surprised that she could. "I deserve to die, I admit. But Dyrra. Dyrra needs help."

"You are trying to heal again?" Scorn all through his words. "You could not leave the power alone?"

"No! I—"

"Look at yourself." Ser Jehnus jerked Sindra's hand to force her attention onto her younger self. "So proud. So confident. So sure of your power. You want it back."

"No. My friend—"

"With a true Healer nearby you dare to offer Nilasah the prayers?"

"The Healer refused—"

"He feared for his own life. You could have offered him safe passage. Your Larek had the mercenaries terrified. Did it even occur to you to drive them off?"

"I..."

Sindra's shoulders slumped. Had the solution been that simple? Could Larek have driven off the mercenaries while the Healer saved Dyrra? Sindra had not even thought of that. She immediately grabbed for her Healer's kit — a kit she should no longer have had — and ran to Dyrra's side.

"I only saw my friend in danger, and the sole Healer around refusing to help."

"You saw the opportunity to take up the mantle again. To Heal again. To hold the power of life and death in your own hand one more time."

"I saw no other option." Tears ran down Sindra's face.

"You looked for no other option."

She looked up at Ser Jehnus. Pleaded with her eyes for under-standing.

"Dyrra needed—"

"Dyrra didn't need you. She needed a Healer."

"Dyrra needed Nilasah! There was no time to bargain or

persuade. There wasn't even time to consult Larek. She needed the soothing touch of Nilasah, and I ... I was the only one there who could beg for intercession."

"Why would you die for her?" The accusation in Ser Jehnus' eyes had changed, become more probing than aggressive. "Because she's your friend?"

"Yes, but there's more. The dragon—"

"Dragons have killed since time immemorial and will kill past the days when your own race is but a memory. Why should these few lives matter? Why should your friend matter? Why should *you* matter?"

Sindra fell to her knees. Not to beg, but out of simple emotional exhaustion.

"Where there is life, there is love," she said. "And love matters. Love is the deepest gift of Nilasah. It is the life that extends beyond life. And the love of my people will survive past even the death of the last dragon for that too is the promise of Nilasah. Love is eternal."

"And what of your own life? Your own love?"

"I..." Sindra looked down at the cleared dirt beneath her. She hadn't thought it was possible to feel even worse, even less deserving, but her next words showed her how complete her failure of her goddess had been. "I have not loved since the night you see around you. How could I, after the pain and suffering I caused through my failure? I do not deserve love. I do not deserve life. But ... I do not petition for myself."

Ser Jehnus' eyes burned through her now, as though flaying her down to her very soul.

"What if I tell you Dyrra will save no townsfolk from the dragon tomorrow? Nor farmers. Neither will Larek. Nor Barth. That none of them will even reach Neton before the dragon next strikes. Would you still offer your life to save her? Not to save hundreds through your sacrifice. Not to have your name spoken of with honor. But only to turn the fate of a single person.

"If I tell you all these true things, will you still offer your life for hers?"

"Yes."

Ser Jehnus faded away, as did Sindra's younger self, and the other wounded, and the assistant Healers, and the tent. Everything all around her faded away. Sindra felt herself sinking into the blackness.

But the blackness was not cold and unfeeling. It felt warm. Welcoming. Comfortable. It smelled of her mother's stew. And a voice shivered through her with the pleasure of parent swaddling a babe.

"Oh, child," said a voice more compassionate and caring than Sindra would have dared dream possible, "if that is not love, what is?"

And then Sindra heard nothing else.

"Chitter," Larek said. "I need the jug! Now!"

Larek knelt at the edge of camp with Sindra dying in his lap. Hair and kirtle, even white shirt matted to her clammy skin. Healer's exhaustion, wasting curse, or something else. He had no way of knowing. He knew only that her pale flesh looked ashen. Not even a reddening spot from his slap. Her pink lips all but colorless. Not a single rise and fall from her breath.

First Dyrra. Now Sindra might not see another dawn.

Barth was doing something. Checking on Dyrra. Searching for breath. But that was at the edge of Larek's vision. Sindra was his focus.

And then Chitter was there with the everfull jug.

Chitter said nothing. There was nothing to say. What Larek was about to do made no more sense than a child saying rhymes. He knew that. If Sindra were dying, a face full of water would not help.

But he could think of nothing else.

Larek hefted the jug. He puffed a quick breath and muttered, "Nilasah, if you ever hear a word I say to you, please hear this: save her. She's only ever tried to do your work."

He uncorked the jug and upended it.

Icy mountain river water flowed from the mouth of the jug onto

Sindra's unconscious face, spilling over onto his legs and the dry earth beneath him.

And Sindra began to cough and sputter. A spasm wracked its way through her body.

Larek quickly capped the jug. Tossed it to Chitter. Helped Sindra turn to her side so she could spit out any water that had gone down the wrong way and get her coughing under control.

That took her several tries, the last of which was followed by a huge gasping inhalation. She blew the air back out as heavily as it had come in, but when she did the color returned to her face.

Her sopping wet face.

Nevertheless, Sindra smiled up at him. A simple, but sincere smile that included her green eyes as well as her lips.

"Thank you," she said, her voice weak. Then her eyebrows drew down slightly. "You know, you never told me why your pretty eyes are red."

That was the last question Larek was expecting. And something about her tone made him uncomfortably aware that he had a beautiful woman lying with her head in his lap. How sweat had matted her kirtle to the curves of her body. How the icy mountain water had drenched her chest, lending transparency to the white shirt showing above her...

"Your kirtle!" He said, pointing. "The symbol!"

"What?" Her left hand flew to her breast ... to the embroidery just above her heart. Sindra sat up quickly, her eyes cast toward the stars above.

The embroidered soothing hand of Nilasah had been restored to its place on her kirtle.

"But..." she said, "does this mean ... I'm a Healer again?"

"I'd say so," said Dyrra, sitting up and adjusting her armor to cover her torso again. Barth knelt beside her, not touching, but ready to lend assistance as needed.

But Dyrra did not look like a woman who needed assistance. Her fingers were swift and sure as she adjusted and re-buckled her armor, while thanking Chitter for repairing the straps and buckles. She sat up straight under her own power, not looking at all like a woman whose guts had been leaking out not so long ago. Her skin practically glowed with health.

Sindra tackled Dyrra in an embrace.

Dyrra returned the hug until she laughed that loud laugh of hers, sitting up and extricating herself. And soon Sindra was laughing too, from the ground beside her. Then Barth and Larek joined in, and the four of them laughed like fools until all the fear and dread of the evening leaked out of them.

Larek managed one more spell to freshen all their clothes, ridding the air of the smell of blood and sweat. And in the process, drying his and Sindra's clothes.

Finally, the four of them, spent, dragged themselves back to their bedrolls around the fire and began to dine at last on such food as required no preparation. Some dried beef, and cheese, and rye bread they could toast on sticks. And a bottle of Sebas' red wine to share.

After Larek told Dyrra about Keon's death and the taking of his body, the group ate in a comfortable silence. Even Chitter seemed content to merely sit. But as they recovered themselves, questions began to arise in their thoughts, until finally Larek gave the most basic of these questions voice.

"I don't understand," he said. "Hours with no change in Dyrra, except maybe getting slowly worse. Then Sindra collapses and starts dying. But then she's not, and suddenly Dyrra's healed? What exactly happened? Are you a Healer again?"

"Nilasah," — Sindra touched the embroidered hand to reassure herself that it remained — "appears to have forgiven me. I've never heard of it happening to a failed Healer before."

"The gods have their own priorities," said Chitter. "And they favor sincere adherence to their precepts above all."

Larek translated for the group.

"So," said Barth, "because your desire to heal was sincere, you were forgiven?"

"It wasn't that simple," Sindra said, her cheeks reddening slightly. "I feel like there was a test. Something terrible I had to face..." She shook her head. "It's there on the tip of my mind, but I don't quite remember."

"Well, thank you for passing it," said Dyrra.

"There's more. Something about tomorrow." Sindra blew out a frustrated breath. "I'm not sure. I think we better get an early start though. I think Blackflame is coming sooner than we expect."

With that dark thought casting a pall over the evening, the four of them turned to their bedrolls. Chitter banked the fire as he took up his watch.

Larek lay there under the light of the stars and the waxing sliver of moon, only just able to hear the sounds of Dyrra praying. And Sindra as well, if he was not mistaken.

"One more thing," said Barth, in a whisper respectful of the darkness, but loud enough for all to hear. "Did Larek and his water help at all?"

"The water, probably not," Sindra said just as softly. But she turned and smiled at Larek again. "But the ... effort? Definitely."

22

THE SUN RISING OVER THE SEVEN PEAKS THAT MORNING WAS THE MOST beautiful sight Sindra had ever seen. Stretches of red and orange and purple like rows of flowers all blooming in sequence. Distant spreads of cloud like rows of rocks, containing and shaping the floral design.

Sindra wished she could smell them, but settled for the subtle, nutty scent of the nearby elm groves and the fading wood smoke of their extinguished fire.

She could hardly call the feel of the sun on her face heat, but it was at least a gentle warmth that chased away the chill of morning dew. Pleasant after a cold breakfast of dried beef and hardening rye bread, washed down with the so-cold water from Larek's magic jug.

Over her shoulder she could hear Larek buckling closed his pack. She knew he would not watch the sunrise. She had asked him about it that second morning, before Dyrra deigned to awaken. How horrible for him to have such beauty displayed throughout the very sky itself twice daily, and yet to see only the fire he dreaded more than anything.

Anything except Blackflame itself. Yet it was to face Blackflame they were riding that day. Such courage, to ride in pursuit of the thing he feared the most.

All of them needed courage to do this. She knew that. She did not dismiss or diminish what each of them risked that day. But for Larek, it must have taken something more. The dragon had almost killed him once already. He had watched one set of companions die under its claws and flame.

And now he was doing it again. Risking himself. Risking another set of companions.

And even though her own life would be in jeopardy, Sindra understood the difference between their roles. The depth of their relative undertakings. She could die and the others could still defeat the dragon. Dyrra or Barth could die — even both, depending on the timing — and still bring about the dragon's death.

But if Larek died, or his nerve broke, they were lost. The dragon would kill them all and that would be the end of it. Sindra knew it. And she knew that Dyrra and Barth knew it as well.

And worst of all, she knew that Larek knew it. How much worse must this task have been for him? Knowing that all of their hopes rested on him. Knowing that the others all trusted him enough to ride against the dragon beside him.

And Sindra trusted Larek beyond a doubt. She knew Dyrra did as well. Barth did not know Larek as well, but if he had any doubts, he kept them to himself. He probably at least had faith in Dyrra's confidence.

The only one who might not trust Larek to do the job was Larek.

Larek, who had spent a decade punishing himself for his last failure. Larek, who was thinking about that failure, or the weight that lay on his shoulders, right now. Sindra could tell. She could see it in the extra force he used when buckling his pack. In the way he refused to meet any of their eyes. Not even Chitter's. In the way his shoulders hunched as he worked.

Learning to see these things was part of a Healer's training. Nilasah's calling required them to soothe the mind as well as treat the body. Sindra knew what her training taught her to do in this situation. Knew the words to calm and focus one who was lost to fear or the past. Knew the ways to touch an arm or shoulder, or stroke the upper back, that would lighten tension. The times and ways to grab a jaw and force focus onto the calm, relaxed presence of a Healer.

She could do these things, and calm Larek.

But Sindra wanted to do more than calm him. She wanted to give him hope. She wanted to give him something to live for. And she knew just what something she wanted that to be.

And if she read his eyes correctly last night when she was shocked back to consciousness, she knew what hope he wanted as well.

Sindra knelt on the stiff grass beside Larek. She put her hand on his shoulder and said his name softly.

Larek turned, and she kissed him. She kissed him hard enough to knock his floppy hat off, her arms clutching his substantial body to her. Sindra tried to put everything into that kiss. Hope. Fear. And even the spark they might fan into love.

Shock slowed his reaction, but then his arms embraced her and he returned the kiss. Such depth he gave it. Hope. Longing. Desperation. Terror. And there too, hidden among the more immediate emotions, she tasted his own spark that might yet grow into love.

Sindra heard the morning preparations halt around her, but ignored the meaningful silence until the kiss had run its course, had said all that it could say until the dragon was dead.

Then, and only then, she pulled back from Larek. She stroked his scarred cheek, and said softly, "Now let's go kill a dragon, so you and I can talk about what that kiss might mean for our future."

Dyrra smiled at the sight of Sindra and Larek kissing there in the dry grass near the extinguished campfire.

Perhaps there was hope for these eastern women after all. Though why anyone would choose to share a first kiss under the dawning rays of Lucala's Jealous Sister when they could kiss under the sweet, seductive light of Lucala herself, Dyrra would never understand.

But then, these easterners did everything backwards anyway.

Like Barth. His interest was obvious enough. Even now his eyes flicked from the kissing couple to Dyrra and back, though he tried to hide his glances. Dyrra was a known widow, not a wife. There should have been no reason he could know of to hold himself back.

Might be that he hadn't met a real woman in too long. Still. That he should hem and haw like a scholar instead of saying what he wanted like a warrior did not suit him.

If he knew anything about Karwalish women, he should have known better.

Not that Dyrra was interested. Not really. It was true that he seemed to be a good man, and he moved like a warrior should. And it was true that she found his face and form and manner pleasing enough. And it was also true that Ommure, if he could say anything to her right now, would be telling her she needed to move on.

In fact, if Ommure's shade were here, he would probably be pushing Dyrra at Barth.

But Dyrra wasn't sure she was ready.

And she certainly didn't feel the need to start something on the day she was likely to die. Not like Sindra, the backwards easterner, who failed to see the good man before her until he literally held her in his lap, and chose to kiss him for the first time knowing that the kiss might be their last...

She *was* intending to stop at just a kiss. Wasn't she? Goodness knows, the kiss had gone on long enough. Dyrra smiled at that despite herself. She certainly agreed that Larek should not have to face a dragon again without first having a woman show him the deepest pleasures of life.

But here? Now?

If that was Sindra's intention, she should have started things last night. Now the sky was brightening around them, and if the dragon had not already taken wing, it would soon.

Of course, given Larek's decade or so of celibacy, he wouldn't need long anyway...

No. Dyrra didn't want to break them up, but she couldn't let things go that far. Sindra seemed like the type to linger afterward, and they had a town to save.

Dyrra got as far as taking a step forward when Sindra broke the kiss.

Sindra had the look of a woman about to say things other people shouldn't hear, so Dyrra noisily checked her pack again. She considered digging out some of that good, sharp cheese to accent the dried meat and rye bread of breakfast.

Chitter scrambled up her pack, looking just about as pleased as Dyrra could imagine a squirrel looking. He chittered something, and though Dyrra couldn't make out the words of his speech, she had a pretty good idea about the content.

"I'm glad it's happening too," she whispered. "I was starting to think I'd have to strip them naked and lock them in a room together."

Chitter laughed at that, one forepaw on his belly and the other slapping his knee like a human. The high-pitched sound drew the eyes of not only Barth, but also Sindra and Larek.

Sindra immediately blushed like a maiden, no doubt guessing the reason for the laughter. Larek choked out something in one of those ancient languages of his. Sharp. Accusatory, unless Dyrra misread the tone. But it couldn't have been too bad, because Chitter was still laughing when he barked out a reply.

"Kisses are one thing," said Dyrra, "but I draw the line at these secret conversations of yours. And don't try to tell me you're discussing magic. I think we all know what you two are talking about."

Sindra managed to blush even harder.

Oh, Lucala. This little slip of an easterner wasn't *actually* a maiden was she?

"Well, whatever it is, break it up," said Dyrra, deciding she had to be reading too much into the moment and determined not to continue thinking about Sindra's sexual history anyway. "We have a dragon to kill."

"Yes, we do," said Larek, with enough determination to raise

Dyrra's eyebrows. Even Chitter looked impressed. Larek picked up his fallen floppy hat and thrust it down on his head.

"Let's ride!"

Sindra smiled, and Dyrra felt a small smile playing about her own lips. Perhaps Sindra was not so backward an eastern woman after all...

***

LAREK COULD NEVER PRETEND TO ENJOY THE SUNRISE, BUT HE HAD TO admit he found the brightening blue of the clear sky above him cheerful. The land itself seemed to encourage him. Red and purple late spring flowers opened toward the sunshine to show their golden centers, dotting the green fields and hills around him and lending a sweetness to the crisp morning air.

Even the wind was at his back, flapping the brim of his hat as though teasing. Riding beside Sindra, with Chitter on his shoulder and Dyrra and Barth in the lead, Larek began to believe they might defeat Blackflame this time.

Last time he had been fresh from apprenticeship. Barely any real research of his own behind his magic, much less the kind of practice that mattered. And though Taran had been marvelous with a bow, and Inga impressive with her sword, the truth was that neither of them were warriors. They were farmers, filling in for warriors the way Larek had been little more than an apprentice, filling in for a wizard.

But Larek had ten years of study and practice since then. Not a lot on the scale of wizards, but enough to begin building real confidence. He had even defeated Sebas in a duel, a far more seasoned spellcaster.

And Dyrra and Barth were both experienced warriors.

And Sindra, wonderful Sindra, had been re-blessed in her calling as a Healer only last night by no less than Nilasah Herself.

That had been a thing Larek would never have believed he might see. In fact, when he thought about it enough to be honest with himself, he knew he had held doubts about the existence of the gods at all.

He took no stand on the subject, though. Unlike other wizards who had written extensive books expressing their views about the true role of magic in the history of the world, and casting even the most basic role of the gods into question.

Such wizards considered the formal temples of every city and country little more than a front for schools of magic that had been lost to the annals of wizardry. Temples that guarded the truth behind their secrets jealously.

But whatever might be the truth about some of the gods, after last night, Larek could not doubt Nilasah. Dyrra had been as good as dead. Then, all of a sudden, her body was whole and hale and she was talking.

Sindra had looked close to the brink of death herself for no better reason than offering a series of prayers. And just as quickly made a full recovery. A recovery that even restored the embroidery on her kirtle.

No. Larek might not even be the twentieth most experienced wizard within a week's ride of the capitol since the tournament started, but he could recognize spells when he saw them, and their absence when he didn't. What he saw last night could only have been the act of a goddess.

And if Nilasah were real, why not Lucala? Why not Inkaamont, the all but forgotten god of magic?

Just in case, Larek muttered, "*Inkaamontos, nossu farra kannu djen.*"

The words were in Chelas, and roughly translated to *Inkaamont, speed our spells this day.*

"Prayer?" said Chitter from Larek's shoulder.

"What could it hurt?"

"You're worried we won't make it in time, aren't you?"

"Actually, I was feeling really good. But now that you mention it..."

"What did I say about private conversations?" called Dyrra without turning around.

"Chitter was asking if I'm worried about speed. I was about to admit that I am."

"Believe me," said Sindra from beside him, "we're too far from Neton to make it at a gallop. We'd have to rest the horses, and walk them. It would cost us hours. But if we stick to the trot we'll make it by…"

Barth gave a sharp whistle, one finger pointing low over the southern horizon.

A shadow against the blue, blue sky. A shadow that stole some of the cheer from the morning.

A shadow with great bat wings.

Sweat broke out on Larek's forehead. He felt a flutter inside him, too low to properly blame his stomach.

"We may need to speed the horses after all," said Barth.

"No," said Dyrra. "A gallop isn't the answer."

Larek's breaths grew shallow. Quick. His black stallion Fal tossed its head and nickered, picking up on its rider's agitation.

"Not a gallup," said Barth, "but a faster trot."

"How—" Larek's voice broke and he had to start again. "How far did you say Neton was?"

"If we keep a *smart* pace," insisted Dyrra, "We'll be there before highsun."

Larek estimated distances and angles in his head while he stared at the shadow of his worst nightmare. Fal high stepped in irritation at the tremor through Larek's knees. He started to double-check himself. If he was right…

"Not soon enough," said Barth.

"I might be able to do something to help the horses," said Sindra. "Innocents are at stake."

"Look at the shadow," said Larek, his voice sounding more relaxed and confident than he felt.

"We know it's coming," said Dyrra, "but—"

"No! Look at the angle. Neton is in front of us by a good distance yet. But the dragon…"

"I see it," said Sindra. "It's heading behind us, not in front of us."

"Blackflame always hits a place two or three times before moving on," said Barth. "It must be sweeping out to gain an angle."

"No," said Dyrra, shading her watering eyes against the glare. "They're right. It wouldn't need to change angles from so far away."

"It's not heading for Neton," said Sindra.

"It's heading for Lillikan," said Larek.

All that effort to chase down the dragon, and all they had needed to do was stay still and wait for it. And now they were so far away. Not much more than a day, but with the speed of a flying dragon, they might as well have been in Karwale.

"Sindra," said Larek, "if you know a prayer to help the horses, you better speak it now. Because I'm not letting those people die."

23

———

Wind in Larek's face now. Strong enough to squint his eyes.
Floppy hat held on only by a quick spell, its brim bouncing more
than the mane of the galloping black stallion beneath him. Larek
riding in the lead this time across the unburnt green hills and fields
of southern Aeralfast. Red and purple flowers around him now, with
their golden centers, looking like sparks of flame seeking a foothold.

Even the smells of fresh, vibrant life around Larek only reminded
him how much more lay waiting for the ruination of the dragon's
wasting breath.

Sindra, Dyrra and Barth kept pace as best they could, though
none of them had been ready when Larek began the charge. Larek
cried his horse to speed the instant Sindra completed her prayer,
begging Nilasah to grant the horses enduring strength that their
riders might save lives.

But Larek had no attention for his companions. Nor for Chitter,
clinging to the saddle horn. No focus even for the racing horse
beneath him, jarring his spine and legs, shaking the heavy meat and
cheese and bread in his belly. The stallion's hooves pounded almost
as swift as his heartbeat.

Never before had Larek ridden so fast. But never before had his need been so great. He had to trust his steed Fal not to stumble without the smoothness of a road beneath them. For Larek kept only cursory attention on the hills and meadows he sped through.

His eyes kept tracking upward and to the south. Upward toward the shadow, the awful shadow high in the sky. The growing shadow of the dragon Blackflame, sweeping north through the air from some hiding place in the southern mountains. Some hiding place that all the king's scouts had not found.

The dragon that gave him his many scars. The dragon that killed two hundred forty-seven others around him. The dragon that took his life, even though it left him breathing.

Larek's breaths came so fast and shallow he felt lightheaded.

Blackflame. Blackflame was back, and once more Larek rode toward it instead of away.

Why take this risk again? Why not grab Sindra and find some-place they could have a life together instead of riding toward his own death?

Why did the dragon leave him alive last time?

That was the question the songs never asked. They made up excuses. Hiding places. Mounds of corpses. A dragon's full belly. But it was the question that had haunted Larek's heart during the most sleepless of nights. During the week around the anniversary of that fateful day, an anniversary that Larek observed every year without fail with fasting and silent mourning.

Larek had lain unconscious and helpless among the soot and ashes of a land scorched by dragonfire, the only thing near him not burnt away to specks. The air itself charred from the heat, trying to burn his lungs and nostrils past the protection of his spell.

Blackflame could not have missed him. It could not have missed that a single living man lay among its carnage. Could not have failed to hear him draw breath, or failed to smell his body's evacuation.

And yet, Larek had awakened. The dragon gone and the world burned away.

No future for Larek. Everyone quick to decry him a failure. To chronicle the errors he had made, that they would never have committed. Every wizard told of the spells they would have cast in his stead. The victory they would have won. The lives they would have saved.

At first Larek had questioned these other wizards. Challenged them. How easy to claim victory from the fireside. How much harder to wrest it from a living dragon. But they laughed at his questions. His challenges. The old stories made it sound so easy.

And everyone knew the stories. So everyone listened to the bragging wizards.

Even Larek himself.

So easy to question each decision when he relived them constantly as he did for the first year. So easy to conclude that the others were right. That Larek had failed from his own ineptitude. Larek, a raw wizard, with no deeds beyond a successful apprenticeship to speak on his behalf.

And Larek *had* lived. If he had been good enough to save his own life, how could he have saved no others?

Those other wizards all believed they could defeat Blackflame. They gathered at a tournament to prove it, not much farther from Lillikan than Larek had been when Barth had first spotted the dragon's shadow that morning.

So why was Larek galloping to fight in their stead?

No easy answer came to him. The moment the question formed, his mind tumbled through images of Taran and Inga, dying. Of years of scorn and countless insults. Of endless nights spent reliving the horror. Of days spent practicing the spells he never expected to cast again.

But those were only the habitual thoughts his mind turned to when he imagined the dragon returning. They came quickest. Easiest.

This time other thoughts found their way in as well.

As Larek sped northeast toward Lillikan, the chaos in his head included recent developments. Dyrra threatening the crowd of Lillikans at sword point on his behalf. Sindra's willingness to sacrifice herself to save Dyrra. Chitter's unswerving faith in him.

Sindra's kiss.

Life.

After a decade of little more than living death, Larek had a chance to live again. To love, perhaps.

He had that chance, where two hundred forty-seven others did not. They were ten years dead, claimed by the dragon.

Larek could not suffer that to happen again. Not if he could stop it.

Even if he couldn't stop it. Even if he arrived too late. Even if he died in the attempt.

He had no right living while the dragon continued to kill.

<hr>

FOR A WIZARD, LAREK COULD RIDE. DYRRA HAD TO GIVE HIM THAT. Two hours at a full gallop and he still held his lead over the rest of the group. She had thought that the downward slopes of hills or the threat of rocks would give him caution, but it seemed that caution slipped behind him like that floppy hat of his should have done hours ago.

Even that fool spirit squirrel of his seemed caught up in the moment. Holding onto the saddle horn, and watching the land ahead of them...

Of course.

Of course none of them had hit a stray rock on their way through untamed meadows where the wild grass grew past their horses' knees. Nor on the broken parts of hills where old, inconsistent rain had left runnels exposing stone below the soil. Nor even the odd broken or low-hanging branch when they raced past groves of elms, and alders, and oaks.

Chitter the earth spirit was keeping their path as safe as the best part of the king's own road. And with Sindra securing Nilasah's blessing to keep the horses strong, Dyrra's roan stallion, Glint, had yet to even break his sweat. And that despite hours of feeling the stallion's muscles bunch and spring beneath her.

With allies like these, how could they fail against the dragon?

Larek's spells keeping the fire off of them. Sindra's prayers healing the wounds inflicted by great claws. Barth's steel swinging a complement to her own. Lucala, blessing her sword arm as ever, even though they fought under the burning glare of Her Jealous Sister.

Surely, together they would defeat Blackflame.

True, they would not all survive, but that was the way of battle. Every Karwalish warrior learned it from childhood. Even Barth, an easterner, likely understood that not all of them would live to see the next moonrise.

Dyrra's eyes flicked upward at the great shadow of the dragon. Bigger than the last time she had looked. Even at such a height, the shadow looked as wide as her outstretched hand. Blackflame had to be covering ground at ten times the speed their horses could manage. Perhaps faster. The odds were good that it would reach Lillikan ahead of them. Some would die before they had a chance to challenge the beast.

That could not be helped.

If Dyrra's time came today, she was ready. She had killed Keon herself. Avenged her dear, sweet Ommure. Made her own peace with Lucala by Her fading rays.

And more, Dyrra knew she was not alone. Sindra had been forgiven by her goddess. If she died today, she would do so knowing she had atoned for her great failure. Barth, Dyrra did not know as well, but he had the look of a warrior seeking a final fight, a good death. If he survived victorious, he might lay down his steel for all time. And if he died, he would die happy.

And Larek, Larek might accept death as repentance for his "failure" to die so many years ago.

He might accept that.

But Dyrra would not.

Blackflame had to die, and Larek had to live. Those were her priorities, in that order.

She would say nothing to the others. Sindra would agree with the list, Dyrra was certain. Barth would focus only on point one. And

Larek, well, Larek was fool enough to try to reverse them. To throw his life away for Sindra, or Dyrra, or Barth.

Perhaps, in doing so, he might even find some measure of peace in his final moments.

But no. Larek did not understand the warrior's death. His death could only be that of a martyr. Something scholars would talk of and bards would sing of, and none of them would truly see for the tragedy it was.

No. Larek could not die. Not when he was so close to finally having a life. The dragon had to die, and Larek had to live.

And Sindra.

That thought was enough to make Dyrra spit a little of the rye bread taste from her mouth.

If Larek lived and Sindra died, for the rest of his days he would see only what could have been and not what was. He would cleave to Sindra's memory and forsake all others.

No. Sindra had to live too.

That settled the matter in Dyrra's head. If death had to come today for more than a dragon, it had to come for a warrior. Not a wizard or a Healer. Dyrra would see to that.

And as she rode, she tried not to think about an envelope left to them by the mercenary Healer who rode with Keon. An envelope that waited in Sindra's left saddlebag. An envelope that contained the name and location of the temple where Dyrra's daughter trained in the ways of the warrior. A letter inside that envelope that included the girl's name.

Suwala.

Dyrra tried not to think about the stories Suwala would be told after her first battle. Stories about her mother. About Ommure. The early victories, yes, but those were not what gnawed at Dyrra's thoughts. It was the later stories, in their abbreviated, incomplete versions.

The truths Dyrra would never have a chance to share with her daughter, not if the dragon took her life today.

Dyrra tried not to think about these things. But the ride was long, and from time to time she could not help but picture a little girl who had gray eyes like her mother.

Sindra glanced up at the sun. Past its apex, though just how far past she had trouble gauging from the back of her speeding chestnut gelding, Nut. Still, likely two more hours to Lillikan at their current speed.

The horses would last. Nilasah's blessing had seen to that. Nut had finally broken a sweat some time ago, but every time Sindra leaned down and pressed her ear to the great gelding's side, his heartbeat sounded strong. Steady as his hoof beats. Tireless. Nut seemed as though his long legs could hold that speed forever, though even Nilasah's blessing had its limits.

Unlike her own heart, which raced as it sorted through a flurry of emotions that she had no time to face. Elation at the restoration of her calling. Terror at the dragon she would confront. Fear for the lives and homes of those the dragon might slay before the five of them arrived. Hope at the prospect of a future with Larek. Dread that even the death of Blackflame might not wipe away the stain it left on his mind. That he would be unable to move on.

She risked a glance at him again, but he looked no better than last time. Resigned to meet his end, even as he sped toward it with single-minded resolve. She had seen that look on warriors going into battle.

Not one of those warriors had lived to see the next sunrise.

But watching him struggle inside would not help. Better to cast her eyes on the twisting little creek to her right, making its way down a small hill toward the river Quar. Better to watch the small forest of oaks on her left for signs of hunters she could cry a warning to about the dragon.

As though its shadow in the sky were not warning enough.

The birds had long since gone into hiding for the day. Those great bat wings. That long, sweeping tail. So many weapons. Dragons were pure destruction given form. As much elementals as Chitter was, though with a more specific focus.

No god would claim them. Even Urandeth the Darkness was said to have "unleashed" the dragons, not formed or created them. As though the dragons were a primal force unto themselves. Chaos spreading chaos, until sufficient strength of order eliminated them.

And they had to be eliminated. Dragons could not be tamed. Could not be broken.

Some had tried. All had failed.

Sindra tried to distract herself from the task before her — and from her worries about Larek — by remembering all she had been taught in the temples about the great beasts, but could think of nothing useful. Their fire consumed everything to ash so fine it melted to the touch. Their claws and teeth could rend castle walls as easily as flesh. Their tails could crush whole companies.

And yet. And yet. And yet the skalds' stories were not alone in their recipe for killing dragons. The histories agreed with them. Always a small group. Always warriors and a wizard. Never any consistent word of the tactics they used or the weapons or spells they relied on. Only the names of the heroes, and the result.

And the lists of those who failed. Those could be found only in the histories. It seemed that the skalds deemed their stories unworthy of recounting, despite all the time and words they devoted to poor Larek.

Larek, with his jaw still clenched. His knuckles white on the reins. If only Sindra could touch him. Stroke the unscarred parts of his cheek. Whisper a few words into his ear. Something to remind him that he was not alone. That this time he did not ride with two would-be warriors he barely knew.

That this time he rode with friends.

Whether they lived or died today, Sindra could not predict. Nilasah gave succor to survivors and strength to those who would aid them. But She was no goddess of heroes. She gave no grace to ensure victory in battle.

But if they must fall today, at least they would likely fall together.

Not a helpful line of thought. Sindra blinked away tears and flicked her eyes around for something better to focus on as they continued to ride at a pace that would leave her sore for days.

The land flattened out ahead. That was something. No sign of Lillikan, though. Still too distant.

Movement up ahead though. Horses and riders at an unsteady, slowing gallop. More than a score of them.

Keon's mercenaries? Yes. There was the yellow kirtle of their Healer.

One of the horses dropped. Then another. They must have pushed their horses too far. Too long. They had begun to drop dead, and the rest would follow shortly.

Had their Healer not sought Nilasah's blessing?

Or perhaps the blessing was denied. Perhaps they had been riding to save their own skins from the beast and not to save the people of Lillikan.

Sindra risked closing her eyes to utter a prayer to Nilasah on their behalf. Of course they had no noble goal. Not only were they mercenaries, but they were *unarmed* mercenaries. Larek had said he made them leave without their weapons, to ensure they did not return for Barth. And now, with the dragon coming, they had no means of defense.

"Look!" cried Larek, the first word he had spoken in hours. He was pointing at the dragon's shadow.

No.

He was pointing at the dragon.

It must have started swooping lower at the sight of so many men and horses available as an appetizer.

Sindra pressed her gelding for as much speed as he could manage, knowing Larek was about to do the same. If he hadn't already. Dyrra and Barth followed suit.

Still they were too far. A mile or two too far, even at this speed.

They would be too late.

Because the dragon dove.

24

LAREK LEANED FORWARD TO KEEP HIS ARMS FROM SNAPPING BACK HIS stallion's reins. If he halted now, he knew he couldn't begin again. Fear had already begun to lock him down.

The dragon. Blackflame. Not just a memory for sleepless nights. Not just a rumor in the taverns. Not just a prize for a tournament.

Not even just a shadow in the bright blue afternoon sky.

He could see it now. The scales like flakes of obsidian. The wings that could cover a small forest. The claws that could each snatch up a team of horses. The jaws that could devour a small keep. The tail that could level a hill.

Twice the size — or more — of the dragon Larek had faced ten years ago. Larek had grown in his power. The dragon had merely grown.

With the roar that had echoed through Larek's countless night-mares, the great dragon Blackflame dove.

And as it dove, Larek's stomach followed suit, turning his insides to ice. Drenching him in fear sweat. Chattering his teeth. Shaking his elbows and knees, even through a wave of calm emanating from Chitter.

A wave that likely kept Fal from panicking. From noticing what doom it sped toward.

Sped too slowly.

Larek's heels jabbed into Fal's sides, spurring the black stallion for a final burst of speed. Those mercenaries were going to die. Die with no weapons to defend themselves, because Larek took those weapons away. Nowhere to hide in the green, open meadows.

High wild grass would not save them from dragonfire.

The dragon landed heavy, rumbling the earth and shaking the mercenaries and horses to the ground. Even from so far away — with Chitter steadying the ground beneath him — Larek could feel the tremors.

Larek's mind raced for a spell. He was too far away to fight, but there had to be a useful spell. Something to distract the dragon. Or shield the mercenaries.

Anything.

But his mind came blank.

Larek could hear only the screams of those ten years dead. He could smell their burning flesh once more. Feel the searing heat trying to claim his own flesh that day. He could all but see those people dying all around him.

The dragon didn't wait.

Blackflame's great jaw swept forward, carried by its long, sinuous neck. Gobbling up screaming mercenaries and horses alike, while sweeping out with its tail and forelimbs to contain the others.

They would all be dead in seconds if Larek did nothing. His mouth grew dry as burlap. His shallow breaths jagged. His chattering teeth tried to bite his own lips as his mind cast about for any way he could help.

Suddenly Barth charged past Larek, his gray stallion Baron finding speed that even Fal could not match. And Dyrra followed, no more than a tail behind. Her bow was drawn and aiming high for a shot she could never make. Barth had his shield on one arm, and spear raised in the other.

Too far. They would never close to firing range in time to make a difference.

Blackflame slammed the earth with its tail, and even the rising mercenaries fell back to the ground. Half of them were dead now, sliding down the dragon's gullet.

There had to be a spell. *Something* Larek could do.

But he could think of only one.

Not a battle spell. Nothing to harm the dragon or bring it pain. Nothing to frighten it, as though anything could. Not even a spell that might shield a few mercenaries. Or hide them.

Larek knew so very many spells. And he could only think of one.

Fanfare.

A stupid spell, paid for by a stupid noble, who would rather pay a wizard once than musicians regularly. He had paid Larek to lay a spell on his ring so that every time he turned it, a chorus of trumpets would announce his entrance.

The enchantment itself had been tricky, and taken weeks. But the fanfare spell was a simple matter.

And a simple matter was all Larek's frozen brain could handle.

His knuckles cracked as he forced them to release the reins. His voice broke twice before he sounded the first syllable of the spell. But moments later the spell was cast.

And from the sky above came the chorus of a hundred trumpets, blasting out the eight note sequence signifying the entrance of the Baron of Tewen to the accompaniment of a like number of drums.

The music echoed all directions, with far more power and volume than Larek had bothered with for the baron's enchantment. But to hear those notes now, reverberating through his skull and down into the vale ahead of him...

Some part of Larek relaxed. A spell, perfectly cast by him. More than he had accomplished the last time he faced Blackflame. Perhaps this time would be different after all. Perhaps this time, they really could slay the beast.

And farther down the slope, the dragon stopped devouring

mercenaries and horses, even though a full quarter of the company remained.

Instead it turned at the sound of the music.

Larek's heart tried to stop again. The dragon was not just looking for the music.

It looked up the slope. It looked at him.

And the dragon Blackflame smiled.

WHILE THE DRAGON WAS FLYING, DYRRA HAD NO WAY TO GAUGE ITS scope. She knew it had to be big. Everyone knew that dragons were big. But it wasn't until that thing shook the ground a mile away with its landing and began devouring men and horses whole that Dyrra realized exactly *how* big Blackflame was.

Big enough to swallow a fist of these eastern knights at a time — in their full plates of armor and riding their warhorses — without needing to chew.

And she was riding right toward it at the fastest gallop she could coax out of her roan stallion.

Fear shivered along Dyrra's spine. That momentary sense of impending death that every true warrior felt from time to time.

Dyrra smiled. She'd missed that feeling.

This was an enemy worth risking her life against. Its scale immense. Her prospects bleak.

Live or die, the effort would be glorious.

Barth charged right past her, his gray stallion's hooves thundering even louder than her rowan's. His shield ready and spear in a throwing grip. Must have been thinking the same thing she was.

Good. A true warrior by her side.

And neither of their horses so much as tossed their heads at the screaming terror of the mercenaries' steeds in the distance. Could have been too distant yet, but Sindra's gelding nickered a protest behind her. Could be that Barth picked out a proper warhorse for her.

Even better.

Much better than those mercenaries. Even unarmed, Dyrra would have tried to fight back. Surely one of them had to have a dagger. A spare mace or short sword. Something. But they all either wept in resignation or tried to run.

As though they could have outrun that thing.

Still, she supposed the running kept them alive a moment longer. That was important. If the dragon finished off those mercenaries before she, Barth and Larek came close enough for a meaningful attack, it might take to the air again and be off to raid Lillikan.

That would be it, then. Yes, Glint had galloped faster and longer than any horse she had ever known, thanks to Sindra's prayers. As had the other horses around Dyrra. But with this final burst of speed, its legs churning and mouth beginning to froth, this would be it.

Glint might survive this charge, but it would need rest. One way or the other, the day's ride was almost done.

Must have been why Barth readied his spear. Too far away yet to throw, even at so large a target. But he wanted to be ready the instant he reached his range. And range was only seconds away, however long those seconds felt.

Well Dyrra had no spear, but she did have her bow.

Dyrra dropped her reins and trusted to Glint to obey the press of her knees, the tapping of her heels. She pulled her bow out and knocked an arrow.

She began arching her bow, gauging her speed, the slope of the land, stiff wind from her left.

Too far yet. Time had slowed for her as it did sometimes in battle. The smooth, steady pump of her heart louder in her ears than the hooves of the four speeding horses. Even the sound of her own breath, a desert wind.

Blackflame seemed to take forever to swoop its head forward at the end of the long, long neck and devour a half-dozen mercenaries whole.

Of all the times to experience battle slowdown, this was not when Dyrra would have chosen. Battle slowdown was wonderful when sand dancing. Feeling as though she had forever to dodge a swing, to kick a knee, to exploit an opening.

But here on horseback, where she could only watch men die while waiting to close to striking distance, the slowness seemed to mock her. To swear that for all her efforts she would be too late.

Then, out of nowhere, trumpets. And drums. More than even the king employed for the tournament. Blaring the fanfare of one of Aeralfast's central barons. Dyrra couldn't remember which, only that he was a muttonhead.

Hundreds of horns and drums, blasting loud enough to make her wince more than Lucala's Jealous Sister above, Dyrra's body echoing their noise from her pelvis to her skull.

Larek. Had to have been.

And the dragon turned. Its great, wide mouth stretched as though smiling.

Well, Larek had its attention now. And all around it the half-dozen remaining mercenaries scrambled for their feet, desperate for one last run for their lives.

The dragon rocked back on its haunches and gave its wings a mighty flap. The wind it generated knocked those hopeful mercenaries to the ground.

The dragon roared.

What had sounded impressive at a good mile distant now all but deafened Dyrra. Shook her to the bone.

This was no monster. This was death itself, come for them all. Come for the whole world, one piece at a time.

The battle was a waste. They had no prayer. No hope. There was no victory against such a thing, no matter what the skalds promised.

Dyrra felt herself lower her bow. The roar still ringing in her head. Ahead of her she could see Barth relaxing his grip on the spear. Their horses slowed to an uncaring walk.

The mercenaries had the right of it. No use it taking arms against that thing. No use in fighting it. Better to stop now. Better to lay down and die.

No one would miss her. No one waited for her. Her daughter

wouldn't care. Death in the jaws of a dragon was a better end for Dyrra than Suwala could have hoped for her shamed mother.

Ommure would be waiting for her on the other side. Sweet Ommure, with his quirked smile and strong hands.

Dyrra's shoulders slumped forward. This was the end then. Certain death after so many near misses. But how could this day end otherwise? Against a creature that was more force of nature than killable foe?

Even Larek would underst...

Larek would...

No.

If Dyrra surrendered, Larek would die.

Larek was not allowed to die today. Not for the dragon. Not for the mercenaries. And not because Dyrra gave up—

Something inside Dyrra snapped. Her head came up. Strength flowed through her again. Anger. Will.

Damn that dragon and damn its roar. And damn the skalds for not warning her about it.

Dyrra kicked her horse to spur it to speed, but Glint only lay down in the grass. Ahead of her Barth's stallion did the same. Barth's spear hung loose in his hand. His shield and head dangled in surrender. Behind her the other horses joined Glint in lying down. Sindra looked pale with terror. Larek looked lost in the horrors of his own mind.

The roar was still upon the others.

Only one hope for it.

"KEENARACH!" screamed Dyrra, calling deeper for the cry than ever before. From her love for Ommure. From her love for her friends. From her need to tell her daughter the truth. From the depths her soul itself.

And as she screamed, Dyrra loosed an arrow and reached into her quiver for another.

THE SIGHT OF THE DRAGON HAD BEEN BAD ENOUGH, BUT WHEN IT roared Sindra found herself back on the streets of the temple district, the day she had been cast out of her order.

She knew better. She knew she was in the green hills and vales southwest of Lillikan. She knew she was surrounded by Larek, Dyrra, Chitter, and Barth, and that they all sped on horseback beyond the means of any normal horse, helped along by the blessings of Nilasah.

But then that great beast faced them, rocked back, and roared. That roar was more than just the sound pummeling her ears and bones. The moment she head the roar, it was as though no time had passed since that moment in the streets of the capitol. She could even smell the dirt and grime of the temple district around her. Her life was lost and empty, and there was no point to anything. Least of all, opposing so omnipotent a creature as the dragon before her.

Better to surrender to the resounding roar in her head. To lie down and die. To seek the oblivion at the end of the dragon's gullet, and move on to whatever came next.

Better just to die here and now.

On some level, Sindra knew what was happening. She had read a small mention of it in one of the histories, forgotten until she faced a roaring dragon herself.

She knew the power of that roar. The effect that it had. That the braver the listener the worse the result.

And yet for all this knowledge she could do nothing against the power, even when her gelding, Nut, abandoned its gallop and seemed resigned to walk to its fate, rocking her up and back with each clop-ping step, until even that proved too much effort.

Her gelding lay down there in the grass. The other horses around it did the same.

The other riders looked as lost as she felt, caught in horrors of their own.

But then Dyrra screamed her war cry. The power. The defiance. The sound seemed to grab Sindra by the shoulders and shake her, slap her back to herself.

The dragon was coming. It had taken to the air with slow, steady flaps. Just enough to keep it airborne, as though walking to them would have sullied its talons.

And she saw its eyes. Those awful orange eyes. They focused on Larek ahead of her.

Blackflame recognized him.

Sindra doubted that was good.

Dyrra launched arrow after arrow at the beast. Each struck home. A few even stuck where they hit. None of them seemed to have any effect.

Barth was shaking his head, coming back to himself. He jumped from his fallen horse and flung his spear at the dragon. It stuck halfway down the torso.

The dragon took no notice.

Larek still had his head down. Still looked defeated. Lost in the past.

Sindra flung a needle coated in Nilasah's Tears at the dragon, catching it at a point between the scales of its neck.

Nothing.

"Larek!" she cried. "Wake up!"

Dyrra had her sword out now, and Barth drew his. They began to charge the dragon, even though with it airborne, the most they could hope to do was stab its tail. They both screamed their defiance as they ran.

Sindra disentangled her feet from her stirrups. She had to get to Larek. Had to snap him out of it. If he couldn't help them, they were as dead as the roar promised they would be.

The dragon's ribs expanded in a mighty inhalation.

Sindra stumbled over herself in her haste to reach Larek. To kiss him. To slap him. To do *something*.

Because in moments it would be too late.

DRAGONS ONLY STRIKE WHERE YOU'RE WEAK.

Those damned words came back to Larek the moment the dragon smiled. Even before it roared.

Ice. All through Larek. His arms. His legs. His guts. His mind. Nothing moved. Nothing functioned. Blackflame was before him again at last. Remembered him. Smiled. Flew closer before unleashing its roar.

So much bigger than last time. So much more dangerous. And yet, Larek could do nothing. Frozen in place as much by those words and the memories they conjured as by the dragon's smile. By its echoing roar.

Dragons only strike where you're weak.

Had it followed Larek this time? Drawn him close so it could finish him off as it had not done so many years ago?

Or was it simply that wherever Larek stood was the weakest place to strike?

Dyrra screamed something. Loosed her arrows. And still Larek stood helpless.

Sindra shouted at him. He could hear her closing footsteps, and still he could think of nothing but those six words, read in that one history text of his master's. The only text that spoke at length about dragons. The only text that warned of their roar. A roar it had not bothered with last time.

Dragons only strike where you're weak.

The dragon sucked in enough air to make even its huge rib cage expand.

Dyrra and Barth charged, weapons in hand. Just as Inga had. Dyrra had fired off her arrows. Just as Taran had.

And now the dragon would breathe its fire and kill them all. Dyrra. Barth. Sindra. Chitter. The horses.

The dragon's fire would consume everything. Just as it had the last time.

No.

It couldn't have them. Not Sindra, restored to her path. Not Dyrra, who had a daughter to find. Not Chitter, Larek's only steadfast friend these long years. And not Barth, who rode beside him for a battle, not a slaughter.

The words of the spell leapt to Larek's lips. The same spell he had cast ten years ago. The same spell that had failed him. In the intervening years, Larek had studied it. Torn it to its roots and components and researched them. Dissected its aspects and traced its history. Understood the portions derived from the Aarkadian, the Thelmastii, the Chelas, and others.

Larek had gotten to know that spell better than he knew himself.

He understood that spell as thoroughly as possible — for a man with no way to test his work. For the spell worked only against dragonfire. It was useless against normal fires. And though the component study had taught Larek more about the magic of fire than he ever wanted to know, much less cast, he had never once gotten the opportunity to test his findings in any meaningful way.

He could only hope that he had it right this time. He had to protect his friends. Their horses. Those remaining mercenaries. Succeed or fail he would try to save every life he could.

Larek threw up his arms and shouted.

"Ahn harakan ne insi! Ne karansi! Ne tok toh!"

The dragon loosed its flame.

The world became a sea of black fire, licked within by hints of purples and blues. It smelled acrid, of bile and death, a smell that clung to the tongue and throat as well as the nostrils. That tried to call back up the beef and heavy cheese of breakfast that were long since gone from Larek's stomach.

And the heat...

...was missing.

Larek remembered the heat of last time. Even under the aegis of a half-worked spell the heat had felt as though his bones boiled within him. As though his very flesh had skipped ash and burned straight away into vapor.

The pain had been too much for Larek's mind to handle. It locked away the depth of the sensations, bringing them out only in hints, when the time came to waken him from the worst of dreams.

But this time those flames kissed like the wings of a butterfly, tapping the skin from a perching spot on the knuckles.

And then the flames were gone.

Larek stood not on a grassy hillside now, but waist deep in ash so fine that it seemed to melt around him. Far too much ash for the grass to have produced. The dragon must have burned away hillside as well.

The air smelled of char and charnel, but so far as Larek could tell, no living thing had died under the blast of flame.

Ahead of him, Dyrra and Barth stumbled, but continued their charge, hooting as though victory had already been won. Beneath him, Fal shook himself and more ash seemed to melt away, leaving the black stallion's sweaty coat tinted dark gray.

To his left, Larek could hear Sindra fall and recover, no doubt her yellow kirtle now as black as his steed.

He could hear the other horses snorting and shaking as well.

But wait. If the hillside were burned away beneath them, why had they not fallen?

Chitter's work? Where was Chitter?

Chitter's head emerged from the ash like a swimmer from a lake. "Deny it the air!" he yelled, and submerged, leaving a tunnel in the dragonash.

Larek refocused on the dragon above him. A dragon that looked as though the fiery breath had shrunk it a little. Made it less imposing, despite its size.

A dragon that no longer smiled. That gnashed its teeth, with eyes narrowed in anger.

Dragons only strike where you're weak.

Perhaps that meant they could not stand against united strength.

Larek's turn to smile.

DYRRA HOOTED WITH JOY AS SHE RAN THROUGH DEEP ASH. ASH THAT

continually dissolved with her every step and movement, but kept her from seeing or feeling the ground beneath her.

But she was not part of the ash. Nor was Barth, though his progress toward the dragon came more stilted than her own.

Likely all of her friends were alive and whole and fighting.

Even with her nose full of fire and death, Dyrra had trouble imagining a more joyful moment.

She didn't worry about her steps. Her training as a sand dancer taught her how to fight across ground she could not see. Even ground she could not feel.

Dyrra twirled her sword of war in her hands, crying out old Karwalish taunts to try to draw the dragon's ire. But the beast had eyes only for Larek.

And the hate in those eyes was a palpable thing. She could feel it radiating against her skin more than she had felt the heat of those all-consuming black flames. How much worse that feeling must have been for Larek, its target.

But though the eyes sought out Larek, the tail seemed to have ideas of its own.

The serpentine tail swept at her. A great bullwhip ready to crack.

Dyrra smiled. Let it come.

She watched the swing. Judged it. Dove clear just before the crack, eyes and mouth closed tight.

Dyrra rolled through the silence of deep ash. Breath held. Sword point safely to one side.

She came up through the melting ash. Blew out her breath. Wiped her eyes clear.

Saw the claw coming for her. Too big. Too fast.

She threw herself backwards in a desperate fall.

The dragon slammed to the ground. The points of its talons missing her face by a scant hand's breadth. Dyrra blinked.

The dragon's cry of protest came high and sharp and longer than its tail. Landing had not been its idea.

Larek to the rescue again? That might have been the harsh syllables of one of his old, dead languages in the background.

Dyrra rolled away from the lifting claw, but the dragon didn't notice her. It focused hard on Larek. Spat a gout of flame at him alone, though this one washed past as uselessly as the other one must have.

Sindra rushed forward? No. Not quite toward the dragon. Off to one side where...

Where was Barth?

No sight of him through the ash, but he must have been caught by claw or tail.

Well, if he lived, Sindra could mend him. And if not, Dyrra could avenge him. Either way, the time had come for the beast to die.

Dyrra now began to crawl along the ground toward the dragon's belly, her sword outstretched to wipe away the ash before her and keep her way clear.

Sindra held her breath as the dragon's tail whipped past the diving Dyrra, then let it out in a cry of despair when the tail-tip cracked against Barth's shield. The shield tore in half. The man was thrown the breadth of the airborne dragon's wingspan.

Barth was down. Possibly dead. Definitely injured. Sindra clutched her Healer's kit tight.

Heedless of the flying dragon, Sindra charged straight past the chanting Larek. His hands waved and gestured while his lips dripped harsh syllables with a speed and confidence he had lacked even during his duel with Sebas.

As she passed Larek, he yanked his hands down, and the dragon slammed into the earth. The reverberations knocked Sindra to the ground, beneath a lake of melting ash. Ash that flooded her mouth and nostrils as she fell.

The dry, acrid taste on her tongue now. Choking her. Clinging to her throat. She thrashed for clean air, and even though the ash around her dissolved with every moment she made, no air came to fill her lungs. None could pass the ash filling her throat.

Expanding in Sindra's throat. Her hands clawed at her nose and into her mouth for air, but none came in. Her belly seized and seized again, trying to expel the ash, but it had become a solid thing.

Heat through her face and bulging neck. Gray sweat in her eyes, carrying more ash. Ash that limned the world. Then coated it.

Then cut it off entirely.

Her body shaking with the need for air. Her eyes blind to the world. Sindra rolled on the ground, more ash melting all around her.

Sindra's blind darkness began to brighten in flashes with her rapid pulse, though still she saw nothing. Her lungs screamed for air. Her fingers clawed and raked above her. Instinctively trying to dig her way out.

No history had warned of this. No skald's tale mentioned the death of inhaled dragonfire ash. But Sindra felt that death coming for her now. Its fingers on her bulging throat.

Panic all through her. Writhing. Clawing. Heaving. No room for thought. No room for regret. No memory flashes. No abandoned hopes. Only the desperate cry for air she could not find. Only her pounding heart speeding her to her grave.

Only the hand of death squeezing the blind life out of her. Shaking her. Ending her.

Only the hand...

The hand...

The prayer came unbidden to Sindra's mind. Her panic overlooked it, as it repeated slowly in the background of her terror. How could a prayer be important at a time like this? The only god that mattered to her body was air, and air was a thankless, heedless god that had abandoned her.

But faith is not a matter of thought. Not a matter of bodily need. True faith is not found in the words that the lips speak, but in the truths that the heart trusts. Deeper than study. Deeper than debate. Deeper than training or habit or opinion.

True faith isn't found in the teaching of a temple. It is earned through devotion and experience. It builds from failure and effort.

And true faith did not abandon Sindra when her need was greatest.

As she lay there, blind and choking and rolling under the ash, a short, simple prayer like an aphorism surfaced within her: *Nilasah, stay Death's hand for me. My work is not yet done.*

How many times had Sindra uttered that prayer for another as part of a healing? Even had she room to think, she would not have known. Never before had she considered that prayer for herself. Death was a fact of life. Every Healer knew a time would come when it could not be stayed. Healers themselves were no exception.

Nevertheless, those words began to run through her head. Small and quiet at first. Unnoticed behind the desperate search for air. The worrying swell of her neck and eyes. The fading brightness of her thready pulse.

And yet, those words were part of her.

And they began to build. *Nilasah, stay Death's hand for me. My work is not yet done.* Over and over they came. Louder and louder they grew. Until at last they demanded even Sindra's dying attention.

Desperation filled her. But not desperation for air this time. Desperation to reach Barth. Precious seconds were ticking by as she suffocated. Seconds she might need to preserve his life.

Sindra repeated the words to herself once more. This time deliberately. Not with the desperation of a dying woman clinging to life — though she was that — but with the pressure of a Healer begging Nilasah to stave off sleep for a few more hours that she might safeguard more lives before she collapsed.

And Nilasah answered.

A tiny gap formed between Sindra's sore throat and the congealed ash. Her abused muscles spasmed and contracted, ejecting it like a lodged peach pit after a helpful clap on the back.

Out the chunk flew, and as it thunked onto the ground her eyes at last blinked clear. Air gushed into Sindra's lungs. The bright morning sky shocked her eyes with its sudden appearance. She realized she could hear again. Larek chanting. The dragon raging. Barth's fading moans.

Sindra sat back on her shaky knees and offered a quick word of thanks to Nilasah. Her mouth still tasted of old coals. Tears filled her eyes. Spit dripped down her chin. She doubted she'd be able to swallow solid food for a day or more.

But she was alive! She wanted to laugh and sing and cry all at once. Life. Life was hers once more. Even if only for a little while longer.

A little while she could not waste.

Sindra snatched up her ash-coated Healer's kit from the ground beside her. She jumped to her feet and ran for the fallen Barth.

If Nilasah was still listening, She heard Sindra praying that she would not be too late.

THE SKY SHOULD HAVE STORMED. LIGHTNING AND THUNDER WERE THE proper elements one should face when squaring off against a dragon. To see it under rich blue, cloudless skies made the wyrm seem all the worse. The north wind should have whipped past them, tugging at Larek's floppy hat, instead of gently kissing his skin.

The feeling was probably a lingering effect of the dragon's glare. That glare had beat down on him like a pressure against his psyche, wearing away at him. Trying to grind him down to nothingness. The pressure eased as the dragon moved, but the sensation lingered like hopelessness taking root where confidence had held so strong.

Or perhaps it was the seeming inevitability of the dragon Black-flame making its slow way closer to Larek on four tremendous, taloned claws. Claws that ripped and tore the ground beneath it, making each step sound like a small avalanche. Its moving bulk dissolved the pungent lake of ash in great spreading ripples.

Or perhaps it was merely that Larek's confidence began to waver as yet another spell failed to cause the dragon to so much as twitch. The sixth or seventh in a row.

Nothing had worked since the binding on its wings had taken. The last spell that proved Larek had any power at all. Even now the dragon's back rippled with effort, but it could not budge those wings from their outstretched pose. Blackflame screeched a protest, but that was all.

So the spell had done something. But not enough. Blackflame might have been out of its element, confined to the ground, but it didn't need to fly to consume them all. Larek was half-surprised it had not swallowed up Barth's gray stallion in passing. But the dragon paid the horses no mind. Nor the fallen Barth. Nor Sindra, who knelt beside Barth, working her healing, her yellow kirtle as crisp and pure as though it weren't surrounded by more ash than any forest fire could produce.

Nor did the dragon seem to notice Dyrra. Not since it was grounded. Larek had worried that this meant the dragon's falling claw had killed her, but he could see a collapsing trail of ash making its way to the dragon's side.

A warrior. Moving into position to stab at the dragon. And yet Blackflame had eyes only for Larek. Even though no damaging spell Larek cast seemed to give it the slightest inconvenience. Not lightning nor ice, not crushing force nor ripping blades.

Spells that could have felled entire keeps did nothing. The battle spells he had learned against his master's advice. Advice that rang out all the wiser as the dragon neared.

Could nothing hinder the beast?

Hinder.

Larek considered the dragon's approach as he drew back a few extra strides in case Blackflame could stretch that neck even farther than appearances suggested. When the dragon had been eating the mercenaries down the hill, it seemed positively lithe in its movements. But now its every step came heavy. Loud. Ponderous, compared to earlier.

Was this because it could not fly?

No! Chitter! Chitter had to be in the earth beneath the dragon, grabbing each leg with his full power as it began to lift. Not enough to stop so vast a dragon, but enough to slow it. To make it awkward.

To hinder it. As Larek had done by binding its wings.

Perhaps magic and spells could not defeat it. Only hinder it.

Larek reached for an Aarkadian looping spell. A variation of the one he used on its wings. If it worked it would tie off the dragon's limbs where they joined the torso. Freeze them in place, no matter how the target might struggle to move them. The one spell had worked on the wings. Perhaps the same principle could paralyze the legs and tail.

Larek's tongue twisted through the odd Aarkadian intonations. Accents never where they looked like they should have been. Instead they changed according to the speaker, the sentence, the meaning, without ever altering the underlying word itself, modified ever so slightly by just the right gesture at just the right time.

And so Larek's voice dripped and ran and rose and fell until the spell was formed and winging its way toward the dragon. Larek's fist clenched to seal the loop, as though yanking it tight.

And still the dragon closed. Each leg showing strain to lift, but the tail whipping back and forth behind it. Another spell failed. The dragon began swaying its head forward, gauging the distance for when the time came to swallow Larek whole.

A time that stalked nearer and nearer with each passing second.

Could they truly have come so close only to fail now?

Barth — if he yet lived — was out of the fight. Sindra was a Healer. Even her most potent weapon could have done nothing more than make the dragon drowse. And Dyrra. Could even her sword of war pierce the dragon's heart, where arrows and a spear seemed useless?

They all lived because the dragon wanted Larek. Would eat him the moment it reached him. And when he fell, the others would follow right behind.

The dragon loosed another slender gout of flame. Just enough for the wizard it wanted to kill. The blue-and-purple-kissed black fire washed over Larek with no more effect than the last three attempts.

That spell held at least.

But Larek knew no spells that would help against a dragon's claws and teeth. As far as he knew, no one had ever devised such protections.

His magic could not kill the beast. Even working with Chitter, he could barely slow it. And now it was coming for him, and Larek could see no way to stop it.

At least the binding on its wings would last for some time. A day. Perhaps two. The people of Lillikan would live a while longer, as would the survivors in Neton. Perhaps long enough for the king's heroes to find and slay Blackflame for all time.

But what could they do that Larek could not? Could their spells of battle be so very much stronger than his?

Or were spells of battle not the answer?

The stories. The histories. They spoke of a team killing the dragon. Not a wizard. Not a warrior. And not just a team. Friends. Always companions who had ridden together before. Faced death together before.

Who knew how to fight together...

Larek had been approaching this all wrong.

Of course no single spell could kill a dragon. Dragons possessed a deeper magic than any wizard. Some said they were formed by magic itself, from the days before even the gods had names.

But where magic cannot crush, perhaps magic can open the way.

"*Dyrra*," Larek yelled, in Karwalish to be certain of her attention, "*strike when your blade is ice!*"

Larek threw wide his arms and chanted faster than he had ever chanted before.

DYRRA HAD FOUND A GOOD RHYTHM TO HER CRAWLING MOVEMENTS. Swipe the sword, twist her torso, push with her legs. Swipe the sword, twist her torso, push with her legs. The last of the ash like dried slime over the crust of burnt earth beneath her.

At not much slower than a stealthy crouching walk, Dyrra made her way closer and closer to the dragon's massive form.

So huge the beast stood. Taller than even ancient trees. Wider than a row of sand dunes. Heat coming off its body in waves that lifted whatever strands of wiry hair had escaped her leather thong. The dragon's scales rustled with each labored step like a thousand shifting snakes.

She could smell it now, even over the pervasive char to the air. The scent was not at all what she expected. She assumed dragons smelled like lizards, dry and slightly musky. But Blackflame smelled wet, like rotten wood floating in a cesspool.

Dyrra might have gagged, but she had kept her breaths short and shallow through her barely open lips. Partially because she didn't trust the melting ash around her. But it was also an old trick she had learned at war. One reaction to a smell could give away an ambush as surely as an early fired crossbow.

And she was close now. Well clear of that swinging tail. Right around the midpoint between the fore and hind legs. Not out of reach of either, but she hoped her path took her closest to wherever such a creature kept its vital organs.

If a dragon had vital organs.

She had almost reached its armored belly when she heard the last thing she expected. Larek, hollering with an easterner's imprecise grasp of Karwalish. She had no idea what he actually meant, but what he said was, "Dyrra, icicle stab, change sword kill."

The dragon stopped walking and reared up, creaking the very ground beneath it. Its long, long neck craning to look around it.

Dyrra had hoped she was forgotten in the beast's press to kill Larek, but his call must have reminded it of the lurking warrior somewhere nearby.

No time to puzzle through Larek's cry. He was chanting now anyway, so whatever he was doing, it had better work.

Dyrra jumped to her feet and ran at the dragon. She leapt as high up that massive belly as she could, but felt like a toddler trying to leap to a parent's shoulders. Still, she drew back her sword of war above her, both hands on the hilt.

A hilt that seemed to turn to ice in her hands. Cold soaking into her bones, spreading up her arms.

The dragon swiped a claw at her, but the battle slowdown had returned. The claw seemed as though it would not reach her for a month. The cold in her arms all but stopped at her elbows, even though she knew it continued to creep its way up.

"Lucala!" she screamed, her own voice echoing into eternity.

Dyrra plunged her blade into the dragon, scarcely a fifth the way up its torso.

But the blade began to cut.

Dyrra's arrows had stuck fast, useless. Barth's spear had stuck fast, useless. But Dyrra's sword, frozen no doubt by Larek's magic, slashed its way into the belly of the great dragon Blackflame with less resistance than a training dummy filled with sand.

Time caught up with Dyrra once more. Her momentum carried her across and down. Across and down. All the while that bone-deep cold spread through her. A painful contrast to the gushing waterfall of scalding black blood.

Her eardrums burst as the dragon screamed.

Dyrra could not see past the flowing blood. She could hear nothing. Pain assaulted her senses from every angle.

But still she clung to that sword for dear life, and slid her way to the ground across the dragon's belly.

Until the ground thumped beneath her feet.

Dyrra blinked her streaming eyes clear in time to see the corpse of the great dragon Blackflame drop its full, massive weight on top of her.

The earth shook with the impact.

25

THE DRAGON LAY DEAD, ITS BLOOD BEFOULING A HILLSIDE SCARRED AND permanently blackened by gouts of dragonflame. But the north wind at last began to gently freshen the air, the smell of fire and decay finally beginning to fade from Sindra's nostrils.

The battle was won, and though the cost was steep, the people needed to know.

To see to that, Larek stood further down the hill, explaining to the remaining mercenaries the task he was setting them as payment for saving their lives. They were to travel to Lillikan and then the capitol and spread the word of what they saw. Word of what Larek, Dyrra, Chitter, Barth, and Sindra had done (though Larek listed himself last), and where His Majesty could find the body. He even presented them with a dragon's scale the size of Barth's shield, to show as proof.

Sindra smiled at the confidence in Larek's voice. A relaxed, certain quality she had never heard in him before. She found it more than a little appealing.

But Sindra had no time for celebration. Her work was not yet done.

Barth lay back on his bedroll before her. She had drenched him with flowing water from Larek's amazing jug, clearing the ash from his body. She never thought a man with so many broken bones — jagged breaks that had torn so many places within him — could possibly have been thought of as lucky, but lucky Barth was.

As he fell, thrown by a blow from the dragon's tail, his head had followed the tattered remnants of his shield. It had concussed him and left a gash across his face, but it had melted the dragonash ahead of it, saving him from the suffocating near death that Sindra herself had suffered when she had fallen face first into the dragonash.

Sindra had spent a precious few of Barth's seconds to spray the area with more water from Larek's jug, clearing as much of the ash away as she dared before settling down to work.

And work it had been. Barth's will to live must have been as mighty as the blow that felled him. Never had she seen a man hurt so badly cling to life. He gave her the time she needed to bring him back from death's grip, to stay death's hand not once, but twice this day.

If only...

But there was no use in such thoughts. The dead were dead and gone, and no one could bring them back. Not even Nilasah. Sindra had to content herself that those who died today had saved the denizens of Lillikan from a similar fate. That they had spent their lives to bring down the dragon.

Still, Sindra had saved Barth, though doing so used up most of her potions, tinctures, and all but one poultice. She would need days to gather and blend new stock. And he would likely smell of astringent and tangy kuruk root well into the night.

And her voice was gone completely. Expelling the dragonash — praise Nilasah — had left her throat raw and rasping. Discomfort in every breath and no voice above a whisper. But even that whisper was gone now. Every painful syllable spent in saving Barth's life, until her final prayers had been uttered from her heart alone.

Now she would have no words until her voice returned. Fortunately she would not need words for her next patient.

Sindra turned to where Dyrra lay, stretched on her own bedroll. She twitched everywhere as spasms worked their way through all the countless spots scalded by the dragon's boiling blood. But the liniments Sindra had applied were doing their work, as were her prayers, and most of that skin would heal good as new.

Dyrra would likely be left with some scarring around her eyes, but Sindra imagined that Dyrra would like that. It would make her more intimidating. Not that she needed the help.

And now it was time to see to Dyrra's hearing.

The death scream of the dragon had silenced the world for all of them in a final burst of blood and searing pain. Fortunately, the treatment was simple enough that Sindra had restored her own hearing immediately and Larek's at the first opportunity. Barth's she had worked into the rhythm of healing his many other wounds.

But Dyrra's had fallen to the bottom of the priority list.

Sindra approached Dyrra, who might well have been seeing double because of the liniments. Her eyes watered, but that was likely from the bright, afternoon sun above her. She blinked rapidly and kept glancing around to see the places she could not hear. She would probably have been sitting up — might have tried once or twice — but the process of healing those burns would keep her on her back most of the day.

Sindra raised her hands in a simple, calming gesture, then pointed at her own ears, then at Dyrra. Dyrra relaxed in a deep sigh, then nodded and eased back.

Sindra rubbed her palms over Dyrra's ears three times and voicelessly prayed, *Sweet Nilasah, bind what has been torn apart. Gather the pieces round. Mend what has been broken here. Restore to her world, sound.*

On the first time through the prayer, Sindra shivered with pleasure as the Healing began to flow down her limbs, like cool water down a sore throat. How she had missed the feel of Nilasah's touch. How she hoped never to go without it again.

But these thoughts were part of her mind's background. Her attention was all for Nilasah, Dyrra, and the healing as she continued to recite the prayer in her heart.

On the third repetition, she felt the flow end. Three times Dyrra had needed it, while Barth had needed two, and Larek and Sindra only one. But three had done the trick. Sindra released her hands. Looked at Dyrra with eyebrows raised.

"Better," Dyrra said. "Thank you. But the dragon. The fall. How…"

Dyrra's voice trailed off, finally realizing that though Sindra's eyebrows crinkled in sympathy, she was pointing to her speechless throat. Dyrra had questions, but Sindra had no way to answer them.

Then Chitter popped out of the ground beside them, squirrel brow furrowed like a human deep in thought. He barked out a phrase that made no sense to Sindra, though she was sure she had heard it before.

And Dyrra nodded as though she understood.

Sindra's jaw dropped in shock, and Dyrra raised a hand to stay any curiosity while she focused her attention on the earth spirit, apparently understanding everything he was saying.

Sindra knew what Chitter was saying. Larek had explained what happened the moment Chitter pulled Dyrra's body — whole but not uninjured — from the ground like a mother lifting her child out of the bath.

Chitter had been in the earth beneath the dragon, fighting it with his own power as much as he could. And he was in the perfect position to save Dyrra from being crushed as the dragon died. He pulled her to safety down through the hillside itself.

Sindra smiled, and shook her head. And now it seemed that she was the only member of their little group who could not understand Chitter. Except Barth, perhaps. If Barth remained with them.

If they remained together at all. Now there was no need to travel south. They had written new tales for the skalds to sing about them.

That thought broadened Sindra's smile further, and she turned at the sound of footsteps, hoping to greet Larek with a celebratory kiss.

But it was not Larek walking up the hill to her. It was Keon's Healer.

"I had to see it for myself," he said, eyes wide with wonder as they tracked past the living, healing Barth and the living, healing Dyrra. "You Healed them, didn't you? You—"

Then he saw the hand of Nilasah, embroidered once more on Sindra's yellow kirtle, just above her heart.

Sindra nodded.

"You could never have had time to... Nilasah Herself did that?"

Sindra nodded.

Keon's Healer dropped to his knees, muttering prayers with his eyes closed. Sindra waited, understanding what he felt. Finally he looked up at her again, as though to ensure he had truly seen Nilasah's hand restored to her kirtle.

"When I saw your horses arrive at such speeds, I wondered. But now I can have no doubts. I, Ren of Tewen, hereby note and witness on behalf of the Order of Healers and Physickers, that you, Sindra, have been restored to our ranks by no less than the goddess Herself, and that you continue to do good works in Her name."

Tears of joy and gratitude began to trickle down Sindra's face.

"No—" Ren stopped himself. He cocked his head to the side and smiled. "You have Healer's Silence, don't you?"

Sindra soundlessly chuckled and sobbed at the same time as her body tried to both cry and laugh together. Healer's Silence. Of course. When a Healer has prayed her voice away tending to others without taking sufficient care of herself, she cannot heal it except through time. Only another Healer can treat it with prayer. Part of Nilasah's requirement of humility.

Ren stood and placed a hand on her throat. He mouthed the prayer softly, and Sindra felt her throat soothe to restoration.

"You should come back to the capitol," he said, and Sindra grimaced, because his hand lingered a touch longer than necessary. He spoke as though he had not noticed her expression. "High Healer Alain will want a celebration in your honor."

"That's all right," said Sindra, smiling down the hill at Larek, approaching. "I have a celebration of my own in mind."

Larek watched the mercenaries leave, six still living from their company with two of their horses walking beside them. The clopping of their hooves was soporific. Larek had to turn away, even though it meant turning away from the fresh air of the north wind and back to the smells of death, blood and fire.

Before him burned the bodies of the fallen mercenaries and their horses, a great pyre in the center of dragonburnt ground that might never see so much as grass growing on it again.

At least that meant he didn't have to watch the fire. It would not spread. There was nothing more near it to burn. He could safely back away from the pyre's oppressive heat, and let it burn itself out when it was ready.

Larek deflated in a sigh that almost finished with him collapsing where he stood. So. Very. Tired. Little sleep. That demanding ride. And the stress and strain of facing Blackflame again. Of calling spells borne of desperation.

Not to mention holding a strong front to those mercenaries. Larek was fairly certain that they would do as he bid. Those who felt no gratitude for their salvation from the dragon had to at least remember their terror at the sight of Larek's ball of fire.

Still, talking to them was not the time to admit weakness, however much his spine had wanted to bow. His lids to droop. Larek knew well that his exhausted mind and body would have been all too happy to shut the world out for a week or so of slumber, without much concern for where it lay.

But even now was not the time. Not yet. He had to know that Dyrra and Barth were alive and healing. That they would recover.

And he wanted to see Sindra's smile again before he slept.

Worried as he might have been about Dyrra and Barth, it was that last thought at the forefront of his mind as his feet trudged their way up the charred earth to where his friends waited.

Keon's Healer was with them. Bowing to Sindra. Now he had his hand on her throat, but gentle.

Larek's brain was too foggy to make much sense of what he saw. But it knew this much. That Healer who had sneered at her. Scorned her. Now stood before her solicitous. Touching her even. Touching

Sindra, who had wanted nothing more than to once more heal on behalf of Nilasah as part of Her holy order.

And now that she could Heal again, Keon's Healer was touching her. And she didn't seem to mind.

Too exhausted to draw further connections. To even truly feel jealousy. Instead Larek was aware of what looked like comfortable familiarity between Sindra and Keon's Healer, and it made his stomach sink, drawing his heart with it.

It took the spirit right out of his feet. They continued their trudge, but without confidence. Without any certainty of what he would find once he reached the group. He might see Sindra smile when he arrived, but would that smile bring him any joy? Or would it merely be another source of pain?

Larek had been hurt by so many through the years. Perhaps one more would not matter.

Then why did his shoulders ride even lower? Why could he feel wetness on his cheeks? Why did his breaths come unsteadily?

With these questions trying to find their way through Larek's spent mind, he made his way up the hillside. A smoother slope now, with so much of the topsoil burned away by dragonfire.

When he reached Sindra and Keon's Healer, Larek opened his mouth to speak. But before the first word could form, Sindra grabbed him in a hug so tight the words got jumbled.

And then she kissed him, and those words lost their way completely.

If the kiss they had shared early that morning had been a promise, then the kiss Sindra gave him now was its fulfillment. It was soft and warm and deep, and spoke of joy at survival, the thrill of reunion, the glee of accomplishment.

And most of all, the simple ecstasy of the kiss itself, of sharing all these things one with the other in an intertwining moment that seemed to last forever, but not nearly long enough.

26

———

Dyrra, Larek, Sindra, Chitter and Barth passed the next several days there on the hillside in Larek's pavilion, arranged just outside the zone burnt by dragonfire.

Sindra had been quite clear that Barth would need days of recovery before he could travel, and perhaps a week before he could ride. And they all knew the horses would benefit from the rest.

Fortunately dragonash did not seem to affect horses the way it affected humans. Dyrra heard Larek wondering about that, even pestering Sindra for details about her experience. And Sindra indulged the questions, providing such coherent details as she could.

Dyrra could not understand that at all. Discussing the finer points of her near-death? When there were other, more pleasurable things they could be doing together to pass the time while Barth convalesced?

Part of the reason wizards and warriors would never understand each other. Not really.

But that didn't matter to Dyrra, especially since Sindra had come to her senses about Larek. Let Larek take his notes for future research. It didn't seem to impede his need to kiss Sindra, which was good.

As far as Dyrra could tell, they had gone no further than that — which was ridiculous in her opinion. Opportunities were meant to be seized before life snatched them away. She herself might well have ravished Barth by now, were he up to the task.

Of course, it was his current state that likely held Larek and Sindra back. She had to be available at need for Barth's treatments. And even after Larek set up that marvelous pavilion, Barth dominated the only available bed for his recovery.

Still, Dyrra would have preferred if Larek and Sindra were sneaking off into the high grass together at night for privacy.

But they had time. And Larek and Sindra seemed to be enjoying getting to know one another further first, which was probably good for their sort of people.

Dyrra supposed.

Even now, just past highsun on the fifth day after the dragon's death, Dyrra had come outside under the pretense of brushing the horses. In truth she was tired of watching Larek watch Sindra sing her prayers over Barth's ribcage. He had a look in his eye that reminded her of Ommure, the times she would catch Ommure watching her train.

And so Dyrra stood under the light of Lucala's Jealous Sister of her own volition, grateful for the puffs of white smoke from Drandle's pipe that filled the bright blue above and diminished the hateful glare.

She took pleasure in the simple smell of horses, the feel of their muscles under her hands and she brushed them down.

The wind blew strong from the north and west, and smelled as though the rains were coming. Days away yet, but coming.

The horses whinnied and nuzzled at Dyrra as she bushed them, grateful for the attention and starting to look fit to ride. She might try taking her roan stallion Glint out later to see how he responded.

"Would you like that?" she said, scratching Glint behind the ears.

Ears that snapped forward. And whatever caused that response, the other horses heard it too.

Dyrra heard it a moment later. The thunderous drumming of hooves. Many hooves.

Dyrra spun around, reflexively reaching for her sword, but checking herself shy of a draw. Keon was dead. No mercenaries were coming for her.

And then she saw the cloud of dust in the distance, and with it the first riders. But she could tell no details. Even shading her watery eyes could not help her enough to see so far in such conditions.

"Larek," she called into the pavilion. "Sindra. Riders approaching."

Larek was first out of the flap, Chitter on his shoulder.

Chitter said something, and Dyrra felt frustrated that she couldn't understand what.

"Two hundred riders," translated Larek. "Four wagons. Two carts."

Nothing to do but wait. Dyrra wanted to grab her bow. Just in case. But she knew better. Against two hundred? No reason to look as though she wanted a fight.

The riders drew closer.

Horns blared. An eight-note pattern, repeated three times. It sounded familiar to Dyrra, but she did not recognize the sequence until Larek dropped to one knee.

The short form of the royal fanfare.

His Royal Majesty, Harlan III, King of Aeralfast, was coming.

Larek had scarcely taken a knee there in the wild grass of the hilltop, just outside the entrance of the Sebas' pavilion, when Dyrra beside him joined him on one knee. Larek was surprised she hadn't knelt first. Warriors had far more reason to memorize the royal fanfare than wizards, especially the short form, or battlefield version.

The king was coming, with some two hundred riders. Larek had never heard of such a thing. Kings summoned people to court. They did not ride out to meet them in the countryside.

"What..." started Sindra, stepping out through the flap of the pavilion behind Larek. But she never finished her question. She saw the oncoming riders, saw Larek and Dyrra kneeling, and joined them.

The three of them waited beside their nickering, hobbled horses, the normally lovely northern wind tainted by the smell of horse droppings.

The huge company stopped well short of the pavilion. In fact, they came to a halt in the dragonburnt portion of the hillside, just beside the great carcass of Blackflame himself. A carcass that had not yet begun to decay, which was a point Larek wondered if he should worry over.

Did dragons go into a sort of torpor? Was it possible to withdraw into a form of suspension? Such as the food in Sebas' pavilion seemed to enter when ... when it was closed...

Something about Sebas and suspension stuck in Larek's head. But nothing he had time to worry about now.

Ahead of him he could see King Harlan III himself, clad in his golden chain mail, with his travel crown and its giant rubies atop its eight spires. King Harlan seemed a vital man, still as capable of battle as any of the score of knights around him, even though those men and women were half his age or less.

The knights encircled the dragon. Half of the soldiers took up a position between their king and Larek, Dyrra and Sindra, though without blocking their monarch's line of sight, if he wished to look at his kneeling subjects up the hill.

Two other riders flanked the king. The first was the robust figure of the Royal Wizard, Tutalak. He had long gray hair and a long gray beard, and filled out his purple robes so full he made Larek look positively emaciated.

The other rider was the wizard in pine green, the dusky woman who had wanted to speak to Larek at the tournament. Who had seemed at the time to try to goad him into entry, though Larek had since wondered about her true purpose.

If any of them spoke, they did so too softly to be heard over the hundreds of yards between where they looked on the fallen dragon and where Larek knelt beside Dyrra and Sindra.

Larek's knees began to ache with the waiting. Sindra frowned at the delay. Dyrra grumbled in Karwalish, beside him. Likely swear words, because he couldn't follow what she said.

Finally, the king turned his mount and began to ride up the crusted hillside, the wizards still flanking him and his knights falling into formation around the three.

The action seemed to settle Dyrra and Sindra, but Larek felt a wave of cold under his chin that rolled down his back. Something about this did not sit right. Perhaps the king wanted to see a fallen dragon for himself, but why was that wizard in green here?

The horses drew rein about a dozen paces away.

"You are Larek, Dyrra and Sindra?" said the king, without waiting for any underling to announce him. He had a rich, baritone voice that sounded as though it should be giving inspiring speeches.

"Yes," said all three of them. Chitter kept his silence.

The king jumped down from the saddle and approached with a broad smile.

"Then stand," he said, "and let me embrace you as friends!"

And the king did just that, clasping each of them in turn. None of them returned the hug, of course. It would not have been proper.

"All my advisors told me that a tournament was the answer," the king said with a laugh. "Only a tournament will draw out the heroes we need." He clasped each of them on the shoulder again. "I should have known. You cannot *summon* true heroes. They *arise* when the need is great!"

"Thank you, Your Majesty," mumbled Larek, still keeping his eyes downcast. "And you must not forget Barth, who heals within the pavilion, and my friend Chitter here, who as an earth spirit gave us immeasurable help."

The king laughed again, as much surprise in his voice as pleasure.

"A humble wizard!" He glanced over his shoulder at Tutalak. "Will the wonders never cease?"

The royal wizard raised a droll eyebrow, but said nothing.

"Then I thank you, Chitter." The King smiled at so formal a bow coming from the body of a flying squirrel. "And I will have plenty of time to meet this Barth, for tonight I will dine with you. As will my royal wizard and my royal historian. You must tell us all what happened in your own words. And then tomorrow" — and for the first time, the king's jovial eyes took on a hint of command — "you must all return to the capitol with us for a proper celebration."

IN DYRRA'S OPINION, ROYALTY SHOULD KEEP TO THEMSELVES. THEY didn't live like other people. They didn't think like other people. They only really had anything in common with each other.

Yes, they were the rulers. As far as Dyrra was concerned, that just meant that they got stuck with the job of making all the big decisions while the little decisions of life and the world — the ones that really mattered — were actually made in the heat of a thousand moments by the people out there doing things instead of hiding behind high walls and eating rich food.

And Dyrra wished this King Harlan were back behind his high walls with his rich food right then, instead of sitting around her campfire like any other traveler.

Well, any other traveler in that ridiculous gilt chain mail. Too thin. Too light. And that much gold was just begging someone to kill him and melt it down.

And honestly. Having his personal cook along to roast geese over the fire? Geese were a terrible camp food. Bland without enough peppercorns to give them zing, and so fatty they kept the fire spitting all night.

Who wants a spitting fire when you're trying to keep warm in these chilly eastern nights?

Well, all right. Dyrra had to give the royal cook this much. He made a separate cooking fire a good two dozen paces away, where his geese could roast without spitting all over the diners. And the man knew his way around seasoning root vegetables. Dyrra had never tasted sweet carrots and turnips before, and they made an excellent counterpoint to the roast geese.

Dyrra also noticed that the separate cooking fire gave King Harlan the illusion of sitting around an actual campfire with his royal wizard, his royal historian, and four actual heroes. And it was four, because His Majesty required Barth to join them, though it meant extra work for Sindra.

It should have been five, but the king barely took notice of Chitter, though both the royal wizard and the royal historian seemed to pay enough attention to the earth spirit to overcome this slight.

And they were heroes, however much Larek, Sindra and Barth seemed to disdain the word when applied to them. Well, let the others keep their humility. Dyrra liked thinking of herself as a hero. And Lucala knew she earned it. Slashing a dragon across the belly while its scalding blood showered her.

Ommure would have been proud.

"Please," said the King to Sindra, his tone practically flirtatious, "Tell me again how Nilasah restored you to Her holy order."

Dyrra was amazed that Sindra did not sigh. She had already told that story three times, pausing and clarifying wherever the royal historian requested.

Dyrra raised her eyes to Lucala's waxing form in the clear night sky above.

Damn that king anyway. Dyrra would be unable to do her sword dance of victory and celebration in praise of Lucala with this crowd around her. Twenty knights standing guard in the background, and nearly ten times that many soldiers. Enough campfires to look like an army on the move, even if they only had enough supplies for a couple of days.

Dyrra had wanted to do the dance every night until Lucala bloomed full and brilliant above her, but it seemed last night concluded it.

She hoped Lucala would understand.

She had been about to offer a silent prayer to Lucala, when she heard the royal historian say something soft to Larek. Something even Dyrra's sharp ears could only just hear between Sindra's recount of her story and the crackling of the campfire.

"Why did you avoid me at the tournament?"

Dyrra almost — almost — turned her eyes to the woman from Lucala's visage above. But that would have been a mistake. The historian would have realized Dyrra was listening, and that would not have done. If this woman intended to move on Larek now that his reputation had been cleared...

Besides. Dyrra did not have to see the woman now to know what she looked like. She filled out her green robe the way a woman should, and her skin had the right dusky hues and tones to suggest that one of her grandparents was Karwalish. Or perhaps from Boll, or Mem.

An attractive combination. Larek might be tempted.

"You looked like another mocking wizard," said Larek, just as quiet. He pointed to the seal hanging from a gold chain around her neck: an open book. "You weren't wearing your badge of office. And I had a job to do."

"Not every wizard spoke ill of you, you know."

"Only the loud ones?"

That seemed to deter the historian. Dyrra smiled. But then the woman rallied.

"Will you walk with me now?"

"Why?"

Dyrra resisted the urge to slap herself in the forehead. Perhaps Larek was not truly so unobservant. Perhaps he knew well why a woman would ask him to walk with her in the evening, and only pretended to ignorance. Or perhaps he even forgot she was a woman in light of her title.

All of these were possibilities, but Dyrra knew which way she would bet.

She heard the historian sigh, and Dyrra's smile broadened. She knew that sigh. That was the sigh of a woman realizing a man was taken. She must have seen something in Larek's body language, or perhaps the way his eyes followed Sindra.

The only question in Dyrra's mind now was whether this historian would respect the situation, or...

"At least to talk to me formally as royal historian. I have questions about the first time you faced Blackflame, and—"

"No," said Larek. "Now please. We're being rude to Sindra."

Dyrra grinned wide enough she had to look away. Her eyes caught Barth's, and though he held his face impassive, she could tell he had been listening just as she was.

They shared a moment of silent humor. The first such moment Dyrra had shared with a man in many years.

She settled back in to listen to Sindra. Her friend.

27

———————

THE CELEBRATIONS LASTED A WEEK, AND SEEMED TO INCLUDE NOT ONLY the capitol itself, but the surrounding towns and farms. Larek had thought the crowds for the tournament were huge, but they were a village market day compared to the throngs dancing and drinking in the streets.

And singing. When Larek was honest with himself, he had begun to find songs praising him almost as tiresome and irritating as songs insulting him. Certainly they seemed to have the same level of accuracy. The skalds seemed to love the image of Larek calling lightning and thunder down from the skies. Not that either would have done much to hurt the dragon.

And they tried so hard to make his spells sound devastating instead of ineffectual, even though the skalds all acknowledged that Dyrra struck the killing blow. Though instead of working with enchantments laid down by Larek, the skalds seemed to decide that the blow was a matter of timing among Larek's thousand thousand spells.

Embarrassing in its inaccuracy.

But none of that mattered at the moment. Larek had finally managed to arrange a little private peace. He had gathered Sindra,

Dyrra and Barth — and Chitter, of course, though Chitter was merely by Larek's side as always — in the sitting room of his small house in the woods.

Four wooden chairs in front of the small, stone hearth. The first time all four had been used at once. Larek had always kept three guest chairs for clients, but in those days his clients never came in more than ones and twos.

A small fire burned in the hearth, just enough to mull some wine for them. A private toast, and a break from the public.

A quiet moment of exposure, Larek realized, as Dyrra and especially Sindra looked around with interest at the place Larek had called home for nearly a decade. Larek was acutely aware of how barren it must have looked. No personal possessions worth noting. A single window, shuttered closed. Not even a bookshelf in here, for he kept all his books in his workroom, which was now, of course, packed into the pouch on his belt.

In fact, the only remaining article of furniture in the room was his small oak cabinet, still full of his few dishes and pans.

"I like it," said Dyrra with a nod. "It suits you."

Sindra looked less certain, but then smiled with realization.

"You always lived in your workroom, didn't you?"

Larek nodded, pouring the mulled wine into four full-sized cups, and a little extra into the special, small cup he kept for Chitter. Chitter began passing out the drinks.

"I can't wait to see it," said Sindra with another smile.

"You mean there's something of his he hasn't shown you yet?"

Dyrra's tone left no doubts about her meaning, and Larek could feel his face try to blush past his scars.

"To us," said Barth, raising his cup and changing the subject. "The skalds may embellish and the historians may twist, but we know the truth. We did what had to be done."

"What had to be done," echoed Larek and the others. And even Chitter drank to that.

"Which raises the question," continued Barth. "What next? I don't know about any of you, but I never expected to live past facing that dragon, and I know I can't go back to being a guard in Lillikan." He snorted and shook his head. "I don't know what to do with myself."

"I think Sebas may be alive," said Larek. "The way he used his workroom with that pavilion suggests to me that he understood suspension better than any other wizard I know of. He might have seen his death coming and suspended himself."

"You want to dig him up?" said Dyrra.

"If he's dead, we can return him to Lillikan for burial. If not, he can go on his way."

"You wouldn't give him back that pavilion," said Sindra. "I love that pavilion."

"No, that's mine by right of victory. In fact, so's his staff, once I dig him up."

"It does sound like the right thing to do," admitted Barth. "Though I never liked the man."

"I want to find my daughter," said Dyrra, bringing the rest of the conversation to a halt. Everyone turned to look at her. "She may have faced her first battle by now. And if she hasn't she will soon. No doubt she'll hear some bad stories about her mother. It's about time she heard a good one."

Larek was still nodding when Barth said, "Never seen Karwale. Wouldn't mind joining you."

"It'd be good for her to hear others talk about her mother as well," said Sindra, her eyes darting to Larek then back to Dyrra. "People who know you."

"Give her a different, but valid perspective," Larek added. "If you wouldn't mind a side-trip to the banks of the Quar first, to dig up a wizard."

Dyrra smiled. "Good! I can finally show you people some decent cooking. You easterners and the way you season. It's criminal—"

"Wait!" said Chitter, jumping into the middle of the wooden floor and waving his arms for attention. When he had it, he spoke in a slower, more careful voice than Larek had heard him use before.

"We have come all the way back to this house, and we are not leaving without that armoire. I miss that armoire!"

"Armoire?" said Sindra. "Did he say armoire?"

"Great Halstaffur," said Barth. "I think I followed that."

"Yes," said Larek, coming to his feet. "The only remaining piece of furniture here that means anything to me. Come on, I'll show you."

Larek led them into his old bedroom and waved one hand high to present to them the vast cedar armoire. Taller than Dyrra, and more than twice as wide as Larek. Sindra ran her hand over the smooth wood of the doors.

"I hope it's full of wizardly robes," said Sindra. "It's time you stopped dressing like a poor merchant."

Larek almost snapped out a denial. A decade of feeling like a failure had made him want to hide. Made him ashamed of who and what he was. But as Dyrra and Sindra began discussing what colors his robes should be, Larek realized that they were right.

It was time he took up the robes again.

SIGN UP FOR STEFON'S NEWSLETTER

Stefon loves to keep in touch with his readers, and loves to keep you reading. The best way for him to do both is for you to sign up for his newsletter.

Sign up at http://www.stefonmears.com/join

If you sign up for Stefon's newsletter, you get...

- Monthly updates about his publishing and travel schedules
- His latest news, in brief, and answers to reader questions
- A free short story for signing up
- List-only offers and occasional specials
- Plus a free short story every month!

ABOUT THE AUTHOR

Stefon Mears still has trouble with modern Karwalish. Stefon has more than thirty books to his credit, and he never stops writing. He earned his M.F.A. in Creative Writing from N.I.L.A., and his B.A. in Religious Studies (double emphasis in Ritual and Mythology) from U.C. Berkeley. He's a lifelong gamer and fantasy fan. Stefon lives in Portland, Oregon, with his wife and three cats.

Look for Stefon online:
www.stefonmears.com
himself@stefonmears.com

www.ingramcontent.com/pod-product-compliance
Lightning Source LLC
Chambersburg PA
CBHW051649180726
48284CB00006B/1927